Alexandra

A Williams Family Journal

Remember: You are never alone!

Alexandra

A Williams Family Journal

Stephanie T. Ayers

10-3-10

Peace!

Stephanie Townsend Ayers

Presswork
Publications

Presswork Publications

ALEXANDRA: A WILLIAMS FAMILY JOURNAL.
Copyright © 2010 by Stephanie Townsend Ayers
Cover photography by Rebecca Haney

www.presassworkpublications.com

Ayers, Stephanie.
Alexandra: A Williams Family Journal / Stephanie Ayers. - 1st ed.
xiii, 306 p., |c20 cm.

ISBN 978-0979299407 (pbk: alk. paper)

2010

First Edition: June 2010

10 9 8 7 6 5 4 3 2 1

This book is dedicated to my family:
the love of my life who has taught me to dream,
Christopher;
and my children,
who have helped those dreams come true:
James, Christina, Madison, Donavon, Caitlin,
Christoph, Faith, William, Juliet, Anna-Grace,
Amelia, and Olivia.

In Memory of my Nanny
&
In Honor of my Bud

THE GATHERING

The sun shone across the frosty air. The icy wind of February cut into her almost as sharp as the pain that ran through her veins. Alexandra ached from the cold, yet she could not make herself move from that spot. Her eyes fixed on the rectangular hole and the pine box covered with pine boughs as everyone else walked back to the house. She could hear the faint murmuring, the sniffling, and Lee's crying. A deep overwhelming sob lodged in her throat and stifled her as she thought of six-year-old Lee and eight-year-old Christine, her brother and sister. How could she and James, her seventeen-year-old brother, take care of them? First it was Pa, then not a fortnight later Ma. Oh, Ma!

As they lowered Ma into her grave, Alexandra felt a scream ... a wail from the very pit of her soul rising to her throat! As hard as she willed herself not to cry, there they were. Tears. Such a rush of tears fell down her face that they poured upon her breast! 'Shame, Alexandra!' she thought. 'What would Ma think? I must bear up for the sake of the children.'

Inside she wanted to take off across the field, through the forest, and run until she fell off the end of the earth! But on the outside, she pulled Pa's handkerchief from her coat pocket, wiped her face, blew her nose, and closed her eyes.

"Forgive me, Lord. Make me strong and guide me. I don't understand, but Ma always said you don't give us more than we can handle. I hope I don't disappoint You. Be patient with me. I promise to try harder to be courageous. Amen," she whispered. As the men threw the last shovel of dirt upon Ma, Alexandra whispered, "Goodbye, Ma. I love you."

With that, she turned and walked toward the house.

The neighbors gathered in the small house trying to soothe and comfort the family. Alexandra stood for a moment on the back porch, straightened her shoulders, tried to smile, and opened the door. She hung her coat and scarf on the hook, and left her boots by the door. It did offer some comfort to see such a bounteous feast upon the table and a roaring fire in the hearth. 'Everyone has been so kind,' she thought.

Christine came over and took Alexandra's hand. These last few days, Christine never seemed to leave Alexandra's side. Alexandra reached down and smoothed Christine's hair. Christine gazed up at her with a fawn-like expression. Alexandra forced a smile, knelt down, and hugged her little sister. "Is there any ham or biscuits left for me?"

Christine smiled. "There is enough to feed even James."

Alexandra laughed, knowing James could eat like a bear most days.

The girls walked over to the crowd gathered around the sitting area, which was also the kitchen. Really, it was one big room divided up by furniture. Mrs. Madison was standing by the table fixing little Lee a plate. She was their closest and dearest neighbor at only a half mile walk. Mrs. Madison was a kindly older lady whose children were grown with half-grown children of their own. She and her husband were like grandparents to the Williams children.

Alexandra and Christine stood by Mrs. Madison as she turned and hugged Alexandra. "You poor child. You are frozen to the bone. Sit by the fire and I'll bring you a plate and some coffee to warm you up. Christine, how about you helping me, dear?"

Alexandra smiled, nodded, and walked to the fire. Christine was pleased to help Mrs. Madison, and Alexandra was relieved to have her kept busy. Alexandra saw James at the mantle gazing hard at the flames popping and flickering in the hearth. Alexandra tightened her jaw and gritted her teeth to keep a sob back. It pained her to see the heaviness and sorrow on her brother's face. Though just a year apart in age at sixteen and seventeen, they had always been as close as twins. She knew together they were sharing the same fears, doubts, and sorrow at this time. Already he seemed older. Whether it was grief and worry or just time, in the last month he had seemed to her to age two years. The moody, immature, and sometimes irresponsible boy of seventeen years seemed to change overnight into a man. There were no more pranks or jokes, no more doing his chores late or forgetting to feed cows. No more daydreaming or tromps through the woods with his buddies, Christoph and Luke. Through fevers, delirium, and coughs, illness had forced her brother into manhood. Alexandra was proud at how James stepped up into this role. How she wished she could be so brave and obedient. James seemed to simply resign himself to the Lord's will.

James broke his gaze, and his eyes caught hers. He

gave her a slight nod and a weak smile. Alexandra tried to smile back. She felt ashamed at her effort. She knew James didn't care much for crowds. 'That is why he has himself over in that corner,' she thought. With his thoughtful look as he gazed into the fire, no one seemed to want to disturb him. Everyone there knew the responsibility that now lay upon his shoulders. What does one say to a seventeen-year-old who now has three mouths to feed besides his own, a farm to keep up or lose, and animals that depend on him, too?

About the time James turned back to the orange glow of the fire, Mr. Alan Jackson, of the Jackson Mercantile, rose to give Alexandra the rocker by the fire. She thanked him with a smile and a nod.

He nervously fingered his hat. "Me and the missus are very sorry for your losses, Alexandra. Please call on us if we can help in any way."

"Thank you kindly, Mr. Jackson. James and I truly appreciate your generosity to our family." She sat down in the rocker.

Mr. Jackson blushed and shook his head. He lowered his gaze as if looking at his shoes. "Aw, never you mind, me and Mrs. Jackson just want to do the Christian thing for your family. Your pa was always upright and fair to me. Your ma was my Susanne's dearest friend. This turn of events cuts us to the quick, but the Lord knows best, Alexandra. Ours is not to question why. You remember what I said now, James." He turned to face James. "Don't let pride stand in the way of you calling. I'll help if ever I can, son." He held out his hand to James.

James straightened up and stood his full height of six feet. He took Mr. Jackson's hand. "Thank you, sir. I'll keep your words in mind, if ever I see fit to need them."

With a smile, Mr. Jackson nodded and turned to
fetch his wife, who stood by the stove, pouring coffee. Mrs.
Madison came over with Alexandra's plate, and Christine
carefully followed behind with a cup of steaming coffee.
Alexandra felt like food would choke her at this moment,
but she didn't want to hurt Mrs. Madison's feelings. She took
the plate onto her lap and carefully took the cup from her
sister. She nibbled on a ham biscuit, and the coffee did seem
to warm her wind-chilled body. Christine sat at her feet and
leaned against her knee.

All of a sudden it struck Alexandra that she didn't
hear Lee's sniffling! Frantically, she searched with her eyes
around the room. Exhaling, she sat back in her rocker. There,
by the front window in another rocker, sat Mr. Madison with
Lee, asleep on his lap, sucking his thumb. It pained her to see
her six-year-old brother reverting back to his baby habits. But
she couldn't bear the thought of scolding him today. Maybe
the thumb-sucking would stop in time.

She slipped the uneaten biscuit plate under her rocker
out of her sight, eased back onto her chair, and finished her
coffee. The warmth of the fire seemed to melt the ice from
her toes and toast her cheeks. As she watched the flames
dance over the logs, Alexandra thought of Pa. She could just
see him swinging his ax onto the log and it splitting right
down the middle in one whack! How strong Pa was.

She could hear his hearty roaring laugh as he teased
James. "One day, boy, if you are lucky, you'll have this kind of
muscle. Maybe even a hair or two on your chin!" Pa would
slap his knee and throw back his head in laughter.

James would puff his chest out and cry out in protest.
He'd grab the ax and start swinging. "I'll prove I'm all man
— even without the chin hairs!"

After most of the logs were split and James sat upon a stump, sweating and puffing for air, Pa would laugh, "Pride, son. A little ribbing and I get my wood chopped in half the time! You fall for it every time!" With his head thrown back, he would roar with laughter!

Alexandra smiled just remembering his laugh. She watched James smiling ever so slightly into the fire. Was he hearing Pa's laugh, too?

Above the fireplace on the mantle sat Ma's prized pewter candlesticks. The set of four had been a wedding gift from Pa. Ma loved to set them out on the table for special occasion meals. Ma would be giddy with excitement when the candlesticks were set out. Alexandra remembered the last time that occurred — just two months before the fever struck Pa and then Ma. The lace cloth had been spread across the table. Baked beans with bits of leftover ham had simmered on the hook over the fire. Ma had even baked two pies of dried apples. Alexandra could still see the twinkle in Ma's eyes as she set all four candlesticks on the table.

"A girl only turns sixteen once." Ma had reached over and hugged Alexandra.

Alexandra could almost feel Ma's arms around her now. She'd give anything to feel that again.

Gingerly, Alexandra reached down and stroked Christine's hair. She looked around and noticed the house was emptying. Lee was awake. Mr. Madison had fixed him a plate and seemed to be doing a good job at getting Lee to eat.

Alexandra noticed Christine watching the table. "Why don't we fix you a little something before Lee eats it all, huh?" Alexandra stood, took her cup and plate, and led Christine to the table.

James had gone to bring in the night's wood with

Christoph Schmidt. The Glens were sweeping the floor and straightening the chairs. Old Widow Stephans was throwing out the dish water. Mrs. Madison was putting away the food and dishes. Alexandra fixed Christine and James a plate. There was just enough cider for the little ones, and Doc Cannon's wife was just setting a fresh pot of coffee on the stove. James would need it when he came back in from the evening air. Alexandra turned her attention to the remaining guests as they paid their last respects, promised help in the future, and said their good-byes. Sighing, she shut the door and turned into the room. As Mr. Madison stoked the fire, James was sitting to the table to eat. Lee was finished, but sipping his cider.

Alexandra noticed Christine was still picking at her plate. Alexandra thought to herself, 'Christine seems to be acting so much younger yesterday and today than her eight years.' She shrugged, walked towards Mrs. Madison, hugged her and said, "You are too good to us. Thank you for all you have done to help. I'm not sure I could have gotten through this without you."

Mrs. Madison took Alexandra's face into her warm, weathered hands. "Oh, child. I wish I could do more than cook and clean for you. If I could take some of that hurt from your eyes I would. Lord knows that I would. You keep praying. He'll make it all work out. That I know. But where He can use this ole grandma to help you, I'll be there."

Alexandra felt that now-familiar lump come back to her throat. Her heart felt it would burst with sorrow. Afraid she would lose control of her emotions if she spoke, she just nodded.

James was up from the table, back by the fire sipping his coffee and talking to Mr. Madison. The older gentleman had his hand upon James' shoulder. James' jaws tightened with emotion. Alexandra said a quick prayer that Mr. Madison would see James was struggling and leave him be. She knew how he hated to show his emotions in front of folks. He would be so embarrassed to shed tears to another man. Only she had seen her brother cry. As Ma had lain near death, she had called to speak to them. Alexandra and James had knelt by her bedside as she had wheezed and whispered her dying wishes. She'd begged James to keep the family together and to try and keep the farm. She'd told them how proud she was of them and made them both promise to seek God's guidance and to remain faithful to His commandments. Ma had praised Alexandra for the lady she was becoming, then made Alexandra promise to be a mother to Lee and Christine, and when marrying time came that it be to a man of God. Then Ma had touched James' face, and told him what a comfort it was knowing he would be left to raise her family.

"Pa is proudly looking from heaven," she had told him. James had begged Ma not to go and sobbed upon her breast. She'd smiled as tears streamed down her cheeks, and told him to be brave and not to deny her a piece of heaven. She'd said Pa was saving her a seat. James and Alexandra had cried through their 'I love yous.' In a weak and quiet voice, Ma had begun to sing "Amazing Grace." Both children had felt a gentle peace settle over them. They, too, had begun to sing. Ma had smiled, closed her eyes, and went to meet Pa. James had reached over and held Alexandra, and they had cried. Oh, how they'd cried! Then her brother had stood up, washed his face, and went out to the barn to build Ma's coffin. While he was out there, Alexandra hadn't known what James did, said, or thought. It had been very late when he'd come in. He had been in complete control of himself ever since.

Alexandra admired his bravery. She only hoped, for his sake, he would be able to control himself at least until the Madisons left. Mr. Madison must have sensed something, for he patted James and turned away. James walked to the table and sat down his cup. He took Lee's hand, and Lee said his good nights to the Madisons. James took him to the back bedroom to get ready for bed.

Mrs. Madison offered to stay for the night, but Alexandra felt they had been kind and generous enough with their time. After promising to stop by tomorrow, the Madisons headed for home.

Alexandra leaned her back against the closed door. Open, it had chilled the room. She pulled her shawl tight around her shoulders. Christine sat in a chair hugging her knees. Alexandra walked over. Hand-in-hand the sisters went to their room. When Alexandra came back out to the sitting area, James was reading from Pa's Bible by the fire.

"Christine finally drifted off to sleep." She sat down next to James on the footstool.

He nodded. "Yeah, I put Lee in my bed, and he agreed to close his eyes. That is about all it took. Quite a day for two small ones, huh?"

With her elbows on her knees, she rested her chin on her hands. "What are we going to do, James?"

James looked down at Pa's Bible. He slid his hand over the opened page. "Here it says, 'My help cometh from the Lord, which made the heaven and earth.' I figure if I keep reading and praying, He'll tell me what to do."

Looking into his lap, Alexandra saw the underlined passage. "Psalms 121. Does it help, James? I hurt so bad I can hardly bear to read. I pray for guidance, but I feel so numb. I know it is sinful, James, but ... I'm ... I feel ... I feel just full of anger! How could God take both Ma and Pa, James, how could He?" Fresh tears blazed her cheeks as sobs heaved in her chest. Shame flushed her, and she hid her face in her hands.

Tears welled up in his eyes as James stroked Alexandra's hair. He flipped through the Bible and stopped at Psalms 23. "Alexandra, we have to pray what Ma taught us when we were too young to even remember. Pray and wait. We can't question God. He is our shepherd. Oh, girlie, I feel like a whole load of logs are resting on my chest and an ox is sitting on my shoulders. I'm scared, real scared, but this here book tells me to trust in Him. Without that, there is nothing. I'd be lying if I said I haven't had some angry thoughts, but that's over now. Tomorrow is a new day. There is work to be done, children to be fed, and a farm to manage. Ma said to take one day at a time. That is the only answer I have for now. Let's get through tonight and in the morning, we will talk about that day, okay?"

He looked down at her and smiled. Alexandra wiped away her tears and nodded. They knelt together, and James prayed. They rose, hugged good night, and Alexandra went to turn in for the evening. James tended to the fire, bolted the doors, and blew out the lamp.

LIFE MOVES ON

The frost crunched under James' boots. With lantern in hand, he hurried across the yard to the barn. When he returned to the house, he could smell sausage all the way on the porch. The rooster was crowing with the first hint of light beyond the horizon. As James set the pail of milk by the dry sink and the basket of eggs on the table, he nodded a frozen good morning to Alexandra. He walked over to the fire to thaw his hands and face. She met him with a steaming cup of coffee.

He held the cup up to his nose. "I like yours better than the ladies' last night. I still can't take it so strong. Thanks."

Alexandra smiled; she appreciated her brother's praise. "Ma said a little brown sugar in a man's coffee takes the bear out of him. Breakfast will be ready in a few more minutes. I let Lee and Christine sleep in a while, just today, okay?"

He sipped his coffee and nodded. "That's fine. I'm sure they are worn out with all the company and such yesterday. Well, tomorrow is here, so I guess we need to lay out our plans. Any thoughts?"

Alexandra stirred the porridge and turned the sausage as she spoke. "I need to plan lunch and supper, do the daily chores, and today is supposed to be wash day."

James nodded in remembrance. "I'll fill the extra barrel with water in the lean-to. Can you get the wash buckets by yourself?" She nodded and he continued, "Okay, well, Christine will need to help. What can Lee do?"

She shook her head and shrugged. "I figured he would help you today. What are your plans?"

James scratched the side of his face as he looked across the room out the window towards the barn. "I was figuring to move the cows out to the west acres and clean some stalls. As mild of weather as we've had, I figure plowing is just around the corner. Pa plowed everything in just one month. I'm afraid it will take me longer to turn over the garden, grain, and corn fields. I've never done such alone before. I reckon I'll try to mend, clean, and do things close to home over the next week or two, then I'll concentrate solely on the plowing. I guess Lee can tag along with me until plowing time."

Alexandra dished up two plates, and they sat down and bowed their heads.

Breakfast was beginning rather quietly in the dim stillness of the dawn.

Alexandra broke the silence. "Have you gone through Pa's papers yet? I was wondering if there were any instructions about the farm. I guess Christine will still go to the summer session of school in town. Lee is supposed to go also this year. Though I might need Christine's help for some canning. Do you think Lee could help with the harvest? I hope the neighbors will turn out to help some, too. What do you think, James?"

James stared at his sister's face for some time, then smiled and placed his spoon down. "Tell me, with so many different thoughts and worries buzzin' around in your head, how did you manage to cook this nice breakfast without catching something afire? Glory be, Alexandra. I thought we decided to take one day at a time. Here you've got fields plowed, planted, tended, harvested, and ready to preserve. You must be exhausted!" He let out a chuckle.

Alexandra's cheeks burned with embarrassment. "I'm sorry. I know my faith is weak. I shouldn't worry so. Ma told me more than once I look for trouble before it even gets here."

James reached over and patted her hand. "Girlie, how about grabbing Pa's Bible for me while I finish this fine feast you have fixed for me." He went back to his breakfast.

Alexandra stood and put her hands on her hips. "Now you're teasing me. Sausage, porridge, and coffee never amounted to a feast, but I guess I'll take a compliment from the likes of you, however lop-sided it is." Smiling, she returned from picking the Bible up out of the rocker where it lay from last night's reading. "You know, it isn't Pa's anymore. It is yours, James. The way you have turned to it lately, I'd say it is rightfully to be called your Bible now."

Now it was James' turn to blush a fine shade of pink.

He pushed his plate back and turned to the front section of the family's recorded history. "Here is the marriage certificate of Ma and Pa. My birth, your birth. Ma even wrote our conversion dates in, too. Here are Julia and Noah's dates. Here are the birth dates of Christine and Lee, also. I guess you need to fill out the rest. Pa always said you had as pretty handwriting as any lady he'd ever seen."

As Alexandra rose to get the pen and ink bottle, she smiled to herself. It had always made her feel special when Pa had said that. Ma would scold not to become prideful over such, though. That special feeling didn't last long.

Alexandra sat staring at the lines on the page. She felt if she didn't put it in writing, it wouldn't have to be true. But she also knew that wasn't reality.

She dipped the pen in the ink and read,

"Edward Charles Williams
born August 19, 1851."

Then she read as she wrote: "died February 7, 1889."

Next she read,

"Grace Leigh Townsend Williams
born December 16, 1854."

Then she read as she wrote: "died February 21, 1889."

Now it was final ... true ... and real. There was no denying it now. It was written in the family's Bible. A single tear rolled down Alexandra's cheek.

"That looks real pretty, sis. Pa is smiling down on it, I just know it." He blew on the ink to make sure it was dry enough to turn the page. About that time, there was a yawn behind him. James turned to see Christine stretching in the bedroom doorway. "Day is half over. About time you got up, sleepy head."

Christine looked out the window at the morning sun's glow. She smiled and rubbed the sleep from her eyes. "You all talking woke me up!"

Alexandra rose to serve up a plate for her little sister. "You run into the boys' room and see if you can stir Lee up. Tell him there is sausage waiting."

Christine shuffled into the other room. Soon the groaning and stretching of Lee could be heard all the way into the kitchen. Christine seated herself next to Alexandra's place, and Lee appeared in the doorway.

"I smell something," he said with a big yawn.

James patted the bench next to his. "Well, if you'll come have a seat, you might get to taste something, too!"

Christine giggled.

James raised an eyebrow at her. "And what is so funny, missy?"

Christine pointed at his head. "Your hair is standing up in all different directions." With that, everyone joined in the giggling.

James sat upright, trying to look dignified. "This, young lady, is the latest hair-do style of the hard-working, toboggan-wearing cow milkers!" With that, the whole house erupted with a roar of laughter. "All right, Miss High Fashion, let's settle down for grace and your meal."

They took each other's hand and bowed their heads.

When James finished prayer, the little ones ate while he looked up a verse in his Bible. "Matthew 11:28: 'Come unto me, all ye that labour and are heavy laden, and I will give you rest.' Well, when we are troubled or upset in our hearts, we need to pray, and God will make it better for us."

Lee finished his milk and glanced up at James with a look full of hope. "Do you mean 'cause it makes me sad Ma and Pa are in heaven, that Jesus will send them back to us?"

Christine looked over at James and seemed to be holding her breath. Alexandra's eyes filled with tears as she saw Lee's begging expression.

James stared at the Bible for a moment, then he turned and put his arm around his little brother. Lee snuggled close. "No, little buddy. That is not going to happen. Ma and Pa are at peace in heaven. No more fever, chills, or coughing. No more pain. It is a place filled with joy. We need to remember that and be happy for Ma and Pa. That verse simply means God will help us know what to do now. Okay?"

Lee nodded, and Christine turned her disappointed eyes to her plate.

Alexandra smiled, reached across the table, and touched James' hand. "That was very nice, James. Thank you."

Once the meal was finished, they all knelt by their seat, and James had prayer to start their day.

THEIR BEST

With James and Lee out in the barn and fields, Alexandra and Christine set about the tasks of wash day. Not just three days ago, Alexandra and Mrs. Madison, with the help of Doc Cannon's wife, Susie, had scalded the walls, floor, and furniture in Ma and Pa's bedroom, along with all their bedding. The clothes they had labored in during their illness had been burned. Doc had wanted the room … *sterilized* … he'd said. It was an awful-sounding word to Alexandra. She had felt like she was wiping all traces of Ma and Pa out of the room. As hard as she had tried not to cry, tears had burned her cheeks the whole time. Neither Mrs. Madison nor Ms. Susie had said anything about that, and Alexandra had been glad. She felt too old to cry in front of folks not family, but try as she might, she couldn't help herself. The next day, several ladies from their small country Mennonite church had come to clean the house for the funeral. Keeping busy had helped Alexandra not dwell on what was happening. Fortunately, last night, everyone had tidied up before they left. Alexandra was glad. After breakfast dishes, she now had more time to devote to wash day.

It seemed to take her twice as long as Ma took. 'Well,' she thought, 'it won't get done just looking at it.'

The water was finished boiling on the stove, so she and Christine lugged buckets of the hot water out to the back porch to commence with the scrubbing. They scrubbed the clothes out on the porch, then came back in to stir and boil the white shirts, petticoats, handkerchiefs, undergarments, linens, and aprons.

Mrs. Madison had taken the Sunday tablecloth home last night. She said there were too many spots gotten on it to leave for the girls to do.

Alexandra lugged the basket of clean, steamy clothes out to the line. Christine handed her each piece, and Alexandra pinned them to the rope. Back inside, they went to get ready for the dark clothes. James came over long enough to take the old water out to the garden sight again. Alexandra wondered what she would do come plowing time. How would she lug those heavy tubs of water to the garden? A small voice whispered in her ear, "lo I am with you alway, even unto the end of the world ..."

Right there on the side porch, Alexandra closed her eyes and prayed silently, "Forgive me, Lord, for my weakness. I know You are taking care of things. Help me to stop worrying so. Even if I must lug that tub of water, I believe You can give me the strength to do it. Amen."

Christine stood watching her sister. "Why'd you stop and close your eyes? Are you tired?"

Alexandra flushed; she felt like she had been caught naked. "No. Well, Christine, to be perfectly honest, I was praying. My thoughts were not good, so I prayed for forgiveness. Sometimes I worry too much. I need to have more faith." Christine simply nodded and stirred the tub of clothes. Alexandra gave her little sister an assuring smile and continued, "I certainly appreciate your help with the laundry. I'm sure I could not have done this without you."

Christine beamed under her sister's praise.

Finally, the dark clothes were finished. It was time to complete the house chores. First, knowing the boys would be hungry for a snack, Alexandra quickly put two ham biscuits in a basket, and Christine ran them out to the boys. She laid Christine and herself out one each at the table. Lunch would not take long at noon, for all she had to do was warm up some of the left-overs. Both girls changed their wet aprons, and Christine hung them by the fireplace to dry.

After their snack, the girls set about making the beds that had aired out for the morning, then dusting the bedrooms, and sweeping the whole house. By the time all that was done, there was just enough time to warm up some venison stew and apple turnovers, and to set the table. Right as Alexandra was sending Christine to ring the dinner bell, they heard the boys washing up on the porch. Alexandra ladled stew into the bowls. Christine carefully poured the coffee. Alexandra had already dipped some buttermilk for Lee and Christine.

James and Lee sat across from the girls.

After prayer, James sniffed the stew. "A good hot stew warms my soul. Everything looks real nice, girls. That wind is a might raw outside. Those clothes ought to be blown dry and stiff by evening."

Alexandra nodded. "I agree. Our hands are chapped from washing in the wind. The house blocked the brunt of it, but it still managed to sneak around the corner. We'll take the clothes in before supper, and then tomorrow will be ironing day. Christine has been a lot of help."

Christine blushed and smiled.

James nodded toward Lee. "I think we have a future farmer on our hands here. Lee has worked hard without complaining. I was wondering if this afternoon we might get something hot for snack. It is right nippy in the wind. I need to rub some salve on Lee's face. It is getting chapped up something fierce."

Lee stopped eating long enough to crinkle his nose. "I don't want that greasy stuff on my face!"

Christine spoke between spoonfuls. "You better or you'll be crying come nightfall about your face burning."

Alexandra smiled at Lee. "I'll put it on good but thin so it won't feel greasy." Turning to James, she spoke. "I'll send out something warm later. Shall I send a half pot of coffee, too?"

James got up to dish himself some more stew. "No. Save the coffee for supper. Water will do us just fine. This stew is good. Do we have anything else left from yesterday?"

Alexandra nodded as she dished Lee and Christine second helpings. "I think there is enough to spread out over at least four more meals, maybe just adding little things to go along. Our coffee supply should hold up a good bit, no stronger than you and I like it. The tea will make it through winter for Lee and Christine." She turned back to the stove and pulled out the turnovers from the warmer.

James leaned back in his chair, bit into the turnover, and sipped his coffee. "If you get time this afternoon, I'd like you to list all our supplies, so we can figure out how long they'll last or how much they'll cost to replenish. We'll look it all over after supper."

Alexandra nibbled the edge of her turnover. "I'll find the time. Mrs. Madison said she would stop by sometime today. She'll know the cost of anything we should need, and she can help me figure how long things should last."

James stared down into his cup. "I'd rather you and I do that on our own. Some folks still think that we are too young for all this and ... well, I just think our business should stay within the family. Pa never told all the town folks the how and when and other details of his providing for us. I ... well ... I just think this should stay personal. Now, don't get me wrong, Alexandra. I really like the Madisons, but we don't have any kin, 'cept some far off uncle and his brood that we haven't seen in ten years. It needs to be you and I that decide things now."

Alexandra fingered her cup. "Whatever you say, James. I'll do as you ask this afternoon."

James stood up to leave the table, and Alexandra took Lee to the bedroom to put salve on his face. Christine began to clear the table.

After the boys left, the girls commenced washing, drying, and putting away the dishes. They decided to surprise the boys with hot fresh gingerbread for the afternoon snack. Christine felt very grown when Alexandra let her stir up the batter. While that baked, the girls wrote down the name of all their goods and the amounts remaining. Then they went to the cellar to list what was left from harvest. Pa and James had done real well with the hunting and trapping.

The girls stopped at three o'clock to carry the gingerbread out to the boys. Lee jumped up in the air and let out a 'whoopee' when he saw his big slice of cake. James thanked Alexandra for the surprise, and the girls headed back to the house.

Christine skipped all the way back. "James said I was turning into a good cook! Lee even looked for crumbs in the basket."

Alexandra smiled. "Yes, I think we gave them a nice surprise."

When they came across the field and entered the

yard, they spied Mrs. Madison knocking at the door. They hollered out, and she turned around and put her hand over her eyes. Once she caught sight of them, she sent a big wave. The girls hurried across the yard to greet her.

"Hello, girls! I came to help with your cleaning, but from the looks of that clothesline, you've been busy this morning."

They stopped running as they neared the porch. Alexandra called out, "Yes, ma'am. I need to pull them in soon."

After hugging each girl, Mrs. Madison turned and followed them into the house. "My, everything is so straight and clean. Do I smell gingerbread, Alexandra?"

Alexandra and Christine grinned at each other. "Yes, ma'am. Christine baked the boys a surprise snack. Can I cut you a piece?"

Christine blushed and looked at her toes.

"No, thank you, dear. You save your sweet-smelling gingerbread for your desert tonight. It does smell like you did a fine job, Christine," Mrs. Madison praised.

Christine replied in a shy voice, "Thank you."

Laying her coat and shawl on the back of a chair, Mrs. Madison took a deep breath. "Okay, ladies, what can I help you with?"

Alexandra looked from Mrs. Madison to the floor. She knew she needed to finish her list for James, but she couldn't share that information. "All that is left for our day is to clean out the ashes, bring in the clothes, start supper, and mend some of the boys' work clothes."

Mrs. Madison put her hand to her chin and crossed her arms in thought. "Well, if Christine can take care of the ashes and you the dry clothes, I'll be glad to take a look at that mending. We'll think about supper within the hour. How does that suit you?"

Alexandra smiled. That suited her just fine. She could finish checking the inventory of the cellar, and then bring in the clothes without much trouble. Both the clothesline and an entrance to the cellar were outside of the house. When she stepped into the lean-to, a door opened out of its back side into a half-underground cellar; that way no matter what the weather, Pa had said, the girls could always get into it. She could take care of both chores without anyone to notice her.

She went to her room and brought out her sewing basket and the items to be mended. Christine took the coal bucket and shovel first to the oven, then to the fireplace. She was taking the last load of ashes out when she saw Alexandra finishing at the clothesline. Christine ran out to help bring in the three baskets.

"Thanks, Christine," Alexandra lauded.

It took two trips to bring in the baskets. Mrs. Madison had mended two shirts, one pair of breeches, two pair of socks, and an apron. Alexandra thanked her profusely and admired her quick, neat work.

"You hush now, girl, or those sweet words might go to my head." Mrs. Madison tossed her head back and laughed. The girls joined in.

Christine lugged the clothes baskets into their bedroom to put the mended items up.

Mrs. Madison led Alexandra into the kitchen. "Now, what are you planning for supper?"

Alexandra looked at Mrs. Madison and wrung her hands together. "Well, I was thinking of dicing some left-over ham and potatoes with an onion and making hash. There are a bit of green beans left, coffee, and the gingerbread."

Mrs. Madison stared at Alexandra and slowly smiled. "I owe you an apology. I underestimated you." With tears in her eyes, she continued, "Your mother, I am sure, is so proud of you. I guess I am not needed after all this evening."

Alexandra reached over and hugged Mrs. Madison. "You have helped so much this afternoon. What you did would have taken me at least four nights to finish. Plus, Christine and I really enjoy your company."

Christine came over and hugged Mrs. Madison, too.

The older lady hugged the girls back and wiped away her tears. "All right, I can see I am still loved. Shall I dice the ham while you do the potatoes before I head back home?"

Alexandra smiled and reached for the knives. "I would really appreciate that."

Christine set the table while Alexandra and their kind neighbor prepared the hash to be cooked. As Alexandra cut up the onion, Mrs. Madison dried her hands and walked to her coat. After the shawl and coat were snugly in place, she wished the girls a good evening and let herself out the door with a promise to visit soon.

By the time James and Lee were heard on the porch, coffee was ready, and the aroma of fried hashed potatoes, ham, and onions filled the house. The hint of gingerbread still lingered in the air. The boys looked cold and tired. Alexandra turned to help wash the dirt off of Lee. Then Christine held the plates as Alexandra served each one, then poured the coffee. Everyone sat and joined hands. After prayer, the boys ate with a serious conviction. Alexandra had to admonish Lee for fear he would choke. Alexandra told about Mrs. Madison's visit and her help with the mending. Lee excitedly described, as Christine listened with wide eyes, about how the cows mooed and tried to go opposite of what James told them. He laughed as he explained how one cow swished her tail, turned her back, and stuck her nose up in the air when they tried to get her to move.

"But James slapped her rump. She kicked, then took off trotting!" Then Lee sat up straight with a serious look. "But it wasn't so funny in the barn. We shoveled at least fifty tons of old straw and manure out of there. I don't see how those animals live like that!" He pinched his nose and continued eating.

Christine laughed. "I'll take washing clothes on a cold, windy day anytime over shoveling manure!" She glanced at her aching, chapped hands.

James caught sight of Christine's grimacing expression. "Alexandra, can't you fix something up to take the sting out of her hands? Yours, too, for that matter," he added as he grabbed her own wrist and held up her chapped hand. "I don't recall Ma's hands looking like this. Did you use too much soap or something?"

Alexandra tucked her hands into her lap and snapped at him defensively, "No, I didn't. It was just the wind, James Edward. I've been doing wash with Ma for near 'bout nine years. I know how to put just enough soap. At bedtime, I'll coat our hands with salve and then put on some old linen gloves. They'll be fine in a day. Ma's hands were toughened from years of work and wash. See how mine aren't as chapped as Christine's."

James watched this outburst with raised eyebrows. "Well, excuse me, Alexandra Paige. I didn't mean to ruffle your feathers."

Alexandra noticed all eyes staring at her. She then realized she had slightly raised her voice. She lowered her eyes to her plate and pushed around her green beans. "I didn't mean to sound so loud. I'm sorry. Do you want more coffee?"

James nodded. "Is there any more hash? It is powerful good. When we hit the porch, I knew if this tasted half as good as it smelt, we were in for a treat."

Lee jerked his head up and down in agreement.

Alexandra dished up more hash, then the dessert. She and Christine washed and dried dishes, put away the food, and straightened the kitchen while the boys rested by the fireplace. When the girls joined them, Lee's eyes were half closed, and he kept yawning.

James chuckled. "If we don't hurry and have devotions, Lee will sleep through them." He opened his Bible and flipped through the pages. After a moment he shut the Book and closed his eyes. He opened them and looked at each person. "How about a song tonight?" Everyone smiled and nodded. "Let us see ... 'Blessed Be The Name.'"

Lee sat in Alexandra's lap and leaned back on her. Christine sat on the floor and leaned against James' chair. After the song, they all knelt. By the end of prayer, Lee was asleep, leaning his head against the chair. James picked him up and took him to the bedroom. Christine hugged Alexandra good-night and headed to bed.

Alexandra kissed her cheek. "I'll be right in to put the salve on your hands. Brush your hair out and wash your face first."

Christine stopped in the doorway and stood facing the door frame. "Can I use Ma's lavender soap tonight?" she hesitantly asked.

Alexandra wanted to scold, "No! That is Ma's for special occasions." But she remembered Ma wouldn't be having any more special occasions.

Gently, she walked to Christine and raised the child's

chin up. "Not today, but for Saturday baths we'll use it to smell of Ma for Sunday."

Christine's eyes beamed. "Thank you, Alexandra!" Off she went to prepare for bed.

After the younger ones were tucked in, James and Alexandra sat at the table using the oil lamp for light. James studied the supply list for a few minutes. Then, with a pencil in hand, he laid down the paper. "All right. I need you to estimate how long each item can last us under normal, everyday living."

Alexandra wrote beside each item her estimate.

"Okay. What are we in need of right now?" he asked.

Alexandra thought hard. "Flour is running low, and so is lamp oil. Other than that, I can't think of anything."

James looked at the list with a glazed stare. Alexandra wondered what he was thinking. She hated to break into his deep thoughts. Finally, he looked at her. "It is eerie, or I guess a better word is amazing."

Alexandra looked confused. "I don't understand."

"Well, you remember what a bountiful harvest we had. Pa kept going on and on about it, then the trapping and hunting were truly a stroke of luck. Pa said it was like three years rolled into one. He was able to dry, salt, smoke, and trade more than he had in the last two years combined. He paid the bank note off for the house and even set a little aside. You and Ma preserved and stored enough for three families our size. It was like the Lord was preparing us for this time. We stand to make out well until next harvest. If I tend to the farm right and you handle the garden, we should fare well."

Alexandra stared at her brother and let his words sink in. "But James, Pa had experience and your help. Even the neighbors came to trade labor with him. How will you do it alone?"

James looked at the table and then into Alexandra's eyes. "I guess just like that. What I can't do alone, I'll trade for labor." He paused for a moment before continuing. "I know the Lord will give me direction and strength. He won't fail me, and I can't allow myself to fail Him or Pa. I have to try my hardest to keep up."

Alexandra couldn't keep her head up. With flaming red cheeks and tears welling up in her eyes, she whispered, "Oh, James. Will I ever learn to trust and have the faith like you? It seems all I am doing lately is praying for forgiveness. I do have confidence in you. And in my heart, I know God will see us through. I'm sorry."

James delicately turned the pages of the Bible. He stopped at Matthew 6:25 and read, "'Therefore I say unto you, Take no thought for your life, what ye shall eat, or what ye shall drink; nor yet for your body, what ye shall put on. Is not the life more than meat, and the body than raiment?'" He looked up at Alexandra. "Ma and Pa are gone, but we are still being looked after. Pa talked a lot last fall while we worked together. Something in him told him his time was near …"

With a gasp, Alexandra interrupted, "He told you he would die soon?!"

James shook his head. "No. He never just came out with it, but looking back, it is like he was preparing me. At the time, I just took it as a father-son thing, but it all feels different now."

Alexandra stared at her chapped hands. Silence hung thick in the air.

Tears fell from her cheeks when Alexandra finally spoke. "Oh, why did I not pay closer attention? Ma sewed feverishly for many nights to get two new quilts made. Remember how we thought it strange for everyone to get new outfits for the holidays? And all that extra canning. I complained so childishly about the extra work. The sweet talks we had as we labored together! I'd give anything to talk with Ma again, no matter how much work was involved!" Throwing her hands to her face, Alexandra sobbed.

James nervously stood up and walked up beside her. He knelt down on one knee and placed his arm around her shoulders. He fought the lump in his own throat as she cried on his shoulder.

"We can't go back, sis. But we can make the most of each new day. Now, here." He took out his handkerchief. "Wipe off your face. You don't want to wake the children. Today was a good day. We won't be this lucky every day. Lee didn't drown me with a million questions. He was so tired, he didn't even cry tonight. Christine seems to be holding her own. Let's you and I try to hold it together, too. I need your help. I cannot be strong by myself."

Alexandra cleaned off her face and sat up. "I'll do better. I guess I'm just plain tired myself. Can you show me that passage in Matthew again? Maybe if I memorize it, it will help me through the rough moments."

Together, they reread the passage, knelt, prayed, and turned in for the evening.

GOING TO TOWN

The next day dawned to a busy household. Lee and Christine rose with James and Alexandra. The morning's sunrise glittered on the frosted ground as the boys crunched across the yard from the barn. Lee kept making little clouds with his breath. James carried the morning's milk and Lee the eggs. Over breakfast, the conversation centered over the remainder of the week's schedule. It looked like a trip to town would be necessary in order to prepare for plowing. James needed some farm supplies, and Alexandra had a small household list. With Ma and Pa having been sick most of January and February, their passings, and then the funerals, Alexandra felt like she knew nothing of the goings on in town. It was decided a trip to town would be good for everyone. Today being Wednesday and ironing day, tomorrow being baking day, then Friday would suit. Friday it was then!

The remainder of the day went as smooth as the day before. The ironing and cleaning were near done, and the meals so far seemed to satisfy everyone. About three o'clock, there was a knock at the door. Christine and Alexandra looked up at each other, then the door. They both wondered who it could be. Christine ran to answer it. There stood Mrs. Stephanie Glen with a crock in her hands and a jar of peaches under her arm.

"Oh! Do come in, Mrs. Glen," Christine said with a

small curtsy.

"Good afternoon, girls. I remembered this was your Ma's ironing day. If you are anything like I was at your age, Alexandra, it'll be a few years yet 'fore you're as quick as your Ma. I was a married woman with a child before I could iron as quick as my ma." She chuckled as she laid the crock by the stove. "I brought supper so you won't have to stop and fix anything. It's just chicken and dumplings, pickled peaches, and I've some stewed carrots out in the buggy still."

Gazing at Mrs. Glen in disbelief, Alexandra's brow glistened with sweat from the heat of the ironing. Her hair was coming down and sticking to her skin. Her sleeves were rolled up, and her apron was dirty. She grinned slightly and nodded. "You are very right about the ironing. I'm sure Ma would have been done by lunch, but I know I've got at least another hour's work here. I'm grateful for you remembering us. You have done me a very nice favor, Mrs. Glen. Thank you."

Christine ran out to the buggy for the carrots.

Mrs. Glen didn't stay long, just long enough to chat about the weather and be on her way.

Thursday kept the girls busy again. Alexandra and Christine did the weekly scrub-down of the house and the ironing and primping of their going-to-town clothes. Alexandra even baked cookies for the picnic they would take.

Friday dawned to a buzzing on the Williams' farm. The boys rose early to do the chores. Alexandra hurried to fry apple turnovers and make biscuit sandwiches. She had put potatoes into the ashes to cook last night at bedtime. Christine busily made beds and scurried about getting ready. After a quick breakfast and devotions, the boys went out to hitch up the wagon as Alexandra did Christine's and her own hair. She combed and fixed Christine's hair into two long plaits and tied red ribbons at the bottom of each.

'Red looks good against her chestnut-colored hair,' Alexandra thought. She looked at her own blonde tresses as she pulled her hair up. She thought it funny how Christine looked so much like James and Lee so much like herself. Somehow, she thought it should be the other way around. She chuckled at her petty, somewhat silly, ideas.

She ran to the fireplace to pull out the bricks and wrap them to lay by their feet in the wagon. The blankets were also there by the hearth warming. She heard James ride up in the wagon, so she headed to the door. The food was packed under the seat. Lee and Christine piled onto some straw and wrapped up snugly. Alexandra sat next to James in Ma's place and James took the reins, just like Pa had. Suddenly Alexandra's heart seemed to skip a beat. This was their first trip off the farm without Pa and Ma. As James shook the reins and started the horses towards town, Alexandra thought of all the firsts that lay ahead for them. With heaviness in her heart, she wondered how Sunday would be. That was the family's favorite day. Their congregation of the Mennonites was still small enough to hold church just once a month in the winter when the minister came to town. He traveled between three small churches right now. Traveling was more difficult in winter, so the other Sundays Pa had read from the Bible, Ma had told a story to the younger children, and many hymns had been sung. The prayer was always shared by all, and the restful day had seemed to bring a closeness that Alexandra had enjoyed. How would this Sunday feel? The cold stung the tears in her eyes.

Easter was just a few weeks away. When times were tight, Ma had always made herself and each girl a new bonnet. In better times, she would sew a new spring dress for each. Last year, Ma and Alexandra had gotten bonnets, but Christine had gotten a new dress. Already by September, Alexandra had to let the hem down. She must remember to speak to James about the tradition. Suddenly, Alexandra felt James' eyes on her. She looked at him, then quickly turned to face straight ahead and look at the road over the horses.

"Out with it. You are too quiet for comfort." He gave her a sly grin.

Flushing, she kept her gaze ahead. "I am sure I don't know what you mean."

James turned his attention back to the path. "I thought you were excited about going to town. Changed your mind? I can drop you off over here at the Madison's."

Alexandra shook her head; she didn't want to dampen the day with her morbid thoughts. She took a deep breath and smiled. "No, sir. I am excited. I just got carried away in my thoughts for a moment. Say ... one minute you complain about a girl's chattering, the next, you say I'm too quiet. Seems to me you, my dear brother, are wishy-washy!"

Lee laughed. "What is wishy-washy?"

James chuckled. "It means you can't make up your mind what you want."

Christine nodded. "Alexandra is right. You boys are wishy-washy."

Lee laughed and shook his head. "Not me. I know what I want. Licorice!" he announced with confidence.

Everyone laughed!

When they reached town, James let the girls off in front of the livery stables. He left Alexandra with instructions concerning the shopping and plans to meet at the mercantile. First, the girls walked down to the grist mill for a while. Then, they walked past the smithy. Christine squealed when sparks flew from the anvil. The hotel seemed as busy as a beehive. There was a buzz coming from all the customers in the dining section, and people seemed to be in a constant stream in and out of its open doors. Across the street, music and laughter could be heard from inside the saloon's swinging doors. Ma had always made a point never to walk down that side of the sidewalk. Pa and Ma spoke sternly against the evils of strong drink, smoking, and such fraternizing. Alexandra made sure she didn't even turn her head in that direction.

The bakery was next to the mercantile. The sweet aromas of the fresh bakery items made Alexandra's stomach flutter. 'It must be closing in on lunch,' she thought. Then she remembered she hadn't eaten much breakfast due to her excitement that morning.

The girls entered the mercantile and immediately turned many heads. A slight hush fell throughout the store. They paused for a moment under the attention. Alexandra took Christine's hand and walked towards the dry goods.

Mrs. Susanne Jackson came from behind the counter. "Alexandra, how are you doing? How are you holding up, child?"

Alexandra wanted to turn and run from all the sorrowing stares, but she looked straight at Mrs. Jackson, stiffened her back and with some effort, smiled. "I'm doing fine, ma'am. We're just in town to fetch some supplies. I'd like to order a few things, and then James will come around in a while and settle up and load the supplies."

Mr. Jackson came alongside his wife. "I can put it on the books and have the stock boy bring it out to your place, if that would help, Alexandra."

She shook her head and handed him the piece of

paper. "Thank you kindly, but it won't be necessary today. Here is the list of dry goods. Mrs. Jackson, I'd like to look at the calicos, if I might."

Mrs. Jackson laid her hand over Alexandra's. "You go right ahead. I need to finish with Mrs. McRoy and Mrs. Evans, and I'll be right over there to assist you."

Mr. Jackson left to go discuss the list with the stock boy, and Mrs. Jackson went back to her other customers.

As Alexandra and Christine crossed the store to the wall of material, Mrs. Cathy McRoy and Mrs. Joyce Evan spoke to them. "Very sorry about your folks, child."

"Yes, so sorry for your losses."

Alexandra nodded a thank you and walked a bit faster. She felt nervous with all this attention. The hop had gone out of their step, and Christine looked very sad. Alexandra forced a smile and pointed to a spring-looking print. It took several minutes for her to regain Christine's interest. Finally, a dark green with tiny pink rosebuds and small foliage caught her eye.

They had moved on to the ribbon section when Widow Stephans walked in. When she spied the girls, she walked right towards them.

She laid her hand on Alexandra's shoulder. "What a joy to see you young ladies in town! I was going to send a messenger out in the morning to your place."

Alexandra and Christine both hugged the elderly lady. "Mrs. Stephans, what a pleasure seeing you."

Widow Stephans put a hand on one of Christine's hands. "I want you and your brothers to dine with me on Sunday. Minister Yoder won't be here until next week, so I thought we would fellowship together."

Alexandra tried not to lose her smile. "I don't know.

I'll need to talk with James first. We ... I mean ... it is, well ..."

"I know, child. Your first Sunday without them both. I was thinking to occupy you all so you wouldn't have to think about it. But I will understand if you'd rather not. Just discuss it and send word to me later today, all right?" She smiled lovingly.

Alexandra smiled back. "Thank you. I'll send word as soon as I speak with James."

Alexandra went to the counter and ordered some thread, a new darning needle, a peppermint for Christine, and a licorice stick for Lee. She even got a few lemon drops for James. As they headed for the door, up pulled James and Lee. Lee hopped out and ran to the candy counter to stare at all the marvelous sights. Christine walked over to admire the dolls along one shelf. Alexandra told James about Mrs. Stephans' offer. He put his hands in his pockets and looked at the floor. They stood there in silence for a few moments.

About that time, Widow Stephans walked by and placed her hand upon his arm. "James, I was selfish to extend an invitation on your first Sunday. I can see how special this day will be to your family. Don't go fretting about me. How about riding out on Wednesday evening to my place instead? You take your family and do as you had planned for the Sabbath."

James swallowed before he spoke. "We don't mean to appear rude, Mrs. Stephans, but Wednesday would suit better."

"Don't give it a second thought, young man. I hope it will be a good day for you all. God bless now. See you midweek."

After she left, James sought Mr. Jackson to settle the bill and load up the supplies.

While Alexandra occupied herself at the fabrics, Mrs. Jackson came up beside her. "Can I cut you anything today?"

Alexandra felt her cheeks getting warm. Oh, how she wished she didn't blush so easily!

"No, ma'am. I was just looking while James settles up. But thank you for asking." Alexandra turned abruptly to go gather the children.

Mrs. Jackson touched her arm. "If you ever need help with your sewing, dear, you let me know. The Ladies' Circle will gladly pitch in to help. Your mother has lent her fine stitchery to almost everyone in our circle at one time or other. We would love the opportunity to pay her back."

Alexandra felt a wave of pride flow through her heart. "I'll keep that in mind. Thank you for the offer."

James had placed the last of their small order on the wagon and was helping Christine and Lee into the back of the wagon.

Alexandra walked up to him. "Everyone has been kind, but I still feel uneasy about all the attention."

James nodded in agreement. He helped her onto the seat and climbed up himself. He drove them to the empty church that also served as their school. They sat under the shelter by a naked tree and set out their lunch. The wind had left since earlier in the week, so the day was bearable in the sunshine. James filled Alexandra in on the town's news that he had picked up at the smithy's. At the same time, Lee excitedly told Christine about the amazing work at the smithy. As soon as they ate, they headed back to unload, finish chores, and rest from their trip.

Once home, Christine and Alexandra unpacked and put away the supplies while the boys tended to the horses and wagon. After the evening chores and a hot supper, Alexandra brought out her surprises. Lee let out his famous 'whoopee' when he saw his licorice stick. He had minded his manners and not asked for it at the store, so it pleased Alexandra that much more to give it to him. Christine nibbled just the edge of her peppermint, intending to savor the candy for days. Lastly, Alexandra handed the tiny bag of six lemon drops to James. She thanked him for taking them along today and for his praying with her during the week.

He smiled and popped a drop into his mouth. "Thanks. I wish you had not gone and wasted your pennies on me. But then again, I do like lemon drops!"

Alexandra laughed. "I know. Ma said it was because you were part sour puss!"

Lee laughed and laughed, which made Christine laugh, which started everyone else laughing!

"Well, it must be Christmas in February. I, too, picked up a few things." James handed Lee another licorice stick and Christine a porcelain button with a rose painted on it. Lee got up and jumped around the room in delight.

Christine held her button in her hand and stared at it. "Oh, thank you, James. It is beautiful!"

James stood from the table and faced Alexandra, who was standing by his side. "I thought you might like this for your hair in the evenings when we sit by the fire." He handed her a silken blue ribbon, enough to tie her hair back. "I don't like it when your hair hangs in your face when you take it down. The flame from a candle might catch it on fire or something."

"Oh, James! I haven't had a blue ribbon in years. Thank you."

"I remember when Ma would tie them on the ends of your braids. Just like you did to Christine's this morning."

Christine grabbed her braid. "But mine are red."

James chuckled. "Yes, but Alexandra's were always blue."

Alexandra hugged James' neck. "Thank you!"

"Now, don't go getting mushy on me," James playfully teased.

The evening was short but leisurely. Alexandra brushed out her hair towards bedtime and pulled it back with her ribbon, tying a small bow on the top. As she looked in her small looking glass hanging above her wash table, she thought about how Ma used to tie her ribbons for her. She could almost feel Ma's presence. Alexandra closed her eyes and envisioned her mother's hand upon her shoulder and Ma leaning in to speak into her ear. "I love the way the blue brings out your heaven-blue eyes, dear." Alexandra could smell Ma's lavender scent. She opened her eyes, but only her own image looked back at her. 'I miss you so, Ma,' she thought.

SUNDAY

Two days later, the sun rose to a bitterly cold and breezy Sabbath. James was up early and had a fire blazing to warm up the room. He quickly left to feed the animals and milk the cow. Alexandra made sure the coffee was ready for when he came back. He hurried in the door and closed it quick as to let the least amount of cold air in with him. Alexandra took his coffee to the fire where he went to thaw.

"The wind is sharp. I feel it will bring harsh weather with it. I need Lee up to help fetch wood to the porch. Christine can help straw and extra stock the animals," he explained.

Alexandra argued, "But, James, it is the Sabbath. Can't that wait until tomorrow morning?"

James shook his head. "The wind and sky don't look kind. We need to set up for rough weather. We will be as quick as possible. I have already ran the rope from the house to the barn door and fed all the animals. One pail of milk went to the animals. The other one is there by the door. If we hurry, we should be done by ten or eleven o'clock. Have a nice big breakfast or an early lunch. I'll get Lee going, if you'll get Christine." Sipping the last of his coffee, he turned towards the bedroom.

A short time later, a well-bundled Lee and Christine headed out the back door.

Alexandra commenced baking biscuits, slicing ham, boiling eggs, and stewing apples. By the time everyone had finished preparing for foul weather, Alexandra had the food and table ready. A very hungry lot sat down.

Once brunch was eaten, the boys made their beds and then sat by the fire. Once the girls had cleaned the kitchen, they joined the boys by the fire, too. With a tired flop, Alexandra dropped into the chair. James reached for his Bible. He read from Luke. Alexandra then told the story of David and Goliath. Lee was seated on the floor in front of her chair. He sat wide-eyed and breathless. She knew it was one of his favorites. They then sang three songs from memory. Together, they knelt for the family prayer. James was silent for the longest time. Heaviness hung in the air.

When he finally spoke, his voice seemed to shake with emotion. "Our dear heavenly Father, I humbly come before You a broken, sinful creature. I feel weak, so undeserving of Your mercy. I fear this responsibility, Lord. I pray for Your guidance and forgiveness." He paused and tried to swallow the emotions lodged in his throat. "I wish some of the hurt would go away. Forgive my selfishness. Oh, how we miss Pa and Ma, but we are glad they're with You. I pray we'll remain faithful, so we'll someday meet them again. Amen."

Lee jumped right in. "Me, too, God." He sniffled. "Tell Ma I love her, and Pa, too. Help me be a good boy and not sass James. Amen."

Alexandra tried to swallow her sob, but it seemed to leap out of her throat anyway. "Dear glorious Father, forgive me for the many times I've failed You this week. I, too, pray for Your leading. I ask for Your comforting to ease my sorrowing. I want to grow more in Your Word, Lord. I've failed in my daily devotions this week, and I ask Your forgiveness. I pray for each of us in our pain, that You'd touch our hearts and ease the hurt. Amen."

There was a small silence that lay heavy in the room, and then a wailing sob came from Christine. "Dear God, I want Ma back so bad! Please don't take Pa and Ma!" She laid against the chair with her head on her arms and wept. James got up and went to her and held her close.

Alexandra tried to control her emotions as she placed her arm around Lee. But her tears just mixed with his.

James spoke softly in Christine's ear. "Hush now. There is nothing we can do to change the past. Ma and Pa are in heaven. Don't wish them back from paradise." He rocked her in his arms and kissed her head. "I know it hurts, honey, but God will ease that. You have got to have faith. God knows so much more than us." He paused. "How about we sing for Ma? I just know she would like that." He took out his handkerchief and wiped Christine's face. She looked up at him and tried to smile. "That's better. Let's dry your face good so it doesn't get chapped. Now you and Lee run bundle up."

They all stood. The small ones went to get their hats, coats, and scarves.

James and Alexandra stood beside each other, blew their noses, and wiped away their tears. James shook his head and spoke softly. "We cannot do this to them again, Alexandra. I'm sorry to have been so weak. I thought the special tradition of Sunday would help, but I had it backwards. It will never be the same without Ma and Pa. Next week will have to be different."

Alexandra watched the sorrow and pain in her brother's face as he looked in the direction of the younger ones.

Bundled and gloved, they walked out to the cemetery.

It seemed too occupied for a family who was so young and had only lived here six years. There were two wooden crosses marked in memory of Julia Charlene, who was stillborn in 1875. They buried her near Pa's folks' place where they had lived then. Another infant, Noah Mathias, had died when he was but six months old in 1879. He, too, was buried back with Julia. Alexandra remembered how her mother mourned for those babies even up until her own death. Ma had told how she looked forward to seeing Pa holding those babies, waiting for her. Then there were the fresh mounds of earth. Two, side by side. Alexandra felt a familiar ache from her head to her toes. There was that urge to run away screaming. Lee squeezed her hand tightly as they stood at the foot of Ma. For what seemed like a long time, everyone was silent. Alexandra felt as if her heart would jump right out of her chest.

James cleared his throat and began to sing. Everyone joined in. The song was weak and the tune choked by emotions, but it came from their hearts all the same.

The cutting wind and dampness of the air put an end to their serenading. After three verses of the hymn, James led them back inside. Everyone agreed to a nap. No one felt much like talking.

That night, as she lay trying to sleep, Alexandra swallowed hard to stop the tears that threatened to spill onto her pillow. Would Sunday ever be happy for them again? She closed her eyes tight and tried to forget her sorrow.

A PIECE OF ADVICE

Alexandra awoke shivering. She pulled the quilt over her head. Christine was snuggled almost underneath her. She willed herself to get out from underneath the warm cocoon of patches. Quickly, she dressed and wrapped the extra quilt at the end of the bed around her shoulders. James was stoking the fire. Its warmth did not seem to be penetrating the coldness of the house.

"Good morning. How about some coffee before I head out into the blizzard?" he called over to her.

Alexandra stood wide-eyed for a moment, then rushed to the window. She rubbed a circle clear but saw nothing but a swirl of white. "Oh, James! How long has it been falling?"

"By the looks of things, I'd say all night. When I turned in last night, I was so tired, I didn't even look outside. It might have already started then."

Alexandra started the coffee and went to wake the children.

Lee rushed to get dressed and flew to the window. "Can I go outside?"

James chuckled. "It looks fun from the inside, but it is all business on the outside. That howling you hear isn't a ghost. That wind has the snow blowing sideways."

Alexandra nodded. "That is why the house seems so

cold. The fire doesn't seem to be thawing us out any."

Christine came into the room wrapped in the bed quilt. "Will it be this cold all day?"

James added another log. "Once the stove heats up, if we maintain a steady flame here, it will thaw out at least."

Alexandra served up the coffee and hot tea for Lee and Christine. Then she set about making breakfast. James headed out through the lean-to. From the porch, he took the lead rope at the front entrance that led to the barn.

The blizzard only lasted until noon the next day. The results were a winter wonderland of white. The Williams family wouldn't make it to Widow Stephans' house for supper this week.

Wednesday afternoon, Alexandra did let the children bundle up and go play beside the house in the snow. She stood on the porch for a moment and laughed at their fun. As she turned to go back inside, bells could be heard in the distance. She turned back and with her hand to her eyes, she searched for the source of the bells. James heard them, too, and had stepped out of the barn looking. A black speck in the horizon grew bigger as it came closer. It was James and Alexandra's friends, Christoph, Luke, and Luke's sister, Mae.

By the time the cutter drew up along the porch, James was standing beside Alexandra.

Christoph pulled the reins and let out a hearty, "Whoa! Hi, fellas! We were out for a ride and thought you might want to join us. Glorious day for a sleigh ride, huh?"

Alexandra and James both laughed at Christoph's booming voice and cheerfulness.

James shook his head and kicked at the porch with his boot toe. "I appreciate the thought, fellas, but I got too much work to do. Alexandra here might just take you up, though."

He nodded in her direction.

Mae leaned forward. "Oh, do come, Alexandra! Don't leave me alone with these two bores to talk to."

Christoph tried to act offended.

Alexandra shook her head also. "Not today, but thanks."

Luke tried his luck at persuasion, but to no avail. With a big wave and shouts of good-bye, they were on their way. As James and Alexandra stood watching them ride away, a wave of envy passed over them both.

"Gosh, Alexandra. I would have watched the children. You should have gone," James replied as he put his work glove back on.

"James, I don't have time for ... for ... well, for such foolishness. There is supper and chores to tend to. Why didn't you go along?" Alexandra retorted.

James watched the sled shrink to a black dot. "Pa never ran off to ride with his friends. Can't say as you would be happy with no milk or eggs gathered. There are a few spots on the barn I need to tighten up that the wind blew loose. They won't fix themselves." He looked at his feet and then started off for the barn.

Alexandra watched his back until he disappeared into the barn. She wondered if she would ever go on another sleigh ride or attend another hymn sing. She remembered how much James loved the last youth activity they attended. A taffy pull! 'James has such a sweet tooth,' she thought. She searched the horizon for the black speck, but it was gone. No more laughing, bells jingling, or crunching of the sleigh against the cold snow. Around she turned, into the house, to start another meal. Alexandra sighed.

Once supper had begun, Alexandra stepped out onto

the porch to call Lee and Christine in to change into some dry clothing. She caught herself chuckling at the lopsided snowman her little brother and sister were putting the finishing touches on. As she pulled her shawl tight around her shoulders, she took a deep breath and thought to herself, 'This is why Ma never minded the extra laundry our playing caused. The happy expressions on Lee's and Christine's faces are worth the extra work.' The smile slowly faded from Alexandra's face as she wondered again if she herself would be able to frolic or just plain feel young ever again.

The next Sunday rolled around to a brisk day. It was an exciting day, the Sunday the preacher was in town. The night before, the Williams had bathed, so they got up and dressed quickly. Between the wind and the sun, the snow had been packed down or blown aside. They got to church early as to have time to talk amongst their friends. James had arranged to eat at Widow Stephans' in place of last Wednesday. He was determined not to relive last Sunday.

Once Alexandra had seated Christine and herself, she looked around to make sure Lee had settled in with James. She noticed that James was seated towards the back with the men, instead of up front with the boys his own age. As she turned and focused her attention to the front, she began to wonder if she should have sat in the back with the grown ladies. Here she sat, right up front, with the youth girls. She decided she would talk it over with James later.

Alexandra had sat beside Tonya Martin. Tonya grabbed her hand and gave it a squeeze. Monica Unruh and Mary Evans leaned up to smile at Alexandra. She thought how nice it felt to see her friends.

Soon Brother Jimmy, Luke's father, got up to lead an opening song. Alexandra wished they could sing all day. She felt warm inside listening to the hymn. Next, Brother Lou, Christoph's father, spoke a few words and led the opening prayer. When Preacher Melvin Yoder stood to address the congregation, Alexandra just had to smile. She really loved church. She thought how much Ma and Pa loved Sundays. She would miss Pa's thoughts and his deep, smooth singing voice. Oh, how Ma could read poetry or tell the children a story. Alexandra tried hard to concentrate on the words of the minister so she wouldn't cry. The preacher spoke about heaven. It seemed so real now to her. How special the Word was to her. She found a peace thinking of Ma and Pa there now holding Julia and Noah.

Alexandra had a longing within her heart about heaven. Before, she of course believed in heaven and wanted to end up there as a Christian, but she never had this longing before. She silently prayed a thanksgiving for the assurance she felt that her ma and pa were in heaven.

Standing around after the service, Alexandra listened to the events in the community. Tonya, aged sixteen years, raved about the new calicos at the mercantile. Monica, seventeen, told about the quilting circle's newest quilt design and the border staying with the Glens. It was their nephew, Joe Samuel. Sixteen-year-old Mary was bubbling over about the hymn sing classes starting in July. Four whole nights of lessons! Christoph's mother, Renée, and Doc Cannon's wife, Susie, were organizing it. Alexandra couldn't wait until then. Immediately a sobering thought struck her. How would she and James ever attend a hymn sing?

Lee tugged her skirt. "James said we'll wait for you by

the wagon."

Alexandra turned to say her good-byes.

"Oh, do come by to knit one day," Tonya pleaded.

Mary grabbed her elbow. "There will be a hay ride the first warm Saturday of spring. Say you will come!"

Alexandra forced a cheery smile. "I'll try, girls, but it's hard to get away now. Lee and Christine need me, and James works so hard at the farm. But, well, just maybe it will work out."

She turned to flee to the wagon, but Monica followed and grabbed her arm. "I'm sorry, Alexandra. We went on and on about such silly things. If we have pressured you about things you are not ready for — well — please forgive us. We are just silly girls. If you need help, please call on me. I really am sorry about your ma and pa."

Alexandra reached over and hugged Monica. "Forgiven. Thanks for understanding. I really mustn't keep James waiting. See you." She turned and ran to the wagon.

James was finishing settling the children in the back of the wagon. "Widow Stephans will be waiting on us." He helped Alexandra onto the seat.

"I'm sorry. I could not seem to tear myself away," she whispered, flushed with shame. She would make sure and apologize to Widow Stephans for her thoughtlessness.

When they pulled up to the house, Widow Stephans greeted them at the door with smiles and hugs. The house was warm and smelled of ham, beans, and fried apples. Seated around the fire were Minister Melvin and his wife, Hazel. They were a comforting couple of about fifty-five years. He was a soft-spoken, yet powerful speaker. She was a meek, loving, positive spirit. Alexandra was glad they would be sharing lunch together. Alexandra sat the loaf of bread and the berry preserves she had brought upon the table. She greeted the Yoders affectionately.

Soon everyone was gathered around the table enjoying the delicious, uplifting meal. The minister asked James several questions about the farm. The two of them spoke at great length about James' responsibilities. Ms. Hazel was very inquisitive as to Alexandra's weekly schedule now. She also inquired about how Christine and Lee were getting along.

With a watchful eye, Widow Stephans sat quietly listening. Suddenly, she laid her spoon down, leaned into the table, and looked directly at James. "I want to know why you didn't go on that sleigh ride you were offered?"

There was silence.

James blinked and looked at her for a moment. "Well, I had chores to tend to."

Lee piped up. "James said he never seed Pa sledding instead of working."

Christine grinned at Lee's awful grammar.

Widow took a deep breath and spoke in a cracking voice. "Son, your pa was a grown-up, married man. You are a boy. Now, don't get me wrong. You are a good, responsible young man — young being the point. Your pa's life ended here on earth, not yours. You and your sister have to keep on living. It warms this old Christian heart to hear how dedicated you both are to doing right by your family, but you must do right by yourselves, too. Now, I want to do my part to help. When you come to town, I'll gladly have Lee and Christine spend some time with me. They are a help and a joy. I am not much at getting out and traveling a lot, but I am sure I can arrange for help to come out to your place when it is needed. Wives and husbands don't grow in the bean batch." She cackled and winked at Alexandra, then continued, "The

Lord can lead, but He can't make you follow. Listen to your heart. There is a time for work, but sometimes there will be a time for play. Next time ask your friends to help with your chores so you can go out with them. If Lee and Christine cannot sit alone or go with you; bring them to stay with someone for the while." She pushed her chair back and stood up. "Well, this old woman has said her peace. How about some pumpkin pie with our coffee?"

James and Alexandra sat there with their mouths opened, and Minister Melvin was deep in his own thoughts. Ms. Hazel began to clear the plates with a smile on her face. Christine and Lee looked at each other and shrugged.

James was quiet throughout dessert. He wasn't sure whether to be offended or thankful at the widow's words. He thought he was doing the Lord's will. He finally decided prayer was needed more than listening to his own thoughts. He would put it aside for now.

Everyone complimented the nice dinner. Christine and Alexandra helped wash and put away the dishes. Alexandra noticed Minister Melvin speaking to James rather intently by the fire. Oh, how she would love to be a fly on the wall! She saw by James' expression that something was troublesome to him. With all his responsibilities now, she wondered if he'd ever have fun anymore. He always seemed so serious.

The ladies finally joined the men by the fire. Ms. Hazel was telling how they would stay for the night with the Unruhs. Alexandra smiled as she thought of them. That was her friend Monica's home.

Widow Stephans nodded as she rocked. "Their youngest girl, Monica, stopped by Monday when the clouds were looking bad. She helped gather wood and did lots of things around here — turned out to be a real joy to me. She said she just felt like helping. Lord bless her soul. She was telling me about a youth prayer meeting this next Friday evening. Seems they will get together and discuss some piece of the Word they agree to read and study ahead of time."

James was staring into the fire. Alexandra seemed to be sitting on the edge of her chair. How interesting it sounded to her.

"I was thinking, James. You would be welcome to drop Lee and Christine off here while you and Alexandra attend the meeting," Widow Stephans offered.

"Sounds like a fine opportunity, son," Minister Melvin added.

James slowly nodded. "Yes, sir. I'll talk it over with Alexandra once we get home. I'll get word to you by midweek, Mrs. Stephans."

Alexandra could not believe her ears! A 'maybe' from James was cause for hope. She could tell he was interested, too.

Minister Melvin seized the opportunity to inject his feelings. "You know, your friend, Christoph Whited, could possibly tell you which passage will be discussed. I feel it would be a fine occasion for an evening of acceptable socializing. I heard through Brother Alan that Brother Robert is leading the group."

Widow Stephans nodded with a chuckle. "Yes, Doc Cannon will lead it, and if I know Susie, there will be lots of fine pies for dessert!"

Alexandra could tell James was uncomfortable, so she tried to change the subject. "Ms. Hazel, will you both be staying in town long this trip?"

Ms. Hazel shook her head. "I'm afraid we will be

heading out tomorrow afternoon. There are a few people to visit, and then we must head home."

The group settled on a light supper of some leftovers and some popped corn before preparing for the evening services. In the winter services, they met earlier so everyone would not have problems get home in the cold. Around four-thirty, everyone loaded up and went back to church.

Later that night, Alexandra and James tucked a weary Lee and Christine into bed. Before turning in themselves, she and James sat at the table.

James fiddled with his fingers as he spoke. "What are your thoughts on the discussion class?"

Alexandra sat directly across from him with her hands in her lap, and she tried not to seem too excited. "I think it sounds interesting. Since it is in the evening, it would not interrupt chores. Well, I ... um ... well, what are you thinking?"

James ran his fingers through his hair. He looked up at his sister. "A part of me wants to jump at the chance to get together with my pals. But, well, we don't have much in common now. Seems like their biggest worry or responsibility is to remember not to giggle at the supper table. How could they understand what my priorities are now?"

Alexandra looked James directly in the eyes. "So that explains why you did not sit with your friends this day at church. Shame on you, James Edward Williams! I don't reckon any of your friends will ever understand your life now. You won't give them the chance. You can't keep everything bottled up inside. The weight of your load will break your spirit. Pride. P-R-I-D-E. You seem to think letting your friends be a friend is some kind of sign of weakness on your part. Even Pa liked to cut loose and laugh sometimes. He was an honest, hard-working man, he was! Yet he knew when to stop and enjoy life, too!" She paused to temper her emotions. "This house was a home because of the love, security, and laughter that filled it. Right lately, with all the grief and losses, it is just a house. It is time to make it a home again." For a while, James just looked at her. Alexandra tried to steady her breathing.

Then he slowly smiled. "Remind me to think twice before I ask you what you think again, okay?" Alexandra blushed and smiled. "All right, sis," he continued, "we will go to the meeting, weather permitting, but I don't want either one of us lolly-gagging around Saturday because we are tired. I did talk to Christoph about the Scripture they will be discussing. It is Matthew 7: 1-14. The meeting runs six o'clock until seven-thirty, then refreshments until eight-fifteen. If we help clean up and pick up the children soon afterwards, we can be home by ten or ten-thirty. That will not put us in bed too late. Christoph said all the youth have said they would all come but us. Mae's cousin, Marie, from up north, will be in town. There is also the Glens' nephew. I think his name is Joe something."

Alexandra nodded. "Monica said it is Joe Samuel. Tonya said her brothers, Matthew and Michael, were coming, but Carl felt he was too old. He turned twenty-six last month. Mary's brothers, Brent and Chad, will go, and Monica's older siblings, Faith and Larry. With Luke's and Mae's cousin, Marie, and Christoph's sisters, Joy, Annie, and Amy, it should be quite a discussion!"

James nodded. "All right, I'll get word to Widow

Stephans. But let's not forget what needs to be done this week, so we can go."

After a time of prayer, they both headed off to their beds.

THE YOUTH MEETING

That week the weather stayed cold but fair. Each morning for her devotions, Alexandra read her passage for Friday night and gave it much prayer throughout the day.

Friday came at last! Everyone busily chipped in to do their chores speedily. They took turns taking baths and putting on their second best outfits. Alexandra and Christine even had enough time to make a small pie to take to Widow Stephans' house with them. Christine packed her sampler to take along. Lee decided to take his checker board.

Finally, the time came to head towards town. Once they pulled to a halt in front of Widow Stephans' house, the children hopped out and ran to meet her at the door. Alexandra took her the pie and thanked her for watching Lee and Christine.

Back on board the wagon, James and Alexandra headed across the small town to the Evans'. The Williams arrived at the same time as the Schmidts. When Luke saw James, he let out a big 'whoop!'

Mae popped her brother on the arm. "Please act civilized, you savage!" With a laugh, she waved to Alexandra.

The boys tied up the horses, while the girls ran to greet each other.

Mae hugged Alexandra with enthusiasm. "I have sore missed you, Alexandra. How have you been?"

Alexandra blushed and stood surprised for a moment, not quite knowing what to say. Just then Mary rushed out to greet the girls.

Mary pulled her coat tight around herself. "Girls, come in quick before you are chilled to the bone. Hurry!" And she ushered her friends into her home.

Meanwhile by the stables, Christoph slapped James' shoulder, "Boy, am I glad to see you. It has been too long, buddy."

Shyly James nodded, with his hands in his coat pockets and his collar turned up against the cold. "Nice seeing you, too, Christoph."

The guys stood outside the door for a short time talking, while the girls headed inside to hang up their coats and hats, and to assist Mrs. Evans. Mary and her brothers had helped their mother get just about everything set up already. After a few final touches, the boys were called in to begin. After the prayer and welcome, the night was opened for discussion. Alexandra was excited but also a little nervous. Doc Cannon started the quiet group with some open-ended thoughts. Soon, Luke and then Joe added their ideas to the circle. Mary and Amy also had a few questions to ask and even a point of view or two on the text.

James was quiet for the longest time. When they first sat down, Alexandra had watched how he fumbled with the cover of his Bible and looked more at the floor than around the room. By mid-evening, he had settled in more and was intently studying those who were speaking. Just before the discussion was coming to a close, James spoke up. Alexandra tried not to smile, but she couldn't help herself. James' thoughts were clear and plain, his voice, quiet and calm. Alexandra could just envision "Pa" sitting across from her.

James looked relaxed. He looked so much like Pa. Quietly, she said a prayer of thanks. By the end of the discussion time, Alexandra felt refreshed. Being in the room surrounded by her friends, she felt a glimmer of her old self, the self before so much grief, awakening.

Doc Cannon asked Matthew to close the meeting with prayer. As girls went to help Mrs. Evans and Mrs. Cannon serve snack, they talked and giggled. Alexandra actually found herself laughing as Amy told tales on her brother Christoph and Tonya made fun of her brother Michael's primping for the night's event. She teased that he took longer combing his hair than she took pulling up hers!

Alexandra caught sight of James out of the corner of her eye as he and Matthew stood by the kitchen door, laughing. She did not know what about, but just the fact that James was having a good time made her feel warm all over. James soon walked up and began helping Mr. Evans and his boys put the furniture back where it belonged. Doc Cannon had help from the other boys loading the chairs he'd brought from his house back onto his wagon. The night finally ended and everyone thanked the Evans and departed into the dark.

Saturday dawned to a bright day. It would prove to be a warming weekend. Alexandra thought James walked with a lighter step this morning. As breakfast cooked, she and Christine busily chatted about the evening before. Christine told how Mrs. Stephans had taught her a new stitch for her sampler. She laughed as she described how at checkers the widow had beat Lee four times! After everyone was seated at their places, grace was said, and the boys hungrily dug into the food on their plates.

Alexandra smiled over at James. "It was a nice evening, wasn't it?"

James nodded and answered between bites. "I thought so, too. I was really impressed by Larry's thoughts. You could hear the conviction in his points."

Alexandra sighed. "I thought the visitors seemed real comfortable. I was glad Marie offered her thoughts."

James held up his fork as to stress his thoughts. "But my favorite part ..." he paused.

Finishing his sentence for him, Alexandra burst out laughingly, "was the pies!"

Everyone joined in the mirth.

James looked sideways at Lee. "How was your evening?"

Lee looked over at Christine, who had begun to giggle.

He looked very seriously at James. "Well, to be honest about it, Widow Stephans whooped me bad at checkers." Then he let loose a wide grin. "But the cookies she had made and the pie we sent made the evening end well after all!"

Everyone laughed again. Alexandra thought to herself what an uplift spiritually the meeting had been, and how she did not feel as desolate after being with her friends again.

As the boys started out to work and the girls began to clear the table, a wagon was heard drawing up to the house. Everyone headed to the door to see who was coming to visit. James opened the door to see Christoph hopping off a wagon and helping his sisters, Amy and Joy, down. Luke and Larry jumped out of the back. Larry helped his sister, Monica, down. On the porch, the Williams stood staring at the crowd of new arrivals.

Amy, aged nineteen years, stepped up first. "We are here to help out. We all miss your company, yet we understand your new responsibilities. So, we talked it over, and here we are. Now, Alexandra, tell us girls where we can get busy."

Larry, Christoph, and Luke stood side by side with their hats in their hands. Christoph stepped forward. "Such a pretty day means field work. So, we figured you would need field hands."

James and Alexandra just stared in disbelief. They looked from each friend to each other.

James smiled at his sister, then put on his hat. "Well, I guess we had better get to the field, then!"

Everyone smiled, and a group "yes, sir" was spoken. The girls went into the house, and the guys headed to the barn. Joy, fifteen, went to make the beds, and Christine was assigned ash duty. Monica went about straightening and sweeping. Alexandra and Amy started on the lunch and morning snack. They knew they would need a man-size meal for that crew.

At ten o'clock, Monica and Alexandra toted a warm snack of sourdough biscuits, blueberry preserves, and thin slices of fried yams out to the field. Although the guys were at work, their spirits were light. They talked and laughed as they ate. It did Alexandra good to see James smiling so much. Soon, the young men stood up, graciously thanked the girls with compliments, and went back to work. Alexandra called out to James as to whether he thought Lee should come to the house.

He shook his head. "No. I don't think we could get finished without him."

Lee grinned, stood a little taller, and followed James

back to his appointed assignment.

Lunch rolled around none to soon for the guys. The ladies had prepared quite a feast: fried chicken, boiled potatoes, succotash, stewed turnips, fried cornbread, boiled ham, stringed beans, and fried onions. They set out the sweet potato pie and two blackberry pies Monica had baked the night before. James asked Larry to return thanks.

After a lively meal, James cleared his throat to speak as he poked his fork into his half-finished piece of pie. "I want to thank you all for helping today. Ladies, this was a fine meal. I feel real blessed by your friendship."

There was an awkward silence, and no one wanted to look up.

Finally, Luke spoke up. "If we are totally honest, James, I have got to admit, we are here for selfish reasons." Alexandra and James, confused, just looked at him as he continued, "We have all missed your company. So since you both have so much work here, we figured we would come here, and that way we would get to see you both."

Everyone smiled.

Lee held up his plate. "Can I have another piece of pie and a slice of ham?"

Everyone laughed.

The girls cleaned up the mess left from lunch. Happy chatter filled the house.

Monica busily scrubbed the table. "Before we leave, we would like to help arrange for supper."

Amy nodded. "You know, after such a big lunch, you would not think the boys could eat a snack. But, after chopping all those fallen trees, I know my brother; so let's decide what we will take out at four-thirty."

Joy giggled. "Lee hinted that he had not had

gingerbread in a long time."

Christine stomped her foot. "I made him gingerbread just two weeks ago!"

Alexandra laughed. "Well, to Lee's stomach that must be a long time."

Amy smiled. "Okay, gingerbread and a pot of coffee."

Meanwhile, as the boys walked back to their work, Larry cleared his throat. "James, I owe you an apology."

James looked confused and shook his head. "Not that I am aware of, Larry."

Larry shook his head, too. "Just hear me out. Between your Pa's getting sick to now adds up to near two months. I should have been by to help long before now. But, I guess I have no excuse but thoughtlessness. I didn't ever think about your new responsibilities. Seeing you and your family Sunday hit me upside my head."

Luke nodded in agreement. "Me, too, on the apology, James. I figure if I had shown myself half the friend I thought I was to you, you would have been more comfortable asking for my help."

Christoph nodded also. "James, it was plain heartless of me to drive out here on the sleigh. If Luke and I had an ounce of sense, we would have stayed and helped you work that day. I am truly sorry."

James bit hard to swallow the lump in his throat. "Forgiven. But it isn't your responsibility to take care of us. I would not expect you fellows to give your fun up for this work. That is my duty."

Christoph stopped and faced James. "We are brothers in Christ. Your burdens are our burdens. That is just the way it is."

Everyone went on to their axes and nothing else was

spoken on the matter.

The young men enjoyed their snack, especially Lee. Soon after the snack time, the guys came back, and the girls were helped into the wagon. Monica extended a Sunday invitation for the noon meal; James accepted. The Williams stood on the porch and waved their good-byes and shouted their thank-yous.

A tired but happy crew sat down to eat after washing up.

Alexandra spoke first. "Oh, James, wasn't it a glorious day?"

James nodded. "We fellas got three days of work done. It was awfully good of them to help me. Chopping has never been a favorite chore of mine."

Lee looked up from his plate with a mouth full of food. "Guess what, Christine?"

Alexandra interrupted him. "After your mouth is empty, please."

Lee swallowed hard as Christine looked on impatiently. "Luke let me ride on his back part of the way back from lunch!"

Christine giggled. "I had fun, too. Amy let me mix the gingerbread, 'cause Alexandra told her I made a good cake!"

Lee rubbed his stomach. "I sure think so!"

Everyone chuckled.

James looked at his sister. "I'll be able to work up some of the garden, weather permitting, beginning of the week now. I had figured on chopping until Wednesday or Thursday. But today took care of that. End of the week, I need to start work on the corn and wheat fields. I am not sure how long that will take."

Alexandra got up to refill the cups. "Some of the girls

are getting together to sew soon. I was wondering about Christine and me."

James looked up, not understanding her question. "What about you?"

"Well," she hesitated, "Easter, spring, and summer are coming." She paused, and he waited for her to continue. "Ma usually sewed bonnets and dresses now."

James went back to eating. Christine and Lee watched and waited.

Finally, James spoke. "Look, Alexandra. That is all girl stuff to know. Just say what you think is needed, and we will see what we can actually afford."

She thought that over for a while as she dished out seconds for everyone. Lee was already yawning when they finished and began clearing the table. James went to help Lee wash up by the stove and get ready for bed; then it was Christine's turn to wash off.

Alexandra was laying out their Sunday clothes when James joined her.

"Lee was so beat he almost slept through his washing. I prayed with him and tucked him in. Where is Christine?"

Alexandra shrugged. "I'll go check on her." She came back from the bedroom smiling. "I guess it was a busy day for them. She was asleep on top of the quilt!" She laughed. "I tucked her in."

After they both took their turns privately bathing in front of the stove, they settled down near the fireplace.

Alexandra sat, holding her hands in her lap, looking into the fire. "James, I'd like to make Christine a new spring dress, and a summer dress for school session. Lee has grown so much since last summer, I figure he will need a pair of trousers and a shirt for school."

James nodded. "For material and notions, how much will you need?" Alexandra did the math aloud, and James thought it over for a moment. "I guess they will need a slate and chalk for school, too?"

Alexandra shook her head. "Just Lee. Christine's is fine from last year. I still have a box of chalk for them to use."

James continued to stare into the fire. "When are you girls going to sew?"

"A week from Tuesday," answered Alexandra.

"If we ride to town this Tuesday after lunch, will that be soon enough?"

Alexandra smiled. "Oh, yes, James!"

James explained, "We will eat an early lunch at home and plan a cold supper to make it easier. Will that work with your wash day?"

Alexandra nodded. "I can manage that."

After devotions and prayer, they called it another day.

ANOTHER SUNDAY

Sunday would prove to be as beautiful as Saturday. After a nice devotion, a story of Noah and his ark, and a few hymns, everyone dressed and loaded into the wagon.

Monica came out the door waving as their wagon pulled into the Unruh family's yard. Larry came out to help take the horses and wagon out to the barn. Lee and Christine followed Alexandra into the house. Anthony and Clara Unruh stood behind their daughter, Faith, aged twenty years, and welcomed them to their home. Faith took the dish that Alexandra was holding. Monica's other older sisters, Hope, twenty-five, and Erica, twenty-three, were also there with their husbands. Hope's little boy was crying in the background, so Monica ran in to pick him up. He was a hefty boy of one year. Lee and Christine volunteered to spend most of the day with him playing on a quilt.

Glancing at the food, Mrs. Unruh shook her head and hugged Alexandra. "You shouldn't have troubled yourself."

Alexandra smiled. "It is stewed carrots. We wanted to contribute something to the meal."

The men went to sit by the fireplace, and the ladies all went to finish setting the table. Soon everything was ready and the men were called to lunch. Hope gave instructions as to the seating arrangement. Mr. Unruh cleared his throat and asked everyone to bow their heads.

After the amen, Mr. Unruh welcomed the Williams to his table and invited them to make themselves at home. "I even had Clara make extra so you could eat like you do at home, James."

Christine giggled.

James blushed and grinned. "I'll try and control myself a little, Mr. Unruh, but it looks like that will be hard!"

Mrs. Unruh shook her head and laughed as she passed a bowl of turnips around. "Now, Anthony, you stop picking on James. You help yourself as many times as you like, James. It does the cook good to see someone enjoy her cooking."

Mr. Unruh, being a rather "healthily"-built man, rubbed his stomach. "I'd say you stay happy most of the time then, by the size of me!"

Everyone laughed with him.

After the meal, the host decided to wait dessert into the afternoon. The feeling was shared unanimously. All the men-folk retired to the parlor area to stretch out and relax. The ladies cleared the table and washed the dishes. Afterward, they joined the men.

When fresh coffee was ready, Hope and Mrs. Unruh began to bring out plates of dessert and cups of coffee. With Lee dozing near James' chair, Alexandra was free to talk with Monica about upcoming sewing days. Monica told how all the ladies had voted to have a special day set aside every other month to catch up on regular sewing and tying off quilts, in addition to special times just for quilting. The thought was that the second Tuesday and Wednesday of the summer months might suit. Before lunch would be the sewing; then after lunch would be the quilting . Some of the elderly ladies would just quilt all day. Alexandra said she thought it was a fine plan. Monica went on to explain that Mrs. Cannon was going to ask around for the final consensus this Thursday. Alexandra told Monica to cast her vote for her so no one would have to come all the way out to their farm. Monica promised she would.

Larry and James were sitting in one corner of the room playing checkers. Alexandra could hear them mumbling something about an upcoming youth activity. Oh, how she wished they would speak up! After James finally beat Larry, he stood up and began to say his good-byes, gathering up the family. Lee had awakened a little bit earlier and polished off his dessert. He and Christine had even split a second helping. Mrs. Unruh tried to persuade them to stay for supper, but James said he wanted to head towards home before it got too dark. There were still the animals to be fed, also.

As they were departing, Monica slipped Alexandra the latest copy of *The Youth's Companion*. The youth always passed around the newest edition of this wholesome and encouraging Christian periodical.

After several good-byes and come-agains, they headed towards home. Once they were on the road, Christine began to sing. Soon Lee and Alexandra joined in. It wasn't long before James piped in also! Alexandra felt good in her heart. 'Maybe Sunday could be special again,' she decided.

LAUGHTER

Monday, crisp and fair, opened to roosters crowing, cows mooing, and James whistling. When he stepped out the back of the barn to throw some scraps to the pigs, something caught his eye. As he squinted to see better in the still-dark morning, he made out the shadow of someone sitting on something. Why, it was Alexandra! 'Now what is she doing outside at this hour?' he wondered . Then he realized that she was at the cemetery visiting Ma. He turned back towards the barn. He didn't want to intrude upon such a private time.

Alexandra shivered and pulled her coat tighter around herself. Her mittens didn't seem to be keeping the chill from her fingertips. But that did not dampen her spirit. She continued telling Ma about what a nice Sunday they had with the Unruhs.

"Oh, Ma, the food was delicious. Monica and her sisters and I sang several songs. Mr. Unruh said it helped his digestion." She giggled, remembering. "The fellowship time is doing James so much good. I forgot to tell you about Saturday! Christoph, Luke, Larry, Amy, Joy, and Monica came and helped us work. I could have kissed them! Oh — well — not the boys, Ma, just the girls, I mean." Alexandra blushed.

"I guess my mouth is talking quicker than I am thinking again. Ma, the ladies are going to have a set sewing time every other month — every month for the three summer months. I'll try to sew small, tight stitches just like you taught me. I have taught Christine two more stitches for her sampler. Widow Stephans showed her a new one, too." Thinking about all the help and kindness caused her to get choked up. "Everyone has been real kind to us."

Alexandra felt tears building up, so she stood and picked up her stool. "Well, Ma, I guess I need to start breakfast and get the children up. I miss you and Pa. I love you, Ma," she added quickly, turned, and hurried into the house.

There she washed the tears from her eyes, stoked the fire, and went about making breakfast.

When Tuesday rolled around, it looked like it would be a normal wash day. But just as the breakfast dishes were being put away and the wash water was coming to a boil, there was a knock on the door. Christine and Alexandra looked at each other, wiped their hands on their aprons, and hurried to the door. There stood Mrs. Stephans and Tonya!

Alexandra was stunned for a moment. "Welcome. What brings you out today?"

Tonya giggled. "It is wash day, isn't it?"

Alexandra nodded, but still she did not understand. "Well, yes, but ..."

Widow Stephans interrupted, "Well, that explains why we are here! I'll boil the water and cook for you today, and Tonya came to stir and scrub. Matthew went out to the barn to help James and Lee."

Alexandra put her hand to her mouth for a minute, then smiled. "I am glad to have the help. Thank you."

Tonya smiled. "You had better wait and see if I do a good job on the spots before you thank me!" She laughed and took off her coat and scarf and laid them in the chair.

While the water was finishing heating up, Alexandra ran out to talk to James about their company. They decided to go to town tomorrow instead and not say anything about their original plans to their help.

As the girls did the laundry, Tonya told Alexandra about next month's discussion group. "Some time this week, Mr. Jackson will send word around as to the Scripture to read. The meeting is going to be at Doc Cannon's house."

Alexandra smiled as she scrubbed the collars of the boys' shirts. "I really enjoyed last Friday night. I wonder who will be in town for this time?"

Tonya wrinkled her brow. "Well, Marie will probably be gone home by then. She leaves next Friday, I believe. Joe Samuel has taken a job with Deacon Henry. I saw him working on the new building by the bakery. I hear he is good at carpentry. So, I guess he will still be in town. This town is growing too fast for me sometimes!"

Alexandra nodded.

Widow Stephans laughed. "Oh, if you girls could just see it from these old eyes! My, there seem to be people everywhere. When I was a young girlie, I would go months without seeing a soul other than our household. Now-a-days, I'm lucky if I go an hour without seeing someone!"

The week rolled on. Friday evening at supper time, everyone sat around the table eating and chatting when Alexandra realized James was staring at her!

"Do I have food on my face?" She quickly wiped her cheeks.

James smiled and shook his head. He looked from one sibling to the other. "I have been thinking about all the hard work we have been able to complete this week. With the weather staying nice and the help we have had, things have gone real fast. How about we pop corn by the fire and read from *The Youth's Companion?*"

"Yes!" everyone yelled out at once.

"Okay," he laughed, "but first we boys need to bring in some wood and shut up the barn. After everyone washes up and the younger ones put on their night clothes, we will have a bit of fun."

Alexandra and Christine hurriedly cleaned the kitchen and ran to their rooms to get ready.

By the time Alexandra had the big bowl and the popping corn out, James had the fire just right.

Christine brought over two shiny apples. "These are still firm enough to roast, don't ya' think, James?"

He took them in his hands and looked them over. "I think they will roast up nicely."

Alexandra went over to the kitchen to get some molasses sugar to sprinkle over the apples and some salt for the corn.

Oh, what an evening they had! Lee and Christine squealed with giggles as the corn began to hiss and pop! Alexandra took in a deep breath, inhaling the aroma of popped corn and roasting apples. Everyone enjoyed their treat. Alexandra meant to eat slowly as to savor each bite, but it was so good she gobbled hers down like everyone else!

With their stomachs full and their bones weary, the Williams children settled back to listen to a story from *The Youth's Companion* . By the end of the story, Lee was asleep leaning back on James' lap. Christine was yawning, yet smiling.

"I love stories! When you read, Alexandra, I can see the whole picture in my head. Thank you."

Alexandra smiled. "I enjoyed it, too. It was a wonderful idea, James."

James picked Lee up and headed to the bedroom. "Yes, I enjoyed it, too. Many more helpings of potatoes and I won't be able to lug this heap of boy around any more!"

Christine giggled as she hugged Alexandra good night. Alexandra straightened everything up and cleaned the remains of their snack. James came out to help her. Together, they knelt to pray, and then turned in for the night.

On Tuesday, after Alexandra spent Wednesday through Saturday cutting out clothes to sew for Lee and Christine, James took Alexandra to the Madison farm. From there Alexandra and Mrs. Madison rode together to sewing circle.

The ladies had decided to start each gathering off right with a rotating devotional schedule. After that, everyone pitched in to help each other. This particular day, Mrs. Madison and Widow Stephans said they were not making anything for themselves, so they helped Alexandra with Lee's trousers and shirt and the green calico and a brown gingham school frock for Christine. Several grandmas and great-grandmas from the town quilted all day, continuing into the afternoon following lunch. Each lady always brought at least two food items, and the hostess and her daughters — or appointed helpers if there were no daughters — were in charge of laying out the meal.

After the sewing day, Christine's spring dress just needed hemming, and Lee's trousers and shirt were completed except for buttons and hem. Alexandra was very pleased. By school time, she knew she could have Christine's other dress sewn.

Christine squealed at the sight of her new dress! Alexandra had cut it long so it would last longer. James said it looked real lady-like. Christine liked being called a lady. Lee said it looked like any old dress to him.

James laughed. "One day, you will see it differently. If not, at least you will learn to say it differently!"

THE NEXT STEP

The hard physical labor of spring's chores kept the family exhausted and too busy to concentrate on their sorrows. With plowing, planting, and weeding, there never seemed to be many free moments. Nonetheless, the Williams family did take a minute or two for fun. Once in the middle of cultivating the garden, a sudden rain shower began. The girls and Lee were staking their rows and picking out any twigs that had blown in last winter and fall while James plowed the soil time and time again. Almost without warning, the sky tore open and poured buckets of water upon them. Try as they might to scurry to the house, it was of no use. A rain earlier in the week had made everything soft. It took no time to make everything — mud!

'Slip and slide,' went James, trying to get the horse towards the barn. 'SPLAT!' went Lee as he tripped, landing face down! The girls spun around and ran to help the very upset Lee, only making matters worse. They both slid to a stop and landed feet in the air and behinds on the ground in a splash right beside him! No one could get up — they were laughing too hard!

Once they finally made it to the porch, reality set in. Alexandra took a hard look at herself and the children. Lee whined when she announced a Wednesday bath was in order. And oh! All those extra mud-caked clothes to wash! Then,

Alexandra caught sight of the "mud monster" walking her way from the barn, and she burst out laughing again. She would wash a ton of extra clothes — she didn't care. It was worth it!

Not long after, on a beautiful, warm, bright, and busy late spring morning, Alexandra and Christine were hanging out a load of freshly washed clothes. They could hear the month-old piglets squealing from behind the barn. It was Lee's chore to feed and tend to the pigs. The squealing and Lee's hollering grew louder by the minute. Yet, being hard at work, the girls did not pay much attention to it. All of a sudden, a piglet went pell-mell through Alexandra's legs! Alexandra screamed, lost her balance, fell back, and sat with a 'plop' onto the ground! Christine shrieked, then burst out laughing. Lee dashed by, chasing after the little piglet.

By the time the dust settled around Alexandra, she had caught her breath and spotted Lee running after the piglet. She began laughing — and laughed so hard, she could not get up! James appeared from inside the barn to investigate all the ruckus. What a sight he witnessed: Lee running around the yard yelling after the very confused and very fast little pig, Christine pointing at Lee and her head thrown back roaring in laughter, and Alexandra sitting right on the ground holding her side and just plain belly-laughing! He shook his head, joined in the excitement, and helped Lee chase the pig back to its home.

Both incidents made for quite a few giggles.

During this same time period, the Williams household also found a time or two to attend the monthly youth gatherings. In April, they met at Doc Cannon's house as planned. Alexandra really enjoyed it. It was a little smaller than the first one, because Marie had headed home and Christoph's family all had colds and could not attend. That put a damper on the night for James. But, overall, they found the evening's fellowship and discussion of the Beatitudes very worthwhile. The same proved true for the May meeting, which was held at the Schmidts' home. Luke and Mae's parents, Jimmy and Sonya, were very nice hosts. Mae and Mrs. Schmidt had made sweet caramel rolls for dessert. Discussion was on the life of John the Baptist. Alexandra didn't know who decided on the topics, but she found herself more refreshed and nourished by them than she was by even the delicious sweet rolls!

The next meeting was planned for two weeks following at the Whited home. James was excited about it. He always liked going to Christoph's house. His father, Lou, was a tall, somewhat big, and jolly man. He laughed a lot and had always treated James with much affection. His mother, Renée, was a tiny bit of a woman, who loved to sing and cook. Christoph's three sisters, Joy, Annie, and Amy, were usually giggling, laughing, or at least smiling. It was always fun to be with them. The topic would be about working on the Sabbath. It would be a little different than before, but, like James, Alexandra still looked forward to it.

About this time, Alexandra began to sense the need for spring cleaning. She had put it off as long as she could. Mrs. Madison, Mae, and Monica came to help. All furniture was moved out to the porch and yard. The floors and walls were washed and scoured. Monica spent a good bit of her time scrubbing all the cookware. Christine was assigned the task of polishing the stove. The straw ticks hung on the line to air out. Lee brought fresh straw for the stuffing over in the goat wagon from the barn. He had trained one of the young nanny goats, Missy, to pull it. Alexandra took it upon herself to scrub and clean Ma and Pa's room. It had received a light cleaning periodically, plenty enough to keep the cobwebs out. The thorough cleaning it had received right after the death of their parents had washed every bit of Ma's lavender smell out. It saddened Alexandra to come into their room. Their empty bedstead matched the empty feeling in her heart.

Mrs. Madison walked over and placed her arm around Alexandra. "Child, sooner or later you will have to empty out this room and move forward. Now, I am real proud of the way you have handled everything thus far, but the time is coming when their things will need to be sorted out. If not, the mice and moths will do it for you."

Alexandra felt that old stubborn lump crawling up in her throat and the fire burning in her cheeks.

With tears in her eyes, she looked at Mrs. Madison. "But I don't want to throw Ma's things out." A small sob leaped from her lips.

Mrs. Madison pulled her close. "Oh, Alexandra! I don't mean throw them out. Some things will be special enough to pack up for you and Christine. When you set up your own house, you will have something to put out of your Ma's. The same with Edward's things; I am sure Lee and James will find something of his for a keepsake. The things you cannot use, why, you could give to someone who is in need of that very thing!" Alexandra wiped her face and thought about the suggestion as she looked around the room. Mrs. Madison continued, "This room is larger than the boys' room. It might work better for them to move into here."

It was too much for Alexandra. She picked up her rags and bucket and sighed, "I'll speak to James about it." She hurried out of the room, leaving their dear neighbor to look around the room, then quietly pull the door closed.

After the house was sparkling and the beds remade,

their friends bid farewell to the Williams and went on their way. Mrs. Madison was nice enough to have put a beef and vegetable stew on the hook before she left.

After such an active day, the girls turned in early. Alexandra decided to speak to James at a later date. Right now all she could think of was her nice, soft, clean bed!

CR

The week seemed to fly by with spring cleaning and the gardening. Before they knew it, Saturday was upon them. Alexandra and James had decided to host a meal. They had invited Widow Stephans, the Schmidt family, and Joe Samuel. Alexandra looked forward to Mae's company, and James always enjoyed Luke. James also had enjoyed getting to know Joe at the last few youth meetings. Alexandra was very nervous about cooking for so many people. Mae and Mrs. Schmidt had insisted on making a cobbler for dessert. Widow Stephans had put her foot down about bringing the bread and her delicious scuppernong preserves. So that just left the main course for Alexandra.

She and Christine were very busy from sun up to sun down preparing for the meal. Alexandra had decided on slow-baked chicken and potatoes in a milk gravy, succotash, and fried carrots and onions. Christine had laid out their nice tablecloth and set the table with their good dishes. Later in the evening, she even went out to pick fresh flowers for the centerpiece. When the day was done and everything cleaned and put into place, Alexandra and James surveyed the room.

"Something is missing." Alexandra wrinkled her brow and sighed.

James touched Alexandra's elbow, nodded his head,

and pointed towards the mantle. Alexandra looked from the mantle to James with a gasp. James gently smiled and nodded again. She turned towards the mantle. After a few moments, she walked over and stood there. She felt her chin quiver a little, so she gently bit her lip. Delicately, she touched the candlestick.

"You are right," she hoarsely whispered. "*These* are missing."

James walked over and picked one of them up. "Ma always set them out for special occasions. Tomorrow will be the first time we have entertained alone. It seems like a right time to use them. What do you say, sis?"

Alexandra smiled. "Yes, it feels right." Together, they set one set of the candlesticks in the center of the table on each side of Christine's centerpiece. Alexandra went and hurriedly found two candles. Again, they surveyed the room.

James put his arm around her shoulders. "It looks real pretty; smells good, too. I don't think Ma could have done better."

Alexandra blushed and gently elbowed him in the ribs. "Flattery still won't get you a taste of anything before tomorrow."

James grabbed his side playfully. "Well, a guy can't help but try!" He winked and walked over to his rocker and flipped through the pages of his Bible while Alexandra silently sat looking at her hands. After some time, James cleared his throat, which gave her a start.

With a smile, he looked across at her. "All right, what is it? You are over there struggling with some problem. I cannot help if you don't tell me about it."

Alexandra gave a little smile. "It isn't really a problem. It is just ... well... I was thinking. No ..." She shook her head and still twisted her hands. "I guess really Mrs. Madison brought it up, not that it had not crossed my mind, but it is probably too soon, except for someone who might need something, although it isn't much trouble to clean as it is, but to tidy, you know, yet if you do need a bigger place, I understand."

James grabbed his ear, shook it, and gave her a very confused look. "Alexandra, I did not understand one word you said. Either I am hearing in a different language or you are speaking in one. Now, please, slowly — what are you talking about?" He leaned forward to try and understand her better.

She took a deep breath, closed her eyes, exhaled, and started over. "Mrs. Madison mentioned that maybe it was time for us to sort through Ma and Pa's room. She thought there are some keepsakes for us and some things to be passed on to those who might be in need of them. She also suggested you boys might want the bigger room."

James nodded thoughtfully and leaned back. "Well. It has been near 'bout four months. I guess I had not really thought about it before. It does make sense — their stuff just sitting there wasting away. But room size isn't everything. All we really need is space to sleep in a bedroom." He paused and took a deep breath. "There is more sunlight coming into their room." He leaned forward, exhaled, and whispered to himself, "Maybe she is right." Looking at Alexandra, he shook his head. "Well, we do not have to decide tonight. Let us just think about it and talk it over next week, okay?"

Alexandra smiled. "That sounds good to me."

After sharing devotion time, Alexandra retired to her room. James stayed up in the quiet dark to think and pray. He gave a deep sigh and thought, 'Seems like there are always decisions to be made.' Wearily, he trudged off to bed.

THE HOSTS

Sunday found the birds singing along with Christine. She was still young enough to be excited about the company instead of nervous. After feeding animals and doing the necessary chores, everyone dressed, had family devotions, and then prepared for their company. Alexandra had put on the fixings to warm and started the coffee. Lee anxiously stood by the window.

Finally, he began to dance about. "I see them! I see them!"

James got up and walked to the window. "Sure enough. But calm yourself down. You might stir up dust. Alexandra will have you sweeping and mopping!"

Alexandra removed her apron and admonished, "Really, James! I just wanted everything to look nice. I wouldn't make him polish on a Sunday. But you still must calm down, Lee."

The family went onto the porch. Finally, the wagon and buggy pulled to a halt in front of the house. James helped Widow Stephans down from Joe's small buggy, while Mr. Schmidt and Luke helped Mrs. Schmidt and Mae out of their wagon. While Lee followed James to help the men put up the horses, Alexandra led the ladies inside.

"My, how good it smells and looks, Alexandra," Widow Stephans observed as she laid her bread and preserves on the table.

Alexandra smiled. "Thank you, Mrs. Stephans."

Mae grabbed Alexandra's arm and gave it a gentle squeeze. "The table looks beautiful. Your Ma's candlesticks are lovely."

Alexandra hugged Mae and whispered in her ear, "Thank you for noticing."

The ladies finished setting the meal out while the men talked on the porch. Finally, Christine called them in to eat.

James thanked everyone for coming. "It feels nice having friends to share this fine day with us. Let us bow our heads and return thanks."

After prayer, the food began to be passed around. As the carrots with onions passed to Mr. Schmidt, he smiled. "Lee, this is how I got my orange hair." He helped himself to a large helping of carrots. "All my life, I have loved carrots!"

Lee stared with wide eyes and an opened mouth. "Well, I like green beans! What will happen to my hair?" He laid his hand on the top of his head.

Everyone laughed.

Mrs. Schmidt spoke kindly to Lee. "Don't let him pull your leg, sweetie." To her husband, she admonished, "Really, Jimmy, a falsehood on the Sabbath!"

He laughed. "I am just teasing you, Lee. God gave me this mop top of mine, not the carrots."

Lee gave a long sigh of relief.

The conversation rotated around fields, gardens, and new baby animals on the two farms. Widow Stephans announced that Preacher Melvin and his wife would be in town in two Sundays. Due to a revival somewhere else, he was coming a week late.

For dessert, Mae served a strawberry cobbler, and Alexandra put a small pitcher of cream on the table.

That afternoon, they sang and talked about the possibility of their own revival. Theirs was usually held more towards the winter months. They wondered aloud what might have prompted the other congregation to hold meetings so early. Together, they prayed for the group having their revival.

It was a pleasant afternoon. Widow Stephans let Lee beat her twice at checkers. By four o'clock, Lee was asleep in her lap as she herself nodded. The Schmidts announced their departure — all too soon, from Mae's and Alexandra's reactions. But they gathered to leave all the same.

The Williams waved their good-byes until the wagon and buggy were out of sight.

Alexandra let out a slow, soft sigh. "That was nice, James."

James turned to go check on the livestock. "Yep. Felt real good."

Lee and Christine went in to play a game of checkers. Alexandra stood on the porch alone for a few minutes, and then she decided to go for a short walk. She walked up to Ma's resting place and sat on the grass beside the foot of the grave.

"It was real nice, Ma. There was enough food even for our supper tonight. Mae left us some cobbler, too. Oh! That is what they brought for dessert — strawberry cobbler. James had two helpings!" She laughed. "I used a set of your candlesticks, Ma. I hope you don't mind. They were real pretty with the flowers between them. James thought of it. He is doing really well. Since we have been getting out some, he seems a lot happier. Christine is faring well. I think she is a little babyish sometimes, like how she still follows me around everywhere. If I leave her inside alone, she'll come running shouting my name like I have run away. James says to just give her time. She is so fearful. I dread thunderstorms! She cries through the whole storm. Lee does well, unless he is up past his bedtime. Every now and then, he slips and calls James 'Pa.' James is hoping he'll just stop. He doesn't want to say anything about it that might upset Lee. The men-folk have been real helpful to James. The ladies, young and old, have been good to me, also. Seems like someone is always dropping by to help us. You and Pa sure had a lot of friends, Ma. They have really shown their love to us. What do you think about us going through your things?" She paused for a while. "I really wish you could answer. I don't know how I feel about it. I wish I knew what was right. James says the Lord will lead us in all things — big or small. I pray He will lead us with your room. It seems hard on James, too." She caught sight of something moving out of the corner of her eye. She turned and looked towards the house. "Christine is looking for me now. She just won't let me get too far out of her sight." She began to get up. "I love you, Ma."

She walked towards the house. Christine finally caught sight of her and ran out to meet her. Hand-in-hand, they went inside the house.

SORTING THROUGH

Wednesday of the following week as they finished their morning devotions, James sent Lee ahead to the barn. Christine had gone to scatter the breakfast crumbs to the chickens.

James cleared his throat. "I was thinking Friday morning that we would go ahead and sort through Pa's room. Next week, we will be going to town for the youth meeting. It will be a good time to give away anything we cannot use. Also, Preacher Melvin will be in town that weekend. Anything that cannot be used here, he can take to the next congregation." He looked at the floor and waited for Alexandra to respond.

With her back to him, she continued to wash the dishes and tried to steady her voice before responding. With a slow nod of her head, she replied, "I'll be ready Friday morning." She was glad he could not see the tears in her eyes.

James walked to the door. "Oh, yes. I was thinking about Christine's birthday. Maybe you could help me think of something special to do."

Alexandra nodded again. "Okay." She did not feel like talking. James left for the barn. Tears ran down her cheeks. Alexandra scolded herself, 'Shame. There is too much work to be done to stand and cry in the dish water. It is just a room. If James feels it is time, then it is time. Now, stop this and straighten up!' She closed her eyes and took a deep breath.

'What was it James read this morning for devotions? Oh, yes, Proverbs 16:3.' Quietly she recited it to herself. "'Commit thy works unto the Lord, and thy thoughts shall be established.' I know James prayed about this. If the Lord is leading him, I will follow. Lord," she prayed, "please give me happy thoughts. I do not want to dread this so much."

Christine entered and brought Alexandra the pail to be washed.

Alexandra took a deep breath and put on a smile. "Christine, I feel like a song. What shall we sing?"

Christine's smile lit up the whole room. Oh, how she loved to sing! And as the girls sang, they got everything ready and began their ironing. Alexandra felt much lighter, and she loved the peace in her heart.

Friday morning after chores, all the children solemnly walked to their parents' room. James put his hand on the latch and pushed the door open. They all crowded in the doorway and peered in. They stood there wide-eyed and silent.

James broke the silence. "I don't know what we are all gawking at. Their things won't get up and sort themselves."

Christine whispered to Lee, "I hope they don't!"

James walked in and stood over Ma's trunk at the end of the bed. Alexandra went over to the dresser and ran her fingers across Ma's box. It was a simple but lovely wooden rectangle, waxed over the beautiful maple. Pa had spent many an hour carving the edges and sanding the wood until it shone like marble. Carved on the lid's center was a simple but lovely heart. Pa had given it to Ma for their second wedding anniversary. Alexandra knew inside was a lock of each child's hair tied with a small piece of ribbon.

With a heavy sigh she turned to face the others. Alexandra took a deep breath. "Okay. Where do we begin?"

James lifted the lid to the trunk. "I guess this is as good a place as any." He laid the two new quilts Ma had made on the bed. Next came a small quilt. Ma had used it when they were all babies. Ma's three bonnets — summer, winter and Sunday — were tucked in the side. There were a pair of baby booties, two tea cups and saucers that had belonged to Ma's grandmother, and wrapped in paper was the Bible that had belonged to Ma's father. Next, James pulled out a few baby day-gowns, along with Ma's wedding dress and journal.

Christine and Lee stood by the bed and stared at all the items. Alexandra chuckled as she told them about each of them wearing the booties.

Lee held a bootie against his foot. "Are you sure my foot was that small?"

James smiled. "Yes. I can hardly believe it myself." James and Alexandra looked over the items on the bed. James ran his fingers through his brown hair. "I guess you will want to put the baby things up for future babies of the family?"

Lee's eyebrows went up and his eyes got big. "Are we getting a baby!?"

Christine giggled.

James turned red. "No, Lee. I mean later. Like when Alexandra marries."

Alexandra blushed. "Please! Such talk, boys." She laid all the baby items back into the trunk except the booties. Those she gently laid inside Ma's special box.

James picked up the two quilts. "What about these?"

Alexandra shook her head. "We don't need them now, but come late fall and winter you boys can use one and we girls the other. For now, they will store better in this cedar chest."

James laid them back in the trunk.

Alexandra picked up the Bible. "This was Grandpa Townsend's Bible."

James nodded. "I have Pa's Bible. Do you want that?"

Alexandra shook her head. "No. I don't think I should take this. Ma got it because there were no sons in her family. I think Lee should have it." She laid it in Lee's hands. Lee smiled and seemed to hold his breath as he looked at the book.

James agreed. "I think that is a fine idea. But it will be put up until you learn to read from it, okay?"

Lee looked a little disappointed, but he nodded his head in agreement and laid the Bible back on the bed for now. Lee pointed to the bonnets. "I don't think I want one of those." He crinkled his nose.

James laughed. "I am glad to hear that."

Alexandra smiled. "I don't need a Sunday one; Ma made me one last spring. Christine, I'll put it up for you someday."

Christine whispered, "Oh, thank you!"

Since there were two teacups with saucers, they decided to put one up for Christine. Alexandra would put one in her hope chest. James told Alexandra that Ma's wedding dress was hers to do with as she saw fit. She decided to put it up for "someday." But they all stared at the journal as if it would bite.

"It might have girl things written in it. You read it, Alexandra." James handed it to her.

Alexandra took it but shook her head. With tears in her eyes, she protested, "Oh, James. I am sure it is all personal. Maybe we should burn it."

James spoke firmly. "I'll not burn Ma's words and thoughts. People keep a journal to record special thoughts and moments in their lives — a reminder of the past. If it wasn't to be read, then it would not have been written. Now you keep it."

They placed it in the wooden box with the locks of hair and baby booties.

Next, they emptied the chest of drawers onto the bed. Pa's special drawer contained a pocket watch, his two pocket knives, a leather pouch, a straight razor, three handkerchiefs, and his bandanna. James took the larger of the knives and presented Lee with the smaller. Lee's eyes lit up, and he gingerly stroked the knife. Alexandra and Christine each took a handkerchief, and so did James. Lee was awarded the bandanna. Immediately, he tucked it into his back pocket. The leather pouch was put away for Lee later. James already had a razor, so it, too, was packed away for later. James stroked the watch and popped the lid open.

As he gazed at the time, he said dreamily, "I can still picture Pa flipping this closed after checking the time." James chuckled. "I always thought Pa looked rather dignified in his suit with his pocket watch." Slowly, he tucked the watch into his shirt pocket.

In one drawer, six pennies were tucked under Pa's wool socks. James gave three each to Christine and Lee. From their reaction, one would have thought he gave them a nugget of gold! Ma's undergarments were given to Alexandra, and James received Pa's. Ma's aprons were divided among the two girls. James and Pa were the same height, but Pa was thicker built. Alexandra thought she could alter some of his clothes to fit James. A few of his much-worn work clothes Alexandra decided to make into a patch quilt. Pa's one Sunday suit would become a second one for James. Alexandra thought she could make a shirt for Lee out of one of Pa's. Lee liked that idea. James already had a very good work jacket for late fall and early winter. So they agreed to give Pa's to someone who needed it. The winter coat, gloves, and scarves were packed up in the trunk.

Ma had three dresses. Alexandra felt she could wear them. After six children, Ma was shaped a little different than Alexandra, but they were close enough to the same size. A few alterations and the dresses would be like new for Alexandra. Ma's winter coat and work boots would go to someone who might need them. Alexandra had a fairly new one herself. Ma's foot was larger than Alexandra's. Ma's soap, brush, comb, and mirror were taken to the girls' room. Ma's trunk was moved to the boys' old room. The dresser was left in the room for the boys to use.

Alexandra took down the lace curtains. She hung a set in their own room and packed up the other. To the windows in her parents' old room she tacked up two Indian blankets Pa had traded for some years ago. She tied them to one side on a nail. She also took Ma's wedding quilt from the bed and put it in her own trunk. She then brought the boys' everyday blankets for the end of their bed.

Together, they stepped back and surveyed the room. It looked so different. When a project was finished, there was usually a sense of accomplishment that went with a job well done. But they all stood there numb.

Finally, James put his hand on Lee's shoulder. "It will be nice to have a big room for us. Since you have insisted on sleeping with me lately, the bigger bed will be good. The curtains are a nice touch, Alexandra."

Alexandra nodded, but she could not find her voice. Christine leaned hard against Alexandra. Alexandra looked down at her and tried to smile. "Let's you and I go pack up our keepsakes." Alexandra gingerly reached over and picked up Ma's wooden box filled with its treasures to take to her own room.

Christine looked around for something — or someone. "Okay."

After a time of setting all the items in their new places, everyone pitched in to help with lunch. It was a quiet table, but the evening supper table was filled with their everyday chit-chat. When the meal was over, Lee got up to go get ready for bed. He headed towards his old bedroom. Christine turned his way and just stared.

Lee came back out of the room with his head down and his hands in his pockets. "Oops. I forgot." Slowly he made his way across the room to his new bedroom. As everyone watched, he stopped in the doorway. James stood up from his chair and clapped his hands together. Everyone jumped.

James laid his hand on his little brother's shoulder. "Let's go into this fine, big room our sisters decorated so nicely for us. With the Indian blanket curtains, you can pretend you are sleeping in a teepee." Lee tried to give him a brave smile. As they went into the room together, Alexandra could still hear James talking. "What Indian name shall we give you?"

Lee gave a weak "I don't know."

"How about Soaring Eagle? Or Little Red Fox? Or — I know — Little Buffalo Chip!"

With that Lee started to giggle. Alexandra let out a deep sigh. She had not even realized she had been holding her breath.

Christine was smiling. "What about an Indian name for me?"

Alexandra chuckled. "All right. Let me see. Skinny

Chicken? Or Noisy Duck? No, I have it. How about Wiggle Worm!?" At that, she reached over and tickled Christine, who shrugged away, giggling.

James came out of the room wearing a fake scowl. "What is all the racket?"

The giggling girls went back to their dishes.

When it was time for bed, Christine shyly approached Alexandra. "Could I wear one of Ma's gowns tonight?"

Alexandra looked up and wrinkled her brow. "Don't you think it might be too big?"

Christine shrugged. "I don't care if it is too long."

James cleared his throat. "I think she would be real pretty in the one with the purple bow at the neck."

Alexandra nodded. "All right. But it is lavender, not purple, James." He shrugged and winked at Christine. Christine skipped to her room. Alexandra shook her head. "She will be too hot in such a big gown."

James smiled. "She won't die from it. It makes her happy, and it is such a small request to fuss over."

Christine came out a short time later to hug them good night. The gown looked like it had swallowed her whole, but the grin on her face kept Alexandra from saying anything. When Christine went back to the bedroom, James and Alexandra covered their mouths to stifle their laughter!

CHRISTINE'S SURPRISE

The next week would prove to be active for the Williams. Besides the regular weekly schedule, school was to begin on Wednesday. Lee grumbled all day Monday and Tuesday that James would need his help in the fields and with the animals. James kept reminding him that his friends, Roger and Grant McRoy, would be there to play with. That satisfied him a little. Christine remained sober and quiet. Alexandra asked her if she felt well.

Suddenly, Christine grabbed Alexandra around the waist and burst into tears. "Don't make me go!"

"Why, Christine? You have always loved school. You are a very good scholar. Don't you want to see Amber McRoy and Martha Jackson? Even Martha's sister, Kelsey, will attend this year," Alexandra tried to comfort.

Christine wiped her eyes against the back of her hands. "I don't know. I just don't want to leave you."

Alexandra hugged Christine tightly. "I will walk a little ways with you each morning. And I will be here waiting on you each and every day after school. You will have to be big and helpful for Lee's sake this year."

Christine nodded. "At least I won't have to walk alone. I wish you could still go to school with me."

Alexandra smiled. "You know I graduated. But I still might show up one day to help out. Would you like that?"

Christine smiled. "I'd like that very much!"

Alexandra straightened herself up. "Let's make sure your new dress is ironed and ready, shall we?"

James and Alexandra chatted excitedly to Lee and Christine Wednesday morning. Both were so nervous neither could eat much breakfast.

Alexandra picked up the lunch bucket from the sideboard. "I thought you might not eat much breakfast. I have packed a big slice of gingerbread cake to go with your lunch. Maybe it will fill the emptiness in your stomachs come lunch time."

James and Alexandra walked part ways with them to the edge of their land. Alexandra had made a tote of some canvas she had found for them to carry their slates and any books they would have. Soon James and Alexandra stopped and waved them on. About a thousand feet off, Lee turned, and James waved good-bye again. Christine gave him a small tug, and they continued on their way. James and Alexandra turned and headed home. Thus began the ritual of the next ten weeks.

Schooling kept Lee and Christine busy. After school each day, there were chores to do. Lee was still in charge of the pigs. Christine took good care of the chickens before and after school. While Christine was in school, Monica planned to come every other week throughout the school season to help Alexandra on wash day. The alternate weeks, Amy planned to come. Usually, Christoph would bring Amy and he would help James at those times. Monica would arrive with Larry. Mr. Unruh had arranged to come at a set date along with Larry. James had offered to trade labor with Mr. Unruh for help he might later need.

Sunday was fast approaching. Alexandra was happy she would again see Preacher Melvin and Ms. Hazel. She and Christine had packed up the items for the minister to take to those in need in the other congregations. Also, for this Sunday, the Jacksons had invited the Williams for the noon meal. They had three smaller children, Miriam, aged eleven years; Martha, nine years; and Kelsey, five. Mrs. Jackson had said the McRoys would join them, too. They also had younger children: Amber, ten; Grant, seven; and Roger, six. Alexandra was a little nervous about no other youths being there, but she knew both families well. Ma and Mrs. Jackson had been close friends. Alexandra had volunteered to make the dessert. She decided on a blueberry spice cake.

But Saturday held delights of its own. James and Alexandra had decided to surprise Christine with a picnic for her birthday. Alexandra fried a chicken and made a molasses cake. When the basket was filled with goodies, they loaded the wagon and headed to the stream. Under the shade of the beautiful trees, James spread out the blanket, and they set out all the food.

"I see you thought the whole town was coming," James teased Alexandra.

Alexandra grabbed some grass and tossed it at him. "I know how you eat, mister!"

Christine was being chased around by Lee, giggling and screaming with delight. Alexandra and James sat laughing at them as Lee would almost catch her and then stumble into the meadow grass.

Soon they all sat down to eat their lunch. James gave the prayer with thanks for the food and Christine's birthday.

Everyone enjoyed the food and especially the cake. Then James gave the children permission to wade in the water, but cautioned them not to get too wet. Alexandra helped Christine tie up the skirt of her dress. James and Alexandra leaned back against the tree watching and laughing. It did not take Lee long to realize it was more fun to try and splash his sister than to simply walk in the edge of the water. Christine was not to be outdone! Before long, they both got carried away and ... 'SPLASH!' Christine got off balance and sat in the water. Alexandra gasped. James roared with laughter. Lee stood wide-eyed and open-mouthed for a fleeting second, then with one hand on his knee and the other around his stomach, he burst into a belly laugh! Christine was not amused. Her bottom lip started to quiver, and in no time she was crying!

Lee tried to stop laughing, but he could not. "Look here, Christine. See!" He jumped into the air and landed with a big splash of his own. Christine stared and sniffled with her mouth hanging open.

James hollered, "That a boy, Lee. Seize the moment!"

Christine tried not to smile and to keep pouting, but she couldn't. She threw her head back and laughed out loud.

After a while of the children pretending to flop around in the creek like a couple of minnows, Alexandra called them out to lie and dry in the sun. There was enough food left from lunch for a snack.

Christine sighed. "It has been a great birthday. Thank you, everyone."

After a quiet rest, everyone loaded up and rode back to the farm. Once there, the boys headed to the barn to attend to the chores, and the girls went inside to finish their own work. Christine carried the picnic blanket. She entered the room and spotted three gifts wrapped in brown paper and tied with twine lying on the table. Throwing the blanket on the floor, she rushed over. Then she whirled around to Alexandra. "For me?"

Alexandra laughed. "Well, do we have another birthday girl?"

Christine grinned and shook her head. "No, ma'am!"

Alexandra set the basket on the table and began to unload it. "Well, I guess they must be for you, but you must wait for the boys to return. Hurry and finish your chores so you will be ready when they get in."

Christine jumped with joy. She hurriedly sped through her chores. She was helping Alexandra set the food on the table when the boys came in from washing up

Christine ran to James and grabbed his arm. "Can I open my gifts before I eat, James?"

James looked at her, pretending he did not know what she was talking about. "Gifts?"

Lee nodded. "Yeah, you know, James, the ones we wrapped two nights ago."

Alexandra covered her mouth and chuckled.

James laughed out loud. "Yes. Tell everything you know, why don't ya'. I guess you can after prayer."

Christine and Lee smiled big at each other.

After the thanks were given for the glorious day shared and the food that had been prepared, Christine picked up one of her gifts. Carefully, she untied the twine and unfolded the paper. Inside laid a handkerchief, an item only grown ladies normally possessed, the corner of which was embroidered with a pink and orange flower.

Christine looked up at Alexandra with her mouth opened. "It is beautiful! Thank you!"

Alexandra smiled. "I thought you were grown enough to carry your own to church now."

"I'll take good care of it." Next the birthday girl unwrapped James' gift. It was a wooden goat he had carved for her. "It looks just like Missy! You did a wonderful job, James."

James blushed and pointed to the next gift. "What is that one? Who could it be from?"

Lee put his hands on his hips and frowned at James. "Now, you know that is from me."

James ruffled Lee's hair. "I am just teasing you, squirt."

Lee turned his attention back to Christine. Almost shaking in his place, Lee grinned at her. "Go ahead. Open it."

Carefully, she unwrapped the tiny package. She gasped, "Oh, Lee! It is one of your pennies! You could have bought licorice sticks with this."

Lee smiled broadly. "I have two more. I wanted you to have that one."

Christine got up and hugged everyone. "Thank you, thank you!"

James pointed to the table. "Can we finally eat?"

Christine sat down and everyone began dishing out the food. It had been a great day.

But at bedtime, Christine was heard sniffling from in the bedroom!

James called over to Alexandra, "*Psst*. Alexandra."

She looked up from the table where she had been reading. "What?"

He pointed to the bedroom. "That sounds like Christine."

She listened for a minute, then quickly got up and went in to check on her. Alexandra found her curled up under the sheet crying. "What is wrong, sweetie?"

Christine whispered through a sniffle, "I wish Ma and Pa had been here today. I got all these nice things, and Ma doesn't even know it." With that thought, she burst out in tears.

Alexandra took her up in her arms and held her tight. "Oh, you are wrong. Ma and Pa saw it all. You can tell Ma all about today by praying."

"I still missed her today."

"Yes, I missed Ma, too. Pa would have laughed hard at you and Lee in the creek!"

Christine giggled a little. "We were funny, weren't we?"

Alexandra smiled. "Yes, you were."

"Thank you for such a nice day. I really did like it all. I wish I didn't feel so sad." Christine looked up at Alexandra and tried so very hard to smile.

"Well, it is all right. Why don't you just close your eyes and tell Ma all about your day until you fall asleep?"

"Okay." Christine rolled over, sniffled a few times, and closed her eyes in prayer.

Alexandra kissed her on the cheek and tucked her in. She went back out to join James. She flopped in the chair beside him.

James was leaning forward. "Well?"

She sighed and wiped away the tears. "She was wishing Ma and Pa could have been here today. I knew it was coming. She had not mentioned them all day."

James sat back. "I was hoping that she would have so much fun she might ..." He trailed off without finishing.

Alexandra looked at him in surprise. "Oh, James! I hope none of us ever forget Ma and Pa."

James shook his head. "That is not what I meant. I was just hoping it would end pleasantly for her."

Alexandra rocked. "I think it will be a nice day in her memories. She is tired, and she misses her ma. She'll be all right."

James also rocked and stared at the empty fireplace. He whispered, "I miss Ma, too."

THE WEDDING

Sunday broke to a cooler dawn; an overnight storm had blown through and left behind lower temperatures. Alexandra was glad. She also appreciated that the rain had settled the dust on the road to town. Everyone ate a cold quick breakfast so as to hurry on their way.

It was so nice to see everyone milling about in front of the church. As Christine hurried to see her friends, Tonya, Monica, and Joy waved and smiled to Alexandra. Martha and Amber were already there talking to Lisa. Lee stood with James as he spoke with some of his friends. Little Casey Martin came over to say hi to Lee, along with Roger and Grant. Soon everyone began to file into the church.

Brother Sam, Lisa's father, led the opening song. Brother Arthur, Doc Cannon's oldest son, gave the opening remarks and prayer. A song was raised by Brother Matthew, Tonya's brother. Finally, Preacher Melvin stood to address the congregation. The next hour flew by for Alexandra. She drank every word spoken. It seemed the older she got, the more she understood Ma and Pa's love for church. The message was refreshing to her spirit. Brother Chad, Mary's brother, led the next song. Then Preacher Melvin stood to dismiss church with prayer, or so she thought.

Instead, he cleared his throat, pulled out a tiny sheet of paper from his jacket pocket, and read, "I have the pleasure this morning of announcing the wedding of Carl Martin and Miss Elizabeth Kanagy. They plan to say their vows before the Lord and this congregation on ..."

Alexandra and Mary, sitting next to her, gasped. To think — a wedding! There had not been a wedding since Jessica Kanagy married Leon Dyck almost two years ago. Now in just three weeks there would be a wedding right here.

Alexandra watched as Elizabeth stood to say a few words and ask for prayer. She blushed as she sat back down. Next, Carl stood, staring at the floor, and spoke about how God had placed a special love for Elizabeth deep in his heart. Alexandra quickly wiped a tear from the corner of her eye. The preacher then gave the closing prayer and dismissed church. Needless to say, the talk of the afternoon was all about the wedding to come.

The next week was busy sewing, sewing, and more sewing. The Ladies' Circle got together Tuesday, Wednesday, and Friday. They busily sewed along with Elizabeth bed linens, a wedding dress, two table cloths, and two dresses. The two dresses she owned now would turn into her work dresses. They also tied off a quilt for her. The men built a small cabin on the piece of land Carl had purchased near his pa's land. On Saturday, the youth boys got together and chinked the logs and finished the fireplace.

The next week was a little quieter. The families of Carl and Elizabeth helped them set up for housekeeping. The final week before the wedding was full of baking, cooking, and getting ready. Preacher Melvin and Ms. Hazel would make a special trip back for the ceremony. Some of the out-of-town relatives would be coming in for the event also.

Alexandra greeted Tonya in front of the church on the lovely day of the wedding. "You look beautiful, Tonya. You even have on a new dress! Are you excited?"

Tonya grabbed Alexandra's hand. "I feel like I ate butterflies for breakfast! I am so excited about having Elizabeth as a sister, but I will sure miss Carl."

Alexandra laughed, "He won't be but one quarter of a mile from your back porch!"

Tonya shrugged. "I know; it still won't be the same. But I am happy. I am to sing a song with Elizabeth's sister, Jessica, along with Matthew and Michael. I hope I don't sniffle and cry through it!"

Both girls were giggling as they went into the church. Onto tables set up in the shade the food committee placed the covered dishes, crocks of tea, cakes, pies, platters, and plates of food that people were bringing. There was enough food laid out for two towns!

After a lovely message on marriage, Minister Melvin cleared his throat as if to invite the bride and groom to step up. Instead he said in a clear voice, "I am happy to be a witness and play a part in God's wonderful plan today. I have to admit I love weddings. Faith Unruh has accepted the proposal of Brent Evans. They, too, will exchange their vows today."

Faith stood and expressed her desire, as did Brent. After a few moments, Preacher Melvin called both couples up front. Tonya and Alexandra looked at Monica and Mary, Faith and Brent's sisters. Their wide eyes and opened-mouth stares were greeted by huge grins.

After the two couples exchanged their promises before God, Tonya blew her nose and wiped her eyes as she headed up front to sing with her brothers and Jessica. After their two songs, Mary and her brother, Chad, along with Monica and her brother, Larry, sang two songs. It was all lovely. Faith's oldest sister, Hope, read a poem that made quite a few happy tears fall. All the youth sang the closing two songs. Then Doc Cannon was asked to close with prayer.

The congregation followed the newlywed couples out to the tables for the reception. Neither couple seemed able to eat, so busy were they staring into each other's eyes and smiling!

Elizabeth's father, Henry, gave her a beautiful chest of drawers that he had made. Carl's family presented them with a lovely hand-pieced quilt. Elizabeth cried as she hugged Mrs. Martin's neck. Friends and neighbors contributed one or two canned items to their new pantry. It would be a good start for them.

It was announced that next week, the ladies would sew for Faith, and the men would help Brent. The couple would stay with Brent's folks until their place could be set up. Mr. Unruh announced a dinner in honor of his Faith and her new husband two weeks from today at eleven o'clock there at the church. Already Alexandra could not wait!

The evening service was filled with lots of singing.

James and Alexandra chatted nonstop on their way home about the surprise of the double wedding. Since the minister was shared between the congregations, utilizing him for a double wedding was not unheard of.

James laughed. "Do you remember four years ago when the minister married four couples at one service?"

Alexandra chuckled. "Oh, yes. What a day! Doc Cannon's Ramona was marrying Gene Beachy, and Hope married Bob Dyck. Also, let me see — oh, yes — the Madison's youngest daughter, Lucille, and Doc Cannon's Caroline."

James shook his head. "I remember it well. I could

not believe Doc would let Carolina marry so young. She was just a few months over sixteen."

Alexandra nodded. "I remember hearing Ma and Pa talk about it. Pa said it was only due to Jason's age and maturity that Doc probably allowed it. He is eight years older than she."

James laughed. "Seems to me, he took her to raise."

Alexandra giggled. "I know. But it seems to have worked out fine. They are doing well on their small farm."

James looked sideways at Alexandra. "Are you sure Monica never hinted about Faith's engagement to you?"

Alexandra shook her head and put her hands on her hips. "Of course not. I pinched her at the dinner for keeping secrets," she laughed. "She said the proposal just came Monday, so I guess everyone was busy all week in preparation. How about Larry?"

James shook his head. "Come to think of it, I haven't seen him in the last two weeks. He did today say that he and his pa are working on a gift for the newlyweds. You know how Larry likes to work with his hands."

When the wagon pulled up outside their cozy house, James and Alexandra noticed Lee and Christine were sound asleep. They had talked so much between the them all the way home that they never noticed the silence in the back of the wagon!

Alexandra sat on the porch and watched the stars come out after putting Christine to bed. James took his time taking care of the animals. She wondered to herself how she and James would ever marry anyone. Would anyone want a piece of their huge pie of responsibilities? How could she ever leave their farm?

She shrugged and sighed. 'Another one of those

thoughts that are not mine to think. I trust, Lord, I do trust.'

She thought about the last Friday's youth meeting. Mrs. Renée Whited and Mrs. Cannon had arranged for four Fridays in July to be hymn sing classes. The families would divide up the nights for refreshments. Alexandra had signed up to help the Unruhs, Kanagys, and the Cannons for the first night. She was going to bake cookies. Mrs. McRoy had asked for Lee and Christine to visit with her children during these nights.

Alexandra began to yawn so much she could no longer focus on the stars. 'I have a very busy week ahead of me,' she thought. She stood and went inside for the night.

PREACHER PAUL

Monday morning, Mr. Madison rode over and spoke with James. At lunch, James told Alexandra about the visit.

"Mr. Madison brought word from Deacon Henry that we are to pray about a minister of our own. Minister Melvin talked with folks this last visit and thought we might be ready to nominate. There will be a meeting Wednesday evening at six o'clock at church. They want to keep it short. I guess you need to plan an early meal, and we will eat a snack when we get back."

Alexandra smiled with excitement. "A minister of our own right here. I wonder who?"

James grinned slightly. "I'd say we need a lot of prayer on the matter."

She nodded. "I guess so. I have never thought about it before. It should be an exciting evening."

Wednesday late afternoon, the Williams loaded up the wagon and headed to church. It was a solemn group that came together and found their seats. Minister Melvin was there up front along with Deacon Henry. After songs and prayer, the congregation was addressed by the minister. Slips of paper and pencils were passed around. Everyone secretly wrote down the name that had been laid on their hearts for nomination. It took a while to collect the slips of papers and for the minister and deacon to examine each slip. It was kept private. Everyone seemed to sit on pins and needles.

Brother Jimmy finally stood to lead a song. Someone called out a number.

After two songs, Minister Melvin stood with tears trickling down his cheeks. "Of all the slips, only two are blank. The Spirit is flowing among us tonight, for the nomination made is unanimous." He paused to gather himself. "Brother Paul Martin was nominated."

A small gasp was heard from the back where Paul's wife, Vera, was sitting. Her head bowed in prayer, and tears began to flow down her cheeks. Brother Paul slowly stood with his head lowered. He stood silently for what seemed like a long time. Finally, he spoke in a small, crackling voice.

Alexandra reached beside her and grabbed Tonya's trembling hand. Most of the girls, ladies, and even some men were wiping their eyes. Brother Paul asked for prayer and openly expressed that he wanted to do the Lord's will. He admitted to feeling the Lord leading him into service, but he had not known exactly what that was to be. He did have peace with the congregation's support, but he did not feel worthy. He dedicated himself to the service of God, and he vowed to honor Him.

After more words from the minister and a closing song, the meeting was adjourned. Tomorrow would hold the ordination of Brother Paul Martin! Everyone would bring covered dishes and baskets full and sup together after the ordination.

Alexandra could not believe it ... a minister of their own! Someone she knew so well — Tonya's very own father. Services every week — oh, how exciting! She could not wait to tell Ma — Ma and Pa.

Suddenly, Alexandra thought she would choke. 'They

would have loved this moment,' she thought to herself.

The evening had been so reverent that everyone filed out of the church solemnly and headed home without stopping to talk to each other. James was very quiet.

Alexandra saw out of the corner of her eye that his jaw was tightened. "Are you all right, James?" she whispered.

Never breaking his gaze ahead, he hoarsely answered, "Pa would have appreciated tonight. I just wish he would have lived to see it." He took out his handkerchief and wiped his nose.

Alexandra whispered as she fought back tears, "I know."

James cleared his throat. "But it is a good thing. I am real glad about it all. It will be nice to have church every week."

Alexandra nodded in agreement. They rode silently the rest of the way home. Alexandra thought about the Martin home. She wondered if any of them would get any sleep tonight. She closed her eyes and said a silent prayer for them.

CR

The ordination and supper went smoothly. Peace and serenity flowed through the service.

Minister Paul made a point over the next two weeks to visit each home to speak with individual families. When he visited their farm, he and James spoke privately in the yard where James came to greet him from where he had been working. After a while they came into the house. Minister Paul had prayer with their family and expressed his desire to help them as individuals or as a family if they ever needed him. It was a friendly visit. Alexandra felt shy, but was glad he had stopped by.

⊗

Two Fridays following the ordination, the hymn sing classes at church began. Brother David Evans from the next town over would be conducting the lessons. He was Mr. Kevin Evans' brother, making him Mary's uncle. He had grown boys to work his fields while he dedicated time to teach the four classes. Mr. Evans teased that he could put his brother to work in between classes so he wouldn't go home lazy!

Since it was summer, relatives from the north and big cities sent their young folks to come work until the harvest was done. Marie was back visiting the Schmidts until mid-August. Mae was happy having her cousin back in town. The Unruhs were having two nephews, Joshua, aged twenty-one years, and Christopher, nineteen, and Mrs. Unruh's youngest brother, Jack Nikell, aged twenty years, staying and helping with their farm. The Glens' nieces came to help with the little ones, since Mrs. Glen was expecting by summer's end. Sylvia and Veronica, aged sixteen and eighteen years respectively, would stay until early September.

All this company increased their youth tremendously. Alexandra liked meeting new people. Some of the visitors had visited in the past, but only briefly, and some had been much younger then. She could hardly wait for Friday night.

Once they dropped Lee and Christine off, James and Alexandra headed to the church. Mr. Evans was a very happy-looking man. He smiled from the moment they met him. Yet, there was a seriousness in his manner. He was also very organized. The meeting began promptly.

Alexandra looked over and noticed James was sitting beside two of the visitors. She wondered who they were. Marie was sitting on Alexandra's left and Veronica to her right. She had not seen Veronica in five years.

The evening went smoothly. During refreshments, Alexandra tried to go around and introduce herself to any visiting girls she saw. She met Sylvia, Veronica's younger sister, and Ms. Sarah, the instructor's wife. Most of the visitors were boys. She would have to wait and let James tell her about them later tonight.

The third meeting, Mr. David, as they now called the instructor, sorted everyone into certain groups and gave them each two songs to learn. The songs would be part of the Sunday program in two weeks. Alexandra was paired with Monica, Christoph, and Matthew. James was paired with Amy, Luke, and Mae. All the groups sang through their songs or at least part of each two or three times. Mr. David instructed each on their pieces. The week's refreshments were provided by the Evans, the Glens, and the Whiteds. Mrs. Evans and Mrs. Whited served the group after the lessons. They had brought cold milk and hot cinnamon rolls!

As Alexandra helped clean up, Mrs. Whited wrapped two rolls up and handed them to her. "Here, Alexandra. Maybe this will make the ride home nicer for Lee and Christine."

Alexandra smiled gratefully. "Thank you for thinking of them."

Once they were settled into the wagon, the smiles on Lee and Christine's faces lit up the night when Alexandra presented them with the big glazed rolls.

James shook the reins. "How was your evening with

the Schimdts?"

"We had fun," replied Christine in between bites.

Lee nodded. "Abram and me helped pop the corn. This has been a swell night — two snacks!"

∽

Nine days later was the program Sunday. The evening service opened with Brother Joshua Unruh leading two congregational songs. The school children sang a song next. After that, all but the first graders sat down. They sang "Jesus Loves Me." Alexandra thought it was very sweet. Brother David made some opening remarks about the beauty of singing praises to God. After prayer, the first group got up. It was James' group. Next, Arthur Cannon, Sylvia, Joy, and Jack Nikell sang. The next songs were by Christopher, Annie, Joe, and Veronica. Mrs. Jessica Dyck, Deacon Henry's daughter, read a poem. More songs followed by different groups, including Alexandra's. Next sang Michael, Joshua, Larry, and Chad. Alexandra thought the quartet was lovely. They harmonized beautifully. The final group was a trio of Tonya, Mary, and Marie. Their sweet, peaceful songs were about heaven, the kind that no matter how many times Alexandra heard them she still had to wipe the tears from her eyes.

After the closing prayer by Preacher Paul, everyone stood around and talked. Alexandra noticed James gently laying a sleeping Lee on the bench. She smiled at his tenderness in rubbing Lee's back as he settled on the bench. James then stood to talk with Christopher. And Alexandra thought it kind of Christopher to stand there holding the sleepy, two-year-old Wayne Glen, who had come over with outstretched arms. The boy had taken a special liking to

Christopher since his arrival at the Unruh farm this summer. The Unruh family were neighbors with the Glens.

Wayne had snuggled into Christopher's shoulder and began to nod. Suddenly, as she realized she was staring, Alexandra flushed and quickly turned away. She noticed Tonya talking with Mary, so she went over to join the conversation.

CR

It had become Alexandra's Monday morning pre-dawn ritual to fill Ma in on the past week's events. The sowing had gone well, and in stages the harvesting was progressing. The children had settled into their school routine. At this point, they only had four weeks left. School had done wonders for Christine. She was losing some of her dependence on Alexandra.

Alexandra had promised them that this week she would walk to school and spend the day helping the teacher.

Tuesday morning James drove everyone into town. He had to run a few errands. Alexandra would just walk home with the children after school. When they arrived, the bell was ringing.

When Lee walked in holding Alexandra's hand, one of the little town girls whispered to him, "Is your ma going to read us a story today?"

Alexandra stopped in her tracks.

Lee looked at the floor and shook his head. "I don't got a ma no more. This is Alexandra, my sister." Then he quickly looked up. "But she knows how to read real good. I bet she will read us a story, won't ya', Alexandra?" He looked up at her with pleading eyes.

With a shaky smile, she swallowed hard. "If your

teacher wants me to, I will be glad to read to you."

Smiling, Lee took his seat as Alexandra sat on a bench against the back wall.

After morning devotions, Alexandra worked math combinations with the upper grades. Next, she called out spelling words for the middle grades. At lunch recess, she played ten steps around the school with the children. As she sat down to rest under a shade tree, Alexandra overheard the same little girl from the morning speaking with Lee by the swings.

"How come you got a pa, but no ma?" Juliet asked.

Lee kept swinging. "I don't. My ma and pa are angels now."

"But you said your pa lets you take care of the pigs," Juliet persisted.

Lee dragged his feet under the swing. "I meant James does. He is my big brother, but he is sort of my pa now."

Juliet stopped swinging and stared at Lee. "How can you grow up without a ma and pa? My ma says you have a ma and pa to teach you right from wrong. Who is ever going to teach you them things?"

Lee wrinkled his brow and stood up off the swing with a huff. "My James and Alexandra taught me! When I am naughty, James whoops me good. You ask too many questions. I don't want to play with you no more!" He stomped off towards the back of the school.

Alexandra got up and followed him. She found him sitting with his legs curled up and his arms wrapped around them. His head was bowed on his knees, and she could hear his sniffling. She sat beside him.

After a moment he looked up at her. "Girls are dumb."

Alexandra tilted her head to one side. "You think so? I thought you said I was smart."

Lee wiped his cheek. "You are!"

"But you just said girls were dumb. I am a girl, you know."

Lee shook his head. "No, you aren't. You're my sister."

Alexandra laughed. "Sister or not, I am a girl. You really should not say ugly things about people — like calling them names."

Lee snuffled. "I'm sorry. But Juliet hurt my feelings."

Alexandra nodded. "I heard her ask you a lot of questions. Her family has only been in town but two weeks. She probably just didn't know that Ma and Pa had passed away. I don't believe she meant to hurt your feelings."

Lee sat quietly for a few moments. Looking out across the field, he added, "Them old ladies at church keep telling me I am lucky to have you and James to take care of me. How can I be lucky that Ma and Pa are dead?"

Alexandra had to think on that question for a while. Quietly, she replied, "I guess every situation has a good side and a bad side. It is up to you how you look at it."

Lee looked into Alexandra's face. "If I am lucky to have you and James, then does that mean I am glad Ma and Pa died?"

She reached over and hugged Lee. "Oh, no! That just means you are accepting the Lord's will and making the most of a horrible situation. Ma and Pa dying was and always will be sad, but we have each other, and that is a good thing."

Lee smiled. "I love you."

Alexandra smiled through her tears. "And oh, how I love you, Lee."

Together, they walked around to the front of the

school to go wash up and start the afternoon session. For the afternoon story hour, Alexandra read Lee's grade a very exciting story about a fuzzy black rabbit. Miss Amelia, their teacher, told Lee that it was the nicest story she had ever heard. Lee sat up straight and proud the rest of the day.

FEVER STRIKES AGAIN!

☙

One Sunday afternoon in early August, the Williams were dining with the Glens. The small ones, Bill and Wayne, along with Mrs. Glen, had laid down for their afternoon nap. Sylvia, Veronica, and Alexandra were trying to learn a new song that Sylvia had brought from home. James and Mr. Glen were playing a game of checkers as Lee watched. Keena, Lisa, and Christine were playing paper dolls on a blanket under a tree. Out front a wagon pulled up. Sylvia opened the door to Monica. The Unruh wagon was filled with Larry, Faith and her new husband Brent, Joshua, Christopher, Jack, Erica and her husband Fred. They were going over to sing for Widow Stephans and were inviting Sylvia, Veronica, Alexandra, and James along.

Mr. Glen laughed. "Sounds like a fine idea. Maybe if I play Lee at checkers, I might stand a chance at winning! Go ahead and have fun."

Everyone loaded up and headed to the widow's house. They found Widow Stephans sitting behind her house under a shade tree. She clapped with joy when she saw everyone pile out of the wagon. They sang for over twenty minutes. She cried and hugged every one of them.

She grabbed Erica's hands. "Everyone stay right here. I'll make some lemonade quickly. I know you must be thirsting to death."

Erica and Faith quickly volunteered to help her.

While they waited, Alexandra watched as James, Christopher, and Larry walked over to the porch. She was too far away to hear them, but she saw as they pointed, examined, and murmured something about the porch.

James helped Widow Stephans down the steps when she finally came out, and Christopher offered to carry the bucket of drink. Everyone received a dipper full of cold lemonade. She had even added sugar! Everyone thanked her and waved as they loaded back into the wagon. Oh, what a glorious day!

CR

Tuesday morning, Monica arrived to help with the wash day. Instead of Larry hopping off the wagon, James hopped onto it. Earlier, he had asked Alexandra to pack him a lunch. He and Larry were going to work on Widow Stephans' porches. Sunday afternoon, they had noticed some loose and rotting boards. Mr. Unruh had offered the wood and supplies, and Larry, James, and Christopher offered the labor. Mrs. Unruh had invited Widow Stephans over to quilt for the day to get her out of the house.

Larry hollered out to Lee, who was standing on the front porch to wave to them good-bye, "Would you like a ride to school?"

Lee jumped up and down. "Would I ever!" He ran in to get Christine.

Alexandra followed them out with their lunch pails. She smiled as she watched Larry gently lifting Lee into the back of the wagon bed. Next, James helped Christine get in. Alexandra giggled as James pulled Christine's bonnet off her shoulders onto her head. 'He will make a good father someday,' she thought. She chided herself, 'Not someday — he is being a good father.'

James came to the porch to retrieve the lunch pails. "We will come back after school in time to do some chores. Will you be all right hauling and dumping the water?"

Alexandra nodded. "Monica and I will manage. Go ahead. I'll be fine."

Alexandra watched them for a moment before she heard Monica from inside call out, "The water is starting to boil!" Quickly, she scurried in the door.

CR

It seemed like the months of August and September came as the rush and turbulence of a hurricane and flew by as quick. Things were so busy with harvesting, preserving, and the men-folk doing house mending for the elderly members in town. Everyone had taken some of their canned bounty to the senior members who were getting too old to garden or farm.

School finally dismissed with a program one Friday evening at the end of August. Lee's first grade class gave a beautiful recitation. Alexandra noticed James wipe a tear from the corner of his eye while Lee was reciting. Christine's class did well in the spelling bee. Christine and Lisa recited a cute poem in unison. James and Alexandra felt very happy with their siblings' performances. The teacher, Miss Amelia Erinn, had said very nice things about them both. Alexandra was glad that Miss Erinn had agreed to come back next year.

During refreshments, Marie, Alexandra, Mary, Monica, and Tonya were standing by the blackboard talking. Alexandra noticed that across the room James was talking with Larry and Christopher. 'I wonder why those fellows are here? They don't have any brothers or sisters in school anymore,' she thought to herself. 'I guess they are just showing their support to our little school,' she finally decided.

Lee came over and tugged at her dress skirt. "My tummy and head hurts," he whimpered.

Alexandra bent over and touched his head. "Did you eat too much cake?"

Lee leaned against her shoulder. "No, ma'am. I didn't want any. I want to go outside now," he added with urgency. Quickly, she rushed him out the back door. When they reached the closest tree, Lee was very sick.

Noticing the commotion inside, James had made his way across the room and followed them outside. He was followed by Monica and Christopher. Alexandra sent Monica for a wet rag. Christopher went around to get the Williams' wagon. Lee leaned sideways against a kneeling James and cried.

Alexandra went back in to find Doc Cannon. Once she located him, he told her to meet him the block over at his office with Lee. Christopher helped James by driving the wagon. James, Alexandra, and Lee rode in the back. Monica took Christine home with her for the while. Lee was sick two more times before they could reach Doc's office. Lee only had enough energy to whimper as the doctor checked him over.

"I'll mix him up something. Have him sip the mixture that I will send home with you every two hours. But only sips. Hopefully, it will pass by tomorrow. I will come by around the noon hour." Doc made Lee swallow a spoonful of a thick white liquid. Lee gagged and groaned, but it stayed in him.

While James and Alexandra were inside with Lee, Christopher and Larry had made a thick straw bed covered with blankets in the back of the wagon. When Doc said he was sending Lee home, Larry went and got Christine from his house. As Preacher Paul stopped by and spoke with James, James gently laid a sleeping Lee on the straw bed.

Off and on, Lee whimpered and groaned as they bumped their way home. Alexandra rubbed his head and hummed to him to try and soothe his sleep. Once home, James helped undress Lee. Alexandra wiped his feverish body with a cool cloth. Alexandra instructed Christine to change into her bed clothes. The three of them knelt in the sitting room and prayed. Christine began to cry.

"You have to be strong for Lee. Pray and have faith that God will heal him," Alexandra encouraged her with a hug.

James kissed Christine's forehead. "Off to bed with you. We will need your help tomorrow, so rest for us, okay?"

Christine nodded and went to her room. Alexandra took another basin of water to the boys' room and bathed Lee with it. He was beginning to whimper again. James brought a bucket to sit by the bedside. The poor child was so pitiful heaving that Alexandra silently cried. There was nothing left in him to come out. Alexandra tried to get him to sip the liquid from Doc Cannon. Lee tried, but was so exhausted and feverish he could barely swallow. James paced at the end of the bed. Alexandra prayed silently through her tears.

By dawn, little Lee had only been able to take two of the doses sent home by Doc. Whether it was exhaustion or the medicine, he was sleeping at least. Alexandra went to fix some coffee. James joined her in the kitchen.

He sat at the table looking at his trembling hands. "He looks bad, Alexandra. He is so pale." Fear shone in his eyes as his chin quivered. Alexandra nodded and tried to stop her shaking. James' voice cracked. "God won't take him, will he?"

Alexandra whirled around and just sat right where she stood. "Oh, no, James! Please, NO!" she sobbed.

James ran to her and held her as they both cried. James prayed, pleading with God for a healing for Lee and strength for themselves if His will was to take Lee home. When they finally calmed down, they prayed some more and released Lee to God, whatever His will might be.

Lee's fever was still raging when Doc arrived. Luke, Larry, Christoph, and Christopher came and took care of James' chores. Monica and Mae took care of the house with Christine's help. Doc stayed into the night and helped administer whatever he could to ease Lee's discomfort and fever.

Shortly after supper the next day, Preacher Paul was sent for. Doc felt he had done all that he knew how. It was strictly in God's hands. Lee had started in with delirium shortly after the noon hour. He would scream out in terror over unseen objects and cry for Ma and Pa.

When the minister arrived, Alexandra was rocking Lee's wet, feverish little body by the fireplace. James was kneeling beside them, rubbing Lee's arm. Alexandra was humming through her tears. Monica sat across from them, rocking a very quiet Christine. Preacher Paul knelt beside them, prayed, and read from the Bible. Then he prayed some more. Though sad and frightened, Alexandra and James felt a peace settle in the house. When James took Lee back to bed and Alexandra followed to bathe him down again, Christine jumped up and ran out the front door.

Monica jumped up to follow her, but Preacher Paul stopped her. "Let her go and vent her anger and fears. She is scared, sad, and mad. Give her a little time, then go find her. She can't go too far from home out here."

And she didn't. She ran straight to the barn and up to the loft. Larry and Christopher were feeding the animals and saw her in flight. Christopher followed her up the loft. He heard her before he could finish climbing the ladder.

"Dear God, please don't take my Lee. I feel like I'll just die, too. He is a good boy. Widow Stephans says earth needs more boys like him. I'll help him mind extra good if You'll let him stay. Oh, please, please! I'd rather You take me. I am older and have lived longer. James looks so sad. I've never seen James cry around people like this. Oh, God, please!!" she wailed.

Christopher reached over and gently grabbed her shoulders. Startled, she spun around. He took her in his arms and held her tight as her whole being shook with sobs.

Soothingly, he whispered in her ear, "Shh ... God heard you, sweetie. He knows all about Lee. He'll do what is best for all of us. We have to trust Him."

He rocked her until she could not cry anymore. They prayed together, and then he helped her down out of the loft. He took out his handkerchief and cleaned her face. Monica was on the porch looking for her. When Christine reached the porch, she and Monica went into the house hand-in-hand.

Mrs. Madison brought over supper. She and Monica helped Christine get ready for bed. James and Alexandra were sitting in chairs side by side at Lee's bed. With one hand touching Lee and their heads on the bed, they had dozed off. Doc kept changing the cloth on Lee's head and squeezing small drops of liquid into his lips.

Just before midnight, Doc laid his hands on their shoulders. "James, Alexandra," he whispered as he gently shook them. "Wake up. It's over ..."

They both jumped up with a start.

Alexandra let out a wail — "NO!" — as James reached over to grab Lee.

"Wait!" Doc cried. "It is all right. The fever has broken. The danger is over."

Alexandra and James both dropped like rag dolls into their chairs. Alexandra covered her face with her hands and wept. At Alexandra's wail, Mrs. Madison, Monica, Larry, and Christopher ran to the doorway of the bedroom. Larry had his hand on Monica's shoulder, expecting the worst.

They each let out a sigh of relief when Lee weakly looked up at Alexandra and hoarsely whispered, "Can I have some water, please?"

Weeping, Alexandra leaned over and kissed his pale, sunken cheek. "Yes, sweetie. You may have some water."

Mrs. Madison brought them a cup of water. Doc showed them how to feed him by the spoonful.

About that time, Monica heard something coming from the other room. She scooted by Larry and went to check it out. She found Christine squatting in the corner of her bedroom crying and rocking. Monica rushed to her side. "Oh, Christine! I am so sorry I didn't come right in here. Hush now," she whispered. "Lee is all right. His fever is all gone. Doc said the danger is over. Lee isn't going to die."

Christine looked up at her. "Then why did Alexandra scream?"

Monica hugged her and smiled. "She was asleep and in her sleepiness she misunderstood Doc. But she is awake now, and everyone is happy. Do you want to go see Lee?"

Christine wiped her face with the back of her hands. "I sure do."

Together, they went to Lee.

Doc left instructions to gradually increase the amounts of liquid to Lee. He left a powder to add to his drinking water to help him regain his strength. Tomorrow he could start drinking broth and eating saltine crackers. Monica and Larry offered to sit by Lee so James and Alexandra could get some rest. James went to his old room, and Alexandra went to her room. Christopher rode with Doc back to town. They dropped Mrs. Madison off on their way.

Christine followed Alexandra to bed. As they prepared to lie down, Christine grabbed Alexandra's hand. "Let us pray and tell God thank you."

Alexandra nodded. "That is a good idea. Let's do. I was so tired, I didn't think of it."

Together they knelt beside their bed and prayed. Alexandra's eyes closed and she was asleep before her head ever hit the pillow.

In the other room, James was kneeling at his bedside crying. He could not speak for all the sobbing, but his heart sang praises of thanksgiving to God.

Finally, he took a deep breath and whispered, "In Jesus' name, Amen." He crawled into the bed and fell instantly asleep.

SURPRISES

Lee was very weak and slow to recover. He slept a lot, which kept him from being restless. Mr. Unruh made him a wagon so he could be pulled out in the yard for some fresh air. By the end of September, he was up and playing again. He still seemed to tire easily, but he was alive and well.

With harvesting, the youth did not have any scheduled meetings. Marie had gone back home by now. Mrs. Glen gave birth to a baby girl whom they named Olivia. Sylvia and Veronica would stay another month to help. Joshua, Christopher, and Jack were finishing the harvest with the Unruhs. All of them talked of heading home the last week in October.

The Whiteds invited the youth one Friday night for a taffy pull. Since James felt the ride and late hour would be too much for Lee yet, Mr. and Mrs. Madison offered to stay at the Williams' with Lee and Christine. Alexandra promised to bring the children back a piece of taffy.

As they rode away Friday evening, Alexandra turned back to wave at the children as they waved from the porch.

"We will be back tonight, Alexandra. You act like we are moving away," James teased her.

She turned around and sighed. "I know. Since Lee took sick, I cannot stand to have them out of my sight."

"Let's see ... Psalm 37:5, 'Commit thy way unto the

Lord; trust also in him; and he shall bring it to pass.' Maybe you do not remember who healed Lee. I am sure God will continue to take care of him as He sees fit," James gently chastised.

Alexandra smiled. "Okay; point taken. I bet you are excited about tonight. Try not to eat all the candy." James laughed and shook the reins slightly.

After a moment, he changed the subject. "I hate to see the fellows head back home this month. They have been really good to us and our community."

Alexandra felt her cheeks turn red. "Some have gone out of their way to help us." She turned her face away from James' sight. She wished she didn't blush so easily!

The rest of the way to town, they chatted about the upcoming holidays and how they might spend them. It was a pleasant but uneventful ride.

The taffy pull was a sticky success! Each family took home several pieces. In turn for their hospitality, the youth sang four songs for Mr. and Mrs. Whited. James and Alexandra were home by nine o'clock. They found Mr. and Mrs. Madison nodding in the rocking chairs and Lee and Christine tucked snugly in their beds.

❦

Saturday's skies held a promise of rain. James put the cover over the wagon so they could go to church even if it rained. Sure enough, a light rain was falling come Sunday morning. Alexandra was glad they could still attend church. They were to eat with the Cannons today. Widow Stephans would also be joining them. The Cannons' children — Arthur, aged twenty-seven years, Ramona and her husband, Gene,

Caroline and her husband, Jason, and the youngest, Calvin, ten — would also be there. Arthur was getting married in two weeks at his bride's congregation one state over. He had met her while he was doing some mission work there a few years back. They would live on his land that he had bought two years ago. He had a nice, simple, two-story house on it already.

The Sunday service seemed to fly by. Preacher Paul was settling into his new position and seemed comfortable with the Spirit's leading in his messages. Alexandra was so surprised when he up and announced the upcoming wedding of Jack Nikell and Amy Whited! Then the double surprise as Joe Samuel and Annie Whited's announcement was made! Two weddings from the same family! Then a sad thought passed through Alexandra's mind. Jack lived far away, so Amy would be moving. Thinking of this, she missed hearing what Jack and Amy said.

The next two weeks were a whirlwind with the sewing and preparation for the weddings. The nights had begun to get cooler, and mornings carried a chill in the air.

The Monday before the weddings found Alexandra on a stool next to Ma's place. Through the morning's darkness, Alexandra could hear the buckets clattering as James worked in the barn.

"He is a good man. Do you think he will ever take a bride? He never complains about having to care for us. And the harvest went well, Ma. James says it wasn't as efficient as Pa's, but we will be well off this winter. Lee is finally putting some weight back on. I was so scared. I'm sorry about you losing Julia and Noah. I guess I never understood how deep it must have cut you. I felt like someone was cutting my heart out as Lee lay there on the brink of death." She paused as she reflected on that time. "Ma, I feel ashamed. I have been jealous this week of all these wedding preparations," she confessed. "I've scolded myself about even thinking of such things, but I cannot seem to help it. How can I ever get married? I could not even think of leaving Lee and Christine, and I would not take them from James. Oh, Ma," she sighed, "I will pray more. I just think I am awfully tired." She looked towards the barn. "James is heading in with the milk." She stood and picked up the stool. "I love you, Ma."

Wearily, she trudged back to the house.

Alexandra tried to spend more time reading her Bible and praying over the next two days. Wednesday night, she retired for the night right after supper. James offered to help Christine do the dishes. Alexandra knelt by her bed and poured out her heart to the Lord. Through her tears, she surrendered to His will. Finally, with a peaceful heart, she drifted off to sleep.

She attended the weddings on Sunday with a glad heart and really enjoyed the service. She no longer had impatient thoughts about her future, whatever it might be.

Thursday morning, Alexandra was busily scurrying around the kitchen. Christine was helping and would giggle with excitement ever so often. Lee had gone out to help James with the morning chores. Though a cool morning, the sky promised a beautiful autumn day. Alexandra had secretly baked and done some extra cooking the day before. Then this morning, she and Christine had been up to a few tricks in the kitchen already.

Quickly, Christine carried the last of their surprises

into the extra bedroom. She and Alexandra had breakfast on the table when the boys came in at last. After prayer and a warm meal, they pushed their plates aside and had devotions. When James got up to head out to work, Lee jumped in his way and blocked the door.

"Surprise!" Lee yelled.

James, puzzled, looked at him. "What do you mean, 'surprise?'"

Christine jumped up and down, clapping and giggling. "We have a surprise for you!"

All together they yelled out "Happy Birthday" to him. He grinned and stood there for a moment. Embarrassed, he said, "Thank you very much. You are right. I am surprised. I forgot about my birthday."

"Well, we didn't, did we Alexandra?" Christine grinned.

Alexandra laughed at James' bewildered look. "No, we did not. We have a glorious morning planned. First, we are all packed for a grand picnic. The Lord has provided a perfect day. The sun will soon warm everything up, so we can bundle up on our way, yet have nice weather by lunch time."

James stood there with his mouth opened. "And where was I while all this planning was going on?"

Lee danced around James in excitement. "We have been sneaky, huh?" James laughed and grabbed at him. He threw Lee onto the floor with a playful tickle. Lee squealed with joy.

James teased, "I know just what to do with sneaks!"

Lee begged for mercy.

Alexandra walked over to the cupboard and removed a checkered tablecloth to take with them. "Christine, you and Lee run along and grab the food and the boxes. James, we figured on riding out to the river. I cooked food for lunch and snacks. We made your favorite ... fried chicken!"

Christine came back into the room carrying the picnic basket. "And she baked two pies!"

James laughed. "Come now. Two whole pies for just me?"

Alexandra shook her head. "No. One is a mincemeat pie for the afternoon."

James smiled broadly. "Well, it all sounds like a fine birthday ahead. I will run out and fetch the wagon." He left to pull the wagon out, and the others gathered the supplies and set them out on the front porch. Alexandra packed the latest *The Youth's Companion* to possibly read aloud after their lunch.

It took them over an hour to reach the river. James stopped by a group of trees. They set their blanket out in the sun. Alexandra set out the food as James chased the children around and about the trees. They even took a walk down to the shore. There they watched the jumping of fish near the water's edge make a ring ripple on the surface. James tried to teach Lee and Christine how to skip rocks, but to no avail. Lee liked to watch the rocks splash! The bigger the better, he thought. Finally, James gave up.

They sang their thanks to the Lord and then bid good wishes to James again. Everyone was hungry from all the playing and soon were laid back on the blanket with full stomachs and droopy eyes.

Alexandra leaned against an old stump and began to read a story. Before she could get to the end, James and Lee were snoring. Christine put her hand over her mouth and giggled. Alexandra laid back her head and closed her eyes. Next thing she knew, Lee was tapping her shoulder. She had fallen asleep!

"Can I have some more pie?" Lee asked. "I'm hungry again."

Alexandra rubbed her eyes as James sat up and looked to the sky as he shaded his eyes. "I'd say we had better think about heading home. There are still some chores that need to be done. I don't want to start out my new year by being lazy." James stood and stretched.

Alexandra cut everyone a piece of mincemeat pie to eat as she cleaned everything else up and repacked.

James wiped his mouth. "That was great. Thank you everyone for the wonderful and delicious birthday."

Lee jumped up. "That's not all." He hurried to the wagon and pulled down a box. He ran it over to James.

James looked at the box with bewilderment. "What is this?"

Christine smiled. "Open it up and see!"

James sat back down on the ground and opened the top. First, he pulled out a small white bag.

Lee looked like he would burst. "That is from me!"

James opened it to find five pieces of candy. "Why thank you, Lee. I cannot believe there has been candy in the house, and I did not sense it." Lee laughed. Next, James pulled out a nicely pressed white handkerchief.

Christine rocked with anticipation. "I made that for you."

James studied the piece of cloth. "I can tell you have worked very hard on it. The stitches are beautiful. Thank you, but it is so nice, I almost hate to use it." Christine blushed and grinned. Finally, he pulled out a new pair of wool socks. "Alexandra, thank you. The way winter seems to be moving in, I know I will put these to use."

Alexandra smiled. "You are welcome, James."

James laid his gifts back into the box. "My, this has been a grand day. Thank you all. But if we don't hurry and get back I might lie back down and snore a little longer."

The next week, Mr. Unruh hosted a farewell supper for his nephews, his brother-in-law, and Amy Whited. All the youth and their families were invited. He pit-roasted one of his pigs. Everyone contributed to the meal. Alexandra made two pies, a blackberry and a gooseberry. She also brought a quart of her pickles.

The smaller children played tag. Lee ran over and tagged Christopher, who was talking with James and Larry. Alexandra giggled as he turned and chased after the little children. Of course, he stumbled around as if he could not catch them. Finally, he tagged Larry! Before long, Larry tagged Calvin, Doc Cannon's youngest boy. Calvin tagged little Wayne. Wayne tagged Luke! It did not take long for all the youth boys to join in. Soon, Lee came over to Alexandra and sat beside her. He laid his head in her lap.

"Why don't you rest until we eat?" she suggested.

Lee nodded. "I'm tuckered out." Alexandra rubbed his head. She was so thankful for this sweaty little boy.

When Mr. Unruh stood to ask the blessing on the food, he thanked the boys for all their help. Alexandra felt a pang of sadness grip her heart. Her cheeks burned red. She quickly looked around as if everyone could hear her thoughts. She brushed her cheek and looked at the ground. Surely, she was just sad because Amy would be leaving. She scolded herself as they all bowed for prayer.

THANKFULNESS

Autumn had found its place at the Williams' farm. Oh, how Alexandra loved the fall season. Ma had always said it really felt warm and cozy with the cellar stocked, the smokehouse full, and the pantry bursting. All the beginnings of warming fires in the hearth and leaves changing colors made Alexandra sigh contentedly.

For this early November's Friday night, James had invited the Martins over to roast apples. Preacher Paul, his wife Vera, Matthew, Michael, Tonya, and Casey came shortly after supper. The boys built a small bonfire out by the brown patch of dirt that had served as the garden earlier. When the fire was ready, the ladies were called out. Tonya carried the bucket of apples, and Alexandra brought a pan of molasses sugar to roll the roasted apples in. They sang while they roasted. By the time they finished, everyone had soot, apple juice, and sugar across their faces and over their hands! What a sight! Once they washed up on the back porch, they went in for hot apple cider. After a departing prayer, the Martins were on their way back home.

As James and Alexandra sat by the fireplace, Alexandra sighed. "The simplest things seem to bring the most joy."

James flipped through his Bible. "Especially when we are content with our lives." He shot her a sideways glance.

Alexandra grinned. "I agree completely."

James shared a passage from Proverbs, and they knelt in prayer. When Alexandra finally crawled into her bed, she smiled and thanked God for her patient and kind brother.

As the Thanksgiving holiday approached, Alexandra reflected on last year's celebration. Pa had been so glad of their generous harvest. He and James had gone out in the morning before the day of their feast and brought back a turkey bigger than Lee! They had feasted with the Madisons and the Jacksons. Alexandra took a deep breath. She could almost smell Ma's pumpkin pies. She laughed to herself as she thought of Ma flittering about from the fireplace to the stove, stirring, turning, basting, and stoking. Alexandra always marveled at how Ma could get so excited about company, holidays, or any special occasion, yet stay so gentle and happy. Few times did Alexandra ever remember Ma angry. Yet, Ma was firm when she said something. Even though James towered over Ma by seven whole inches for near about three years, he never crossed Ma when she gave him instructions. Secretly, James and Alexandra swore Ma's whippings were worse than Pa's! With Pa, Alexandra thought the disappointed look in his eyes hurt deeper than the switching ever did.

The Unruhs had invited the Williams to spend Thanksgiving at their house this year. Mr. Unruh's two brothers would be bringing their families also. James and Alexandra talked about the upcoming event over supper.

"Seems like Joshua and Christopher should have just stayed; they will only be home a month before they will return at Thanksgiving," James said matter-of-factly.

Alexandra served more coffee. "Do you know much about their families?"

James nodded. "Christopher and I talked about it. Joshua is the oldest of six. His twin sisters and next sister are all married. The next two are boys about Christine's age and a little older. Now, Christopher is the next to the youngest of eight. He has a younger sister. All are married but those two. From what Larry was saying, those are the only children coming with that family. Joshua's brothers and he will come, but none of the married girls." He continued eating. "Are you interested for any particular reason?"

Alexandra flushed and looked shocked at him. "James Edward! Of course not. I was just making conversation."

James laughed. "Oh, smooth your feathers. I was just teasing you. The blush on those cheeks tells a different story, though." He chuckled at her. "I guess I need not remind you that revivals start next week," he playfully taunted her.

Alexandra stood up quickly and began to clear the table. "Brothers can be so awful!"

James laughed and took his coffee to his rocking chair. Lee and Christine looked at each other and shrugged.

Alexandra tried to be as cheerful and excited as Ma had always been at holidays, but something about the smell of the baking pumpkin pies brought tears to her eyes. No matter how much she prayed, she could not shake the veil of sadness that had gripped her heart. She sent Lee and Christine out to play. Finally, she could not stand herself any more. She went to her room and flung herself across the bed. She did not even try to stop them; the hot salty tears streaked down her face.

Christine had come in to ask for some milk when she heard Alexandra crying. Quickly, she dashed out the door to find James. He came running in. When he got to Alexandra's doorway and saw her lying on the bed wrapped in Ma's shawl, he quietly escorted Lee and Christine outside. He went back in alone and approached Alexandra's bed.

Gently, he sat on the edge of the bed and laid his hand on his shoulder. "Can I help?"

Alexandra shook her head. "Will it ever stop hurting? I am tired, James, tired of fighting memories, struggling with tears, and the loneliness of being without Ma and Pa." Alexandra continued to weep.

James looked at the floor and sat there without speaking for a few moments. He silently prayed for the right words before answering her. "I don't know what to tell you, sis. Maybe we have fought it all too much. Could be crying will help. I wondered myself if we should talk about them more. You have been working hard. Just rest and we will finish up everything later." Again he touched her shoulder and gave it a gentle squeeze.

Alexandra did not realize how tired she was. Before James could close her door, she was asleep.

When she awoke, the room was dark. Slowly, she sat up and oriented herself. She made her way to the great room. Everyone was sitting around the table eating. They all stopped and stared at her.

"Surely it isn't supper time already?" she asked as she rubbed the sleep from her eyes.

Lee smiled. "You slept all day. James said you were a baby."

Christine scolded, "He did not, Lee! He said, 'she was sleeping like a babe.' You always get things mixed up."

Lee shrugged. "I thought that is what I said, like a baby!"

James tapped the table. "Settle down, you two. We saved you some supper: sausage, potato cakes, and pickled peaches. Nothing fancy, but at least I didn't burn the house down."

Alexandra fixed her plate and sat across from James. She bowed her head in silent prayer. She moved the sausage around with her fork. "I am sorry about ..."

James cut her off. "No need. You have been working so hard, and ... well, you just needed a good rest. Enough said." James nodded his head for everyone to continue eating. "We will need to finish all our chores tomorrow. We will get an early start the next morning for the Unruhs'. We had better take some extra blankets in case it is cooler on the ride home. I cannot read the wind. Hopefully any foul weather will hold off a little longer. It isn't even officially winter yet, but you never know snow. It likes to surprise ya'."

CR

Thanksgiving Day opened with a chilly wind. Everyone was bubbling with holiday feelings. The Unruh house was toasty and very much alive. People were singing, laughing, and buzzing about. Eggnog was served to tide everyone over until the meal could be completed. It tickled Alexandra every time Mr. Unruh gave his bellowing laugh. Two large tables were set up side by side to accommodate all the adults. The children were set up in a side bedroom that had been cleared out to hold a table. There was not much elbow room, but cozy felt good to Alexandra.

When everyone settled down around the tables, Mr.

Unruh stood to address the group. He cleared his throat. "I am happy that each of you could be here to share this glorious time with us. It is a real blessing to have this house filled with family. James and his brood have always been special to us. I count it an honor to call them family today. Everyone make themselves right at home and enjoy all this good food that the ladies have slaved so over. I'd like to say I am thankful for healthy children, both at home and those who live away today. I am grateful for a virtuous wife, my good dear friends, my precious brothers and their families, and a merciful God."

Next the other Mr. Unruh, Joshua's father, stood. "I, too, would like to express my thankfulness for a loving, obedient family, God's great forgiveness, and a country I am free to worship Him in."

Another Mr. Unruh, Christopher's father, stood. "Praises be for the salvation offered to us by the shed blood of Christ. I am a fortunate man to have a devoted wife, and all my children serving our Lord. I have never known a starving day in my life, and it looks like I won't today, either!" Everyone tried not to chuckle out loud. He continued, "Back home we have good neighbors and the Lord has provided us with great crops and meat for our winter. I have nothing on this earth to complain about. I pray that we will all remain faithful, so we can one day have a home with Him."

Once Mr. Unruh was seated, James slowly stood. He fiddled with his napkin for a moment. "I feel quite small after such devotions, but I am thankful. It has been a long year, not without its trials, but the Lord has not failed us. He has been our strength and guide, and for that I am grateful. I am thankful for His healing of Lee and for His grace that gives me the assurance that Ma and Pa are at home with Him. We, as a family, want to thank you for including us in this family gathering today. We take it as an honor and privilege to have such wonderful friends." He took his seat.

Alexandra was not the only lady to wipe the corner of her eye. Mr. Unruh stood and asked for everyone to bow in prayer. Lee did not think they would ever get to eat!

Finally, the amen was said and the food seemed never ending. They ate, rested, played, ate some more, played, sang, snacked again, and then shortly before six o'clock, they headed home. James had intended on heading back before dark, but the time slipped away from him. It was truly a day to be thankful for.

THE GIFT OF PEACE

CR

It did not take long for the season's first snow to fall. Three days after Thanksgiving, they woke to a landscape of white.

As Alexandra and James stood on the front porch, James shook his head. "It won't stick around long, but it is still cloudy enough to stay at least day or two."

Alexandra pulled her blanket tighter around her shoulders."The icy rain yesterday helped it stick quicker, I'm sure."

Together, they went in and sat down to a hot breakfast. After the dishes were done, James and Lee came in from the barn. Lee was smiling from ear to ear. "All ready!"

Christine giggled and ran to the bedroom. "Okay." With her arms full of coats, she returned.

Alexandra looked around, confused. "Ready for what?"

James, Lee, and Christine glanced at each other and grinned. Lee pulled up a chair, and Christine led Alexandra to it. Bewildered, she sat with a 'plop'. Christine pulled a sheet of paper from her dress pocket.

Holding it in front of her, she began,

"Happy Birthday to you.
We hope you don't turn blue.
Off for a ride in the snow,

We hope the bad wind don't blow.
But first a song we will sing.
We hope you like its ring.
We want to show our love for you,
For all the wonderful things you do."

Then, the three stood before her and sang two lines from her favorite hymn. Alexandra sat and smiled. When they finished, Christine handed Alexandra her coat, scarf, and gloves. James had the sled and horse hooked up and ready for a ride. They rode around the land for over an hour, laughing and singing. The air was very cold, but at least there was no wind. By the time they arrived back at the house, all their noses and cheeks looked like cherries! Everyone helped put up the horse and wipe down the sled.

As they trudged back to the house, James was hit in the back. He spun around to greet a snowball with a kiss! He brushed the snow from his face.

Lee was lying on the snow laughing and kicking. "She got you good!"

James rushed at a screaming Alexandra, grabbed her, and rubbed snow in her face! They continued to throw snow and chase each other until they dropped from exhaustion onto the porch.

Lee sat there huffing. "I'm hungry!"

Christine laughed. "You are always hungry."

Alexandra smiled, trying to catch her breath. "For once, I agree with Lee. My stomach is hollering for food. Come, let's see if lunch is ready."

James brushed snow from his clothes. "Those baked beans you put on before breakfast ought to hit the spot."

Everyone piled in the lean-to and shed their wet

clothes to hang around the stove to dry. Once in some dry clothes, they all helped get the table set as Alexandra fried some cornbread to go with the beans. James even sliced some cheese and sat out some pickles. After prayer, the room was quiet except for the sounds of spoons digging into the bowls.

Christine looked up at everyone thoughtfully. "Seems like play makes you as hungry as hard work."

Alexandra smiled at each person. "Thank you all so much for the fun birthday."

Lee and Christine looked at each other and giggled.

After second helpings, James leaned back and let out a deep breath. "I think I just have room for dessert before I explode."

Alexandra looked embarrassed. "I'm sorry, but I haven't anything made for dessert. I wasn't planning for this celebration. Tomorrow is my real birthday, and I had thought of making something in the morning, but..."

James smiled mischievously and cut her off. "I know, but the snow might not be left enough to sled on, so we thought we would move everything up a day."

Christine got up and went to James' room. She came back with an apple pie, and Lee ran to the cellar and brought in a small pail of cream.

Alexandra put her hands on her hips. "Now how did you all cook this without me knowing it?"

Christine giggled with excitement. "James did it."

James laughed as Alexandra looked at him with her mouth opened.

"Not exactly. I asked Monica, Sunday after church, if she would bake it. I had planned to run to town today. When the weather began to look bad, Larry brought it out when he helped me with the cows day before yesterday. Since I know you like a hot pie, I thought I would put it in the oven to warm while we do the dishes for you."

Alexandra smiled. "I like that idea very much!"

Christine laughed. "Which part, us doing the dishes, or the warm pie?"

Alexandra sat herself by the fire. "Both!"

Finally, when they had served and eaten the pie, Lee and Christine each brought out a small gift for Alexandra. Lee gave her a shiny thimble. She put it on her finger. "Thank you, Lee. Now I won't stick myself so much."

Lee grinned.

Alexandra opened Christine's gift next. She had made a pin cushion. Alexandra looked at her in wonderment. "Now who showed you how to make this?"

"Mrs. Madison helped me." She grinned broadly.

"It will be very useful. Thank you."

James took a moment to get a box from his room. "Here." He blushed as he handed it to her. Carefully, she opened it.

She gasped when she saw what was inside. "Oh, James. It is too much!"

"It is about time you have a real nice dress, not made from everyday stuff. Happy birthday."

She held up the material delicately. It was a solid blue piece of cashmere.

Alexandra studied the cloth's nap with awe. "It seems too nice to touch. I am afraid to cut it. I don't want to mess it up."

James shook his head. "Nonsense. Ma said you could sew as well as she could. I asked Mrs. Jackson how much to get, and she measured it out."

Alexandra looked at them all with tears in her eyes.

"Thank you all!"

Lee jumped up. "That's not all. James said after supper tonight we could make popcorn balls!"

Everyone laughed at his excitement.

Alexandra went to bed that night with a smile on her face.

CR

December came cold and fast.

"So much cold and snow so early in the season makes me nervous," James said as he watched the snow falling from the front window.

Alexandra stood by his side. "I hope it lets up soon. Christmas is just two weeks away."

James nodded. "Well, at least it isn't a blizzard. I think this winter will be worse than the last two. Our supplies are well stocked. So, I guess we really don't have anything to worry about. I do want to relocate some wood to beside the lean-to."

Alexandra went back to the stove. "Have you decided about Christmas? The Schimdts have invited us to lunch."

James sighed. "I guess a lot depends on the weather. As soon as it clears up enough to run to town, I'll go ahead and make the trip. I would like it if you went along. It might be our last trip to town for a while."

Alexandra smiled. "Maybe we could take the sled?"

James shrugged. "If we do not need to bring home many supplies."

That afternoon the snow stopped.

The next morning, Lee was disappointed. "It barely snowed enough to cover the ground!"

James nodded as he stirred his porridge. "The sun looks like he will pay us a visit today. If that happens, I will want to go to town first thing after breakfast tomorrow. The road should be cleared enough for the horses and wagon. Sorry, Alexandra, no sled."

Alexandra shrugged. "That is all right. I'd like to pick up some flour, salt, coffee, and tea. Then, everything will be set for whatever winter holds for us."

James nodded. "I plan to take the hides in and trade them. But I want to go in and do our business and come right home. We will take a snack to eat on the ride back."

And so went the next day. At the Jackson Mercantile, Lee and Christine stared at the candy counter while James and Alexandra did their shopping.

Mr. Jackson came over to speak to Lee and Christine. "Merry Christmas to you, children!"

Christine and Lee giggled bashfully. "Merry Christmas," they said together.

From behind his back, Mr. Jackson produced a small white-with-red-striped candy stick in each hand. "Do you think you have been good enough boys and girls for one of these?" Excitedly, they both looked from each other to James, who had walked up behind them. James smiled and nodded.

Quickly, they turned back to Mr. Jackson and replied, "Yes, sir!"

He handed them the candy from over the counter.

"Thank you, Mr. Jackson," replied Christine with a broad smile.

"Yes, thank you!" said Lee as he looked wide-eyed at the candy.

Mr. Jackson laughed. "You're welcome, children. James, I hope they are always that easy to please."

After their purchases were loaded into the wagon, they headed home, and none too quick. The sky seemed to get darker by the minute, and the wind steadily picked up. The ride home proved to be a lot cooler than when they set out that morning.

As they unhitched the wagon, James spoke to Lee. "I don't think the worst of this will be here for a day or two. All the same, let's you and I set everything up for the bad weather."

Lee took a deep breath and nodded. It made him feel grown up when James let him help with such important work.

They came in later than what Alexandra expected. She teased, "I thought you got lost from the barn to here."

Lee wrinkled his brow. "It isn't that far. We were just getting ready for the storm."

Christine and Alexandra stopped what they were doing and looked at James.

James rolled his eyes at Lee and corrected him, "In case of a storm. The skies look cold and wet. In case something comes down, I just wanted to be prepared. Nothing to worry about."

Alexandra went back to setting the table.

That night, the snow blew over without visiting the Williams' farm.

At church on Sunday, James spoke with Mr. Schimdt. James explained that the weather just was too unpredictable lately to guarantee they could come for the holiday meal. Mr. Schimdt agreed. Still, he left James with an open invitation. If weather permitted, he would expect them. James agreed.

The few days before Christmas, the house was filled with the aroma of cinnamon rolls, spiced cider, pumpkin pie, baked ham, roasting fowl, stewed turnips, baked beans, fried onions, and Christmas cookies.

"Alexandra, are you sure you are not expecting an army to drop by?" James teased her as he nibbled and tasted things over her shoulder.

"If we do go to Mae's, I would like to take our share of the food. If not, we will have plenty around here!" she retorted.

Christmas Eve night found them sitting in front of the fire reading the story of Christmas. James read Luke 1:1-2:17. They talked about what Christmas meant to them. They prayed and thanked God for His precious gift.

The next morning found Alexandra singing over the bubbling breakfast. Christine and Lee came out of their bedrooms about the same time.

Christine stretched. "What is that noise?"

Alexandra laughed. "Merry Christmas to you, too. It is the wind."

Lee rubbed his eyes. "It sounds like a bear!" Suddenly, the lean-to door flew open. A flurry of white flakes and a burst of cold air blew around the room. In bustled a well-bundled James.

Lee and Christine shouted at the same time, "Snow!" and flew to the window. They rubbed a spot to look out.

James took off his wet things and walked over to Alexandra for a cup of coffee. Then he sat by the fire. "There is plenty of it out there. I knew the sky held snow, but it sure took its own sweet time dumping it. Well, so be it. Merry Christmas, everyone!"

Everyone cried out, "Merry Christmas!" at once.

After a big breakfast of bacon and eggs, everyone stretched out before the fire. Before bedtime the night before, Lee and Christine had placed their packages to the others beside the fireplace. James now grinned as he watched Lee and Christine almost bursting with anticipation.

Alexandra rebuked him, "Stop teasing them, James. Go ahead and let them give out their gifts."

Both children looked pleadingly at James.

"Okay. I guess you have been patient enough," he finally relented. Both jumped up off the floor from where they were sitting and rushed to the small group of packages. Christine picked out the ones she had wrapped and took them to each person. Lee did the same with his. Alexandra went to her room and brought out the gifts from herself. James went to the lean-to and came back with an armful of something draped in a quilt.

Lee opened his gifts first. James had carved him a cow, horse, pig, and a dog out of cedar. Lee walked them on the floor. "Thank you, James!" Then from Christine, he received a new set of mittens. Lee smiled. "You made them in my favorite color — green! Thank you." From Alexandra, he received a stick pony. She had sewn the head of burlap with big button eyes, an embroidered red nose, and a black yarn mane. James had fastened it securely onto a stick. Lee jumped up and 'rode' it around the room, yelling, "Yippee!"

Everyone laughed.

"Okay, cowboy. Settle down while everyone takes their turn," James chided.

Lee sat down so Christine could open her gifts. From Alexandra, she opened a beautiful baby doll quilt. Soft and fluffy, it had been pieced together and was full of carded wool. Christine ran to get her rag doll that Ma had made her last

Christmas.She wrapped it in the quilt. "Thank you. I love it." She sat for a moment and looked around. She just sat there, for there were no more gifts for her. Lee covered his mouth and giggled.

James slowly lifted the old blanket from the bundle he had brought in. Christine gasped. It was a doll cradle!

Lee laughed out loud in his excitement. "I helped sand it nice and smooth!"

James nodded. "Yes. This is from Lee and me."

Christine stroked it gingerly. She laid her doll in it and wrapped it with the quilt. "Oh, thank you all!"

Everyone turned to Alexandra. First, she opened the gift from Christine. She held it up in front of herself, "Oh, Christine. It is a lovely apron. How did you learn to embroider this rose on the pocket?"

"Monica helped me." Christine grinned.

"Thank you very much, Christine." Alexandra stood and removed her old apron and tied the new one on. Next, she picked up the other gift. "This is a little heavy. What could it be?" she said playfully.

Lee bounced excitedly. "Open it! Open it!"

She laughed. "I think I will." She unwrapped the brown paper. "Oh, James! It is beautiful," she whispered. It was a cedar box with a rose burnt-carved into the top. The box was ten inches by six inches, sanded, and oiled smooth. She looked at the box, and then at James. "There aren't any nails. How did you do it?"

James shrugged. "It is mine and Lee's secret. He sanded and oiled it. It was his idea for the rose."

Lee smiled. "Really, I first said a piggy, but James said I need to pick a girl thing."

Everyone laughed, and Lee just looked at them.

Alexandra stopped laughing. "Thank you, boys. Okay, it is your turn, James."

James yawned. "Maybe I will take a nap before I open mine."

Lee and Christine yelled together, "No!"

James chuckled. "All right." He opened Christine's first. She had knitted him a gray scarf. He wrapped it around his neck. "I can take on the cold now! Thank you, girlie."

Christine giggled.

Next, he unwrapped a leather pouch with a leather drawstring. Lee hopped up. "It's for your bullets!"

James laughed at Lee's excitement. "Thank you. It is just what I have been thinking of making. I sure needed this."

Lee beamed.

Finally, James unwrapped Alexandra's gift. It was a new white Sunday shirt she had made him. He held it up. "It is very handsome, Alexandra. I look forward to the next church service so I can wear it. Thank you."

Alexandra served everyone a mug of eggnog, and they sang some songs. They even told some stories of past Christmases. Alexandra felt good talking about Ma and Pa. It brought them back into the home. James said that is where they belonged.

After a full day of playing, singing, a few stories, lots of snow, and hoards of food, Alexandra sat in front of the fire with James. Lee and Christine were snugly off in dreamland already.

"I really felt good talking about Ma and Pa. The stories we remembered made me feel like Pa and Ma were a part of this Christmas, too," sighed Alexandra.

James nodded thoughtfully. "Well, maybe we are all healing. The hurt isn't so raw; the thought of Ma and Pa can now make us smile instead of cry."

"It looks like we will be home alone on Sunday. I am looking forward to it now." Alexandra sat back in her chair and watched the fire.

James smiled. "Me, too. I think it is time. We are coming to the New Year. Do you ever wonder what it holds for us?"

Alexandra had to laugh. "Oh, James. What a question. I wonder, worry, and even dream about our future. I have so many questions, but one thing I did learn this year — leave the future to God."

James leaned forward in his chair. "I have seen many changes in you, sis, all of them good. Ma and Pa would be real happy with how you have grown spiritually."

Alexandra blushed. "I feel the same about you. I hate Pa did not get to see you grow into a man this year. You have been a good provider for us. Thank you."

James sat back and looked into the glowing fire. "The Lord has been good to us. I wonder what He has planned for us now."

A NEW BEGINNING

James stood looking out the front window, steam from his coffee mug swirling under his nose.

Alexandra quietly drew up beside him. Softly, she broke the morning's silence. "Penny for your thoughts."

Never breaking his gaze, James sighed, "I was thinking about our hogs. This nice cold weather means butchering time." He paused to sip his coffee. "That was the last big thing we tackled before Pa took sick. He really looked forward to this time each year. He enjoyed all the neighbors joining together to help and the fresh pork ribs and tenderloins for dinner." He smiled to himself as he sipped his coffee. "I sure am grateful for the meat and lard."

Alexandra wrinkled her nose. "But it is a foul smelling job to tackle!" She leaned her head against James' shoulder and remembered, "Ma always loved the headcheese." She sighed. "It's hard to not feel melancholy thinking about Ma and Pa. It is near 'bout a year since they took sick and died. Yet after such a nice Thanksgiving and Christmas, I am not going to let myself become sad." With a determined spirit, she turned and went back to the kitchen area to finish setting the breakfast table.

Soon after, Lee came trampling in from the cellar through the lean-to door. "I put the milk down to settle, and I found three apples like you asked." He bustled over to the stove where Alexandra was stirring the porridge.

"Thanks, Lee. Go warm by the fire while I fry these up." She gave him a thankful smile and went to slicing the apples.

Christine came out of the boys' room. "All the beds are made and the rooms straightened. Shall I pour the coffee now?"

Alexandra shook her head. "Not yet. I could use some water to heat for dishwater. Can you set a pot on the back burner to warm?"

James set his empty mug on the table. "I'll get that, Christine. I wanted to fill the corner barrel today anyway." He grabbed his hat and coat and headed towards the door.

Alexandra called over her shoulder, "Breakfast will be on the table in about ten minutes, James."

James grinned and tugged his hat on tightly. "Yes, ma'am." He called over to Lee, "Come, Lee, and help me out."

With a hop, Lee grabbed his things off the peg. "Sure!"

By the time the girls were pouring the coffee, the boys were stamping their feet on the back porch. James hustled in carrying two buckets packed with snow; Lee carried one. They dumped them in the corner barrel, and Christine hastily filled a pot with snow and set it on the stove. Soon they were all settled around the table. They all took hands and bowed their heads. James returned thanks for their health and for the food.

"Hot porridge and fried apples warms me right down to my toes." James winked at Christine. She giggled, and Lee nodded as he blew on his steaming spoonful of apples. "If weather holds out, the butchering should commence at the Unruhs day after tomorrow. Yesterday's snow might slow things down by a day, but just twenty-four hours of snow should not hinder things too bad." James went back to eating.

Alexandra looked at James. "Well, how will you know if we are to go or not?"

James sipped his coffee. "Larry was to ride out today and let me know. A cutter could make it. I will just wait out the day and see what it holds. If he does come, then our turn should fall on the New Year. It will be a busy several days around here, but well worth it. We will help with the Unruhs, and in return we will have a day to get ready for our help."

Alexandra nodded. "It always feels good to have plenty of meat set up for winter. I am afraid we are in for a cold season this time around. I do not recall so many snows so early in the season." She got up to refill the bowls. James was nodding and seemed to be lost in his thoughts. Everyone finished eating quietly with the only sound being the crackling from the hearth in the background.

Finally, James pushed back from the table. "Well, ladies, another fine meal you have served us men. Thank you."

Alexandra took her plate to the washtub. "You are welcomed."

She smiled at Lee as he mimicked James. "Yes. Thank ya', ladies."

Christine giggled.

James went into his room and re-entered with his rifle and bullet pouch. Alexandra and Christine were washing and drying the dishes. Alexandra looked over her shoulder with raised eyebrows at James. "All those deep thoughts over breakfast have something to do with that rifle?"

James smiled. "I did not think I was as deep into my thoughts as I was into that porridge! However, yes, I was thinking that with such a clear, crisp day after so much snow, deer might be out and about searching for food. Would you mind fixing some jerky and a biscuit for me to take along? I plan on staying out a while."

Lee hopped up from where he was playing with the wooden animals that James had carved him for Christmas. "Can I go hunting with you, James? I promise to be extra still and quiet!"

James looked at Alexandra. "What do you think?"

Alexandra looked from Lee to James. "If I remember correctly, you began hunting with Pa when you were five years old. I reckon it is past time for Lee to go. But boys, please be extra careful. Lee, I do not want you to get sick again." She shuddered as she recalled last August when Lee took the fever. The memory of him coming so near death during those days still made her heart ache with fear.

Lee ran to his room to put away his toys.

James chuckled, interrupting her thoughts. "We will be careful, sis. Can we have something thick and hot waiting on us when we return?"

Christine was wrapping two biscuits from last night's meal. "A thick vegetable beef stew would be nice. We still have some vegetables left from our Christmas meal yesterday."

Alexandra smiled. "Since you thought of it, I will let you make it. How would you like that?"

Christine grinned. "Would I ever!"

James gave her a serious look. "You trying to scare us into not coming home?"

Christine stuck out her tongue at him. "You sure eat enough of the cookies that I bake."

He laughed aloud. "Testy, just like your sister!"

Lee appeared, tumbling out of the room, bundled tight in a sweater, scarf, and hat. "I just need to grab my coat and gloves and I will be ready."

James stood from where he had knelt to tie his boot, taking his rifle and heading to the lean-to in order to bundle himself.

Lee took the brown paper package from Christine. She leaned over and whispered in his ear, "I stuck in some cookies, too." Lee licked his lips and grinned.

Alexandra came over and made sure everything was buttoned, wrapped, and tucked tight. "I hope you are sharing good secrets."

Lee smiled. "More like delicious secrets." Christine laughed. Lee hurried out through the lean-to.

Alexandra turned to Christine. "Well, what shall we tackle today?"

Christine thought for a moment. "I have two more letters to sew in order to finish my sampler. Let us finish that. You said once I was finished, I could begin my quilt blocks."

Alexandra nodded. "So I did. Get your sampler and we shall finish it. You and I will start the soup right after lunch. There are still slices of pie left from yesterday, too. We will set them in the warmer once we set the table."

The afternoon stretched on as the girls sewed and waited. Shortly after lunch, they heard someone approaching. Out of the window, they spied Larry and Monica riding up. Alexandra and Christine grabbed their shawls and rushed onto the porch to greet them.

Larry pulled right next to the porch. "Afternoon, ladies."

Christine blushed and giggled. She stepped halfway behind Alexandra.

Alexandra nodded her greeting. "How do."

Monica smiled. "Papa sent us out to let you know the

butchering is still on as planned. Do you think you can still come?"

Alexandra pulled her shawl tighter around her face. "We will be there. James and Lee went hunting this morning. I expect them soon. Would you like to come in and thaw out?"

Larry shook his head. "Thank you kindly, but we need to get home and prepare for all the help coming for the slaughter." With a little flick of the reins, they trotted off. Monica peeked out from under the quilt and waved, then quickly reburied herself under the covers. Alexandra and Christine waved a quick good-bye and hastily retreated into the house.

By mid-afternoon, James and Lee could be seen traipsing across the side field.

Christine squealed, "I see them! James and Lee are carrying something!"

Alexandra wiped her hands on her apron and hurried to the window. "Yes. I do see they have had a good hunt. But, I'm afraid not as big as James was probably wanting. Hurry and finish seasoning your stew, and we will slice some bread. I will run to the cellar for some pumpkin butter."

The girls quickly went about their tasks as the boys drew near. James went to the barn to finish dressing out the two rabbits while Lee ran in to get the pan and knife James would need. Alexandra had them sitting in the lean-to waiting on him. Once finished, the boys brought the meat in for Alexandra to finish. Lee's cheeks and nose were bright red. Christine helped him off with his coat, scarf, gloves, and hat. He rushed over to the fire to try to thaw his frozen body.

James sat down on the table bench and began unlacing his boots. "We found a few tracks, but no deer. It is some kind of cold. Trudging through the snow wears you out. After a hot supper, I will be so ready for bed."

Lee turned away. "Not me." However, his big yawn told the truth.

Alexandra helped pull the layers of clothes off Lee. "Let us give the stew thirty more minutes at least. Then we will eat."

James nodded and looked down at his unlaced boot. "Sounds good." He began to re-lace his boots. "I think I will go ahead and feed the animals. It will be time to go back out in an hour, so I might as well go ahead. Hold supper until I finish."

Lee had sat on the floor by the fire with his arms wrapped around his drawn-up knees. "Could we have a snack while we wait for you to get back?"

James was putting on his coat. "Talk to your sister. I will try to hurry."

Alexandra smiled. "I knew you would be hungry. I have an apple turnover in the warmer for you. Since it is so close to supper, how about you and Christine splitting it?"

Lee and Christine looked at each other, nodded, and smiled.

"I will get it for us," Christine offered.

James and Alexandra sat by the fire that night with the wind whistling outside the window.

Alexandra explained, "I put on the rabbit stew for tomorrow. I will carry it with us to Widow Stephans' house. We are supposed to eat and rest there for the afternoon following church until the early evening service." She paused for a moment, then put down her knitting and turned to her brother. "James, you have been sort of quiet since you and Lee came back this evening. The way he went on and on about how great the hunt went, I take it he did not get into much trouble. So, if it is not Lee — what is wrong?"

James slowly shook his head and gave her a sly grin. "Sometimes it is not a good thing to have a sister who reads you so well." He rocked for a moment in silence, then with a soft sigh, he began, "There really is not anything wrong. I saw some signs that winter plans to be very rough. We came across a beaver's dam. It was the thickest I have seen in at least six years." He ran his fingers through his hair and yawned. "Excuse me." He leaned his elbows on his legs. "Our harvest was good, and if we get our three hogs slaughtered, I can trade one for all the winter's dry goods. Ma's quilts and our clothes are fine for anything winter can bring. I do think I want to move our wood completely inside the barn and fill half the lean-to and side porch. I am going to run a strong lead rope to the barn. I might be able to get Larry and Christoph to come out next week, if the weather holds out. I want to make sure the roof and barn are secure against any harsh winds that might come."

Alexandra picked up her knitting. "Well, for someone who is not worried, you seem to have given it a lot of thought."

James shrugged. "No need to worry over something I cannot control. I just want to be prepared."

"What can we girls do?" Alexandra inquired.

James shook his head. "Nothing. Wait, maybe I will leave the chickens to you. Bed them down well and see if the coup needs any more work."

Alexandra nodded. "We can handle that."

"I'm ready for some shuteye. Trudging along in the snow wore me out."

Together in prayer, they knelt. Then Alexandra went to her room as James fixed the fire for the night.

BUTCHERING TIME

Two days later, butchering commenced at Anthony Unruh's house. Anthony, Carl Martin, and his father Minister Paul all slaughtered together. Mrs. Unruh, her daughters Monica and the newly married Faith, along with Carl's bride Elizabeth, Paul's wife and daughter Vera and Tonya, and Christine and Alexandra were there to cook, salt, stuff, wrap, and grind. Besides Mr. Unruh's son Larry and son-in-law Brent, there were James, Lee, Paul's sons Michael and Matthew, and Casey to help with the butchering. Of course, Lee and Casey seemed to play more than help, but after everything began, James found that Lee playing was less of a bother than his help! Mr. Unruh and Minister Paul took care of shooting and bleeding the pigs at the appropriate times. Larry, Carl, Matthew, and Michael were in charge of scalding and scraping. Brent, James, Mr. Unruh, and Minister Paul took over hanging and gutting the hogs. The innards were given to the ladies to sort and prepare. Carl and Larry began to saw the carcass into sections. Monica prepared a kettle to render the lard right away in the back yard.

A late lunch consisted of tenderloins, ribs, cornbread, steamed cabbage, sweet potato pies, and fried turnips. The afternoon was filled with the making of sausage, headcheese, rendering lard, and preparing the meat. By the time the Williams headed for home, they were a tired, quiet lot.

Between his yawns, Lee tried telling Christine about playing with Casey. Christine attempted to listen but soon found she was nodding with each bump in the road.

Two days later, another butchering was occurring at Sam Glen's. Several families were gathered there also. James and Alexandra did not assist this time. They were preparing for their own butchering day, which would follow in two days. Their neighbors the Madisons and Brent Evans were bringing their hogs to the Williams' farm for butchering. Brent had purchased a tract of land just on the other side of the Madisons, since his marriage to the former Faith Unruh. Larry and his family, Matthew, Michael, Carl, Martin, and Brent's brother and sister Chad and Mary would also attend.

James woke early, with anticipation, on New Year's morning. The sky was still as black as tar, and the air was blowing a whispering chill across the barnyard. He stirred the embers to wake the fire. He remained squatting, gazing at the kindling as the small flames licked its edges. 'A new year, a whole year without Pa and Ma,' he whispered as he thought to himself about the new year that lay ahead. He was so deep in his thoughts that he never heard the slight rustling of the quilt wrapped around Alexandra as she crept up beside him.

"It will be a better year. Won't it?" she whispered.

He jerked his face towards her. "You startled me."

"I'm sorry," Alexandra apologized.

He turned back to the fire and added some wood. "I was just thinking of the verse James 4:14-15. Hand me my Bible, please, and I will read it to you."

Alexandra reached over and picked up the Bible from his rocker. "I could not sleep, so I thought I might as well get up when I heard you in here." She sat on the floor beside him.

James leafed through the New Testament until he

found the verses. "Here it is. 'Whereas ye know not what shall be on the morrow. For what is your life? It is even a vapour, that appeareth for a little time, and then vanisheth away. For that ye ought to say, If the Lord will, we shall live, and do this, or that.' So far, not worrying about tomorrow, but trusting Him who knows all our needs has done us well. I do not want to begin this new year with doubts and fears." James closed his Bible and looked at Alexandra. "Life is treating us more than well. We are warm, healthy, well fed, and much loved. What else could we ask of Him?"

Alexandra looked into the fire. "That is why I could not sleep. I thought I should be sad and scared; instead, I feel content. I do trust that God has a plan for me, and I am looking forward to this year."

James drew a deep breath, letting the cool morning air fill his lungs slowly. He exhaled. "I dreamed of Pa last night. I saw him standing across the yard. He walked toward me. Alexandra, he was so close, I wanted to reach out and touch him, but I could not move. He smiled and said, 'Well done, son.' Ma came over out of nowhere and put her hand on his arm. She looked at me and smiled. Her smile went straight to my heart. She blew me a kiss, and they faded away." He shook his head slightly and gave Alexandra a small smile. "They looked so happy. I could not be sad. It felt like twenty pounds lifted off my chest. I awoke smiling." He stirred the fire and nodded as he spoke. "It will be a good day, sis. That I am sure."

Alexandra smiled and wiped the happy tears from her cheeks. Together, they knelt and prayed a thankful prayer for whatever the year held for them.

The day got busy early and quickly. The butchering went well. Though the work was smelly and hectic, Alexandra did not mind, especially when so many good friends helped. The women sang, laughed, and chatted away the busy hours. Mr. Unruh, Mrs. Unruh, Larry, and Monica were the last to load up at the end of the day. Mr. Unruh and James stood over by the well talking as everyone else boarded into the wagon. Alexandra glanced over the top of the wagon where she stood helping Monica load. She saw James was nodding his head and looking intently at Mr. Unruh. They shook hands, and soon the Unruh wagon was on its way. Good-byes and thank-yous were shouted as the Williams clan stood waving from the porch.

Alexandra and Christine went back inside to finish up with a few things. James and Lee went to do evening chores.

After prayer, they wearily headed off to bed.

James stopped. "I forgot to mention over supper that Larry, Mr. Unruh, and Hope's husband, Bob, are coming back in the morning to help tighten up things to prepare for any harsh weather that might try and surprise us. Mr. Unruh feels, like I do, that something will happen soon. He said they would ride out after chore time."

Alexandra yawned. "That will be fine. How long do you expect to work?"

James scratched his thin brown beard. "At least until lunch, maybe a little after, I expect."

She nodded and sleepily disappeared into her bedroom.

A HOWLING SURPRISE!

The roof repairs and some maintenance to the barn the following day were completed none too soon. Everyone woke the day after to a wild, icy wind! Sleet could be heard tapping on the roof and blowing against the windowpanes. Alexandra was busy in the kitchen when James came in from morning chores, shivering and dripping. Alexandra rushed over to help him out of his wet coat, hat, and boots. Christine came out of the bedroom where she had been straightening up. She grabbed her shawl from the hook next to the front door and hurried to James.

Alexandra wrapped it around his shoulders. "You will catch your death of cold. You are chilled through, James! Quick, come to the fire."

"Oh, please! I will warm soon enough. How about some coffee?" he protested.

Christine hurried over and carefully poured a cup full of steaming brew for him. Holding it with both hands around the rim, she hastened it to James. He sipped it and tried to stop his teeth from chattering. "It is freezing cold out there. The Lord has led us safely again. The repairs were finished in time and so was the slaughtering. I left the milk in the lean-to. Alexandra, I was so eager to get next to this fire, I forgot it. I am sorry." He continued to sip his coffee.

"No problem." Alexandra headed to get the milk.

"You need to dig out Pa's slicker from the winter trunk to wear over your coat. I will make a mask out of a scrap to protect your face and neck from the ice." She went to work on the milk as Christine set the table for breakfast.

Lee came yawning and stretching in the doorway of his room. "What is all the noise?"

Everyone looked at him.

"Happy birthday, you sleepy head," Christine shouted.

Lee's sleepy eyes popped open. "My birthday?"

James, who was finally beginning to dry out and warm up, laughed. "Yes, my little buddy, it is your very own birthday, number seven to be exact. How does it feel to be another year older?"

Lee smiled and stood straight. "I feel all grown up!"

Alexandra and Christine laughed. Alexandra shook her head. "Growing, I am sure of, but all grown up, not quite yet. Happy birthday to you, little brother." She went over and hugged him.

Lee grinned, and then he looked very serious. "What is all that noise outside?"

James looked towards the window. "Sleet and wind."

Lee looked disappointed. "We will not be able to go to church today, will we?"

James chuckled. "You will not even get to step outside the door today. I will have to tend to all the chores."

Christine danced around Lee. "No need for you to worry. We have lots of indoor surprises for you today!" she teased.

"Really?" Lee's face brightened.

Alexandra laughed. "Yes, really. Now, run and dress warmly. Make your bed and come to breakfast. You might find your first surprise by then!"

Lee dashed off to get his special day started. Soon a big 'whoopee' was heard from the boys' room. Christine giggled with anticipation.

James looked suspiciously at the girls. "I smell some sneaky foxes in this coop."

Alexandra tried to look very innocent. "Oh, well, I at least hope it is a pleasant stench." She laughed.

Lee came bounding out of his room smoothing the front of his new flannel shirt. "My, it is warm and soft. Thank you, Alexandra."

"You are welcomed. How about trying not to outgrow it too soon?" Alexandra chuckled as Lee walked over and hugged her waist.

Everyone found their place at the table. James thanked God for their warm house against the outside cold, the warm food, and for Lee.

As Lee held his bowl out for a second helping, James laughed. "You will outgrow that shirt at a rabbit's pace eating like that."

Lee grinned. "Can't help it. Alexandra cooks too good! My stomach just keeps asking for more."

Christine giggled as she refilled everyone's cup.

James cleared his throat. "Lee, how about putting another log on the fire, please?"

Everyone tried to watch Lee without being obvious. He gladly hopped up and went to put a log, which was leaning against the hearth, into the fire. He was laying the log in when something caught the corner of his eye. Underneath where that log had been leaning, a toy horse stood reared up on its hind legs.

"Oh, James!" he whispered excitedly as he let go of the log quickly. "Look, Christine!" He held the horse up for her to see.

Christine bounced in her seat and clapped. "I know, I hid it for James!"

Lee rushed back to the table. "Thank you, James!"

"You are welcomed. It is a mustang." James sat back and sipped his coffee.

Alexandra asked to see it and complimented on how wild and strong it looked. Lee beamed with satisfaction. He could hardly wait to play with it! He sat it in front of him and gazed at it as he emptied his bowl.

Christine smiled over at Lee. "I made you a cake this morning. When it cools, Alexandra will whip up some icing, and you can lick the bowl all by yourself!"

"Man! I am glad it is my birthday!" Lee's smile warmed the entire room.

After breakfast dishes were cleaned and put away, everyone sat around the fire to sing hymns. Lee was allowed to choose all three songs since it was his birthday. Alexandra read about Shadrack, Meshack, and Abendego. Lee liked to hear their "sing-songy" names, as he called them. James read Matthew chapters three and four. Then they each in turn prayed aloud.

Later in the day, Lee sat by the fire and played with his set of wooden animals that James had carved for him over the last year. Christine was working on her quilt patches. Since she had finished her sampler last week, Alexandra, who was now knitting and rocking, had started her on a nine-patch quilt. Thinking of another surprise, Christine tried not to smile as she looked at her sister.

Suddenly, James came in from the lean-to with a rush. He hurried over to the fire. Stripping away his coat and gloves, Christine quickly gave him her shawl to wrap around his shoulders. Alexandra was pouring him a hot cup of tea before anyone spoke.

"Thank you, everyone. The slicker did help keep me drier. I left it, my gloves, and boots in the lean-to. The sleet has mixed with a lot of snow. I suspect it soon will be all snow." His teeth chattered between words. He sipped his tea.

"What about the wind?" Alexandra asked as she settled back to her knitting.

James sighed. "Still blowing. The sleet and snow would not be half as rough if the wind did not try to drive through you."

Lee smiled. "I am glad it is so messy outside."

"Lee Charles Williams! What makes you say such?" Alexandra scolded.

Lee sat up and looked at everyone. "Because we are all together and that would be my birthday wish. If the weather was nice, we all might be out doing chores. I like it when we sit here together."

James ruffled Lee's hair. "I do, too. However, if we always sat around, we would not survive. Who would get milk, food, and necessities for us?"

Lee shrugged. "Oh, I know, but it is nice for my birthday."

Alexandra sat straight up on the edge of her chair. "Lee, your feet look cold. Go to your room and get another pair of socks on, please."

Lee looked at his feet. "They are nice and toasty, Alexandra."

James, looking over his steaming cup of tea, said firmly, "Do not sass your sister, Lee."

With a puzzled look, Lee shrugged as he rose. "Yes, sir. I'm sorry, Alexandra."

"Thank you." Alexandra tried not to smile.

Christine struggled to suppress her giggle.

After a moment, Lee let out a chuckle from within his room. "You got me good!" He came dashing back to the fireplace carrying a pair of gray knitted woolen socks with a red band at the top. The pair was neatly tied with a bow in twine.

"Happy birthday!" Christine yelled.

"Come to think of it, my old socks do not seem to be keeping my toes warm enough. I really need to put on this pair!" Lee took off his old pair and put the new ones on. "Thanks, Christine."

Christine blushed. "Alexandra made most of them, but she taught me how to do the band. The red yarn is my work."

"Some cake would go good with this last drop of tea I have left," James teased.

"Funny way of asking for more tea," Alexandra bantered as she got up.

Christine jumped up to help Alexandra. "Maybe we can read a story for Lee's birthday tonight?"

James pretended to think about it for a moment. "I guess so — and maybe some buttermilk with our cake."

Lee's eyes grew as big as saucers as he rapidly nodded his head up and down and rubbed his hands together. "Boy, oh boy, what a day!"

Later, after the younger ones were in bed, James and Alexandra laid out and hung James' wet clothes, jackets, hats, and gloves around the fire and stove to dry.

"Everything will be dry and ready for the new day by morning," Alexandra said as she finally sat down.

James sighed. "I missed hearing Minister Paul today, but we cannot control the weather."

Alexandra nodded. "Yes. Winter does seem to run long without visiting on Sundays. We did have a blessed day, though, for Lee's birthday."

James scratched the side of his thin beard. "Funny how he never mentioned Ma or Pa today, don't ya' think?"

Alexandra looked up at him. "Young children seem to accept life and move on so much easier than we older ones. I know he has not forgotten them. Just yesterday, he was talking about Pa. He has just accepted their absence, that's all."

James nodded. "I am glad. Sometimes I learn a lot by watching him and Christine." After turning the clothes again, he read from his Bible aloud, prayed, and then they both headed to bed.

The rough weather lasted only two days. The icy snow sparkled across the yard. Lee trudged back and forth to the barn to help with the animal chores. Yet, it was a full week later before Christine could begin taking over the chicken chore again. The snow was too deep and the ice underneath too slick for her to brave it alone. James took care of the coup for her. After a week, she was bursting to get out of the house.

"I am ready to throw this quilt square right into the fire!" Christine huffed.

Alexandra raised her eyebrows. "Whatever for? You have been doing very well at sewing."

Christine sighed. "I usually like to sew, but I am tired of sitting and sewing, sewing, sewing. I want to run and breathe fresh air."

Alexandra chuckled. "I understand; Ma use to call this 'cabin fever.' You know, burning your quilt square will not take care of it, though."

Christine grinned. "I am sorry. I know it was foolish. Can I put my sewing away and maybe play with my doll?"

Alexandra smiled. "That would be fine. You have gotten much sewn down on your patches. Maybe James will let you help do the chickens tomorrow."

Christine jumped up. "Oh, goody! I will ask him at supper." She ran to put up her sewing and brought her cradle and doll out to play with by the fire.

James surprised Christine at supper by readily agreeing that it was time for her to take over the chicken duties. Alexandra, too, suffered from the dreaded cabin fever. So she bundled up and helped Christine for a couple of days. She yearned for some fresh air herself. Being able to get outside after having been cooped up made even laundry day seem fun. The girls appreciated any chance to get outside.

The family missed another Sunday in town. Nevertheless, by the following week, the messy residue of snow and ice had packed down good and tight. Everyone dressed and bundled up that next Sunday for the long cold drive to town. Covers and bricks were warmed for their feet. Three years ago, Pa had killed a bear and had used the skin to make a wonderful wrap against the weather. Lee and James bedded down the back of the wagon with straw for the youngest two. James and Alexandra would ride up front.

James and Lee finally came in for breakfast.

As he sat down, James looked at Alexandra. "I want to leave plenty early. After such weather, you never know the conditions of the road. It might be an extra long drive."

Alexandra nodded. "We will be ready whenever you are. We need to clean the breakfast dishes and load the lunch. You fellas need to change and get cleaned up."

Lee looked surprised. "But, I took a bath last night!"

Christine laughed, "But you went and got mud smeared on your nose!" Lee tried to look at the end of his smudged nose. Christine burst out in a fit of giggles at his cross-eyed face.

"All right, calm down, you two. Bow, please." James returned thanks for the meal.

Soon a clean, fresh-faced Lee was being loaded into the wagon along with everyone else. The road had a few ruts and bumps to maneuver around, but overall it went well. Alexandra could not help but smile as they drew near the church. She recognized several wagons and knew who would be inside to greet her. When she finally stepped into the door, there by the stove warming were Mary, Monica, Tonya, and Mae. Soon Joy came traipsing in followed by her brother, Christoph. Alexandra always enjoyed visiting with her friends before church.

"Oh, Alexandra how good it is to see you!" Monica whispered as she gave her a squeeze her hello.

Mary laughed. "We have missed you these last weeks. I hope it is not as bad a winter as the men predict. We will never get to see you."

Alexandra laughed. "Oh, I will be around. How is everyone?"

Monica giggled. "Well, last Sunday, Erica came to church in a shift — a maternity dress, you know! Can you believe it? Our house is very excited. After five years, we were wondering if they would be able to have any children."

Alexandra squeezed Monica's hand. "I am so happy for them!"

Mae laughed. "That is not all. Look who is wearing a shift today!" She pointed across the room. There stood Brent taking the wraps from around Faith's shoulders. Faith was blushing under all the stares and smiles.

Tonya leaned over to Monica. "I bet your mama and papa are bursting at the seams with excitement. Just think of it, two daughters expecting!"

Soon everyone began to find their seats, and the service began.

After the closing prayer, everyone began to file out. Tonya and Alexandra went over together to congratulate Faith. Then Alexandra went over to Erica. Soon, she saw James standing near the door and looking at her. She nodded, said her good-byes, and followed him and the children out.

As they rode to Widow Stephans' house, James commented, "Did you see Widow this morning?"

Alexandra sighed and nodded. "I am afraid I did. James, she looked so ... so ... well, weary. It has been just three weeks since we have seen her, yet I would say she has aged five years!"

James agreed. "I asked Minister Paul about it. Seems Christmas week she was real poorly. She got over it, but seems she does not have her pep back. I know she is eighty-five years of age, but she just never before seemed that old."

Alexandra's forehead creased with concern. "I hope it is not too much on her to have us for company today."

James shrugged. "She is the one that sent Luke out to invite us."

Their afternoon with the widow was a quiet one. After warming up lunch, they sat and talked.

Widow Stephans chuckled. "Alexandra, I wish you would erase those worry lines from your brow. I know I look a sight, but I am not dead yet."

Alexandra blushed and touched her forehead. "I am

sorry. I am just concerned about you living here all alone this winter."

Widow Stephans' eyes filled with tears, and she smiled lovingly at Alexandra. "That is real sweet of you, dear. I am glad to have you thinking of me, but I am fine. At my age, each day on earth is an added blessing to my many years of memories. When I got so old, six years ago, that I could not keep up the farm, I sold out and moved to town. Now I have many neighbors and friends who treat me like a child." She sat back and chuckled. "I like it, too!" Everyone laughed with her. "You know I only cook one or two days a week. That is because I like to. Everyone takes me to their house or brings meals to me. That Monica and her family spoil me. While I was sickly, Clara and Hope doctored me good-fashioned."

James sighed. "I am glad to hear you are being looked after."

Widow Stephans smiled. "Always. I think everyone adopted me as their grandma long ago. With Jacob being gone on before my good sons, my Ruth, and me —" she paused to wipe a tear from the corner of her eye — "I am lucky that I have my two granddaughters and their families in town. Any big cold spells this winter, and I reckon I will stay with one of them."

James nodded. "Do you ever get to see Ms. Ruth?"

Widow Stephans blew her nose. "No, child. You know she is near seventy years now. Ruth lives out west a far bit. That is too much traveling for her to come home and the long ride back. But she is a good daughter. She writes me most every single month of the year. For Christmas, she sent me a new feather quilt." To Christine, she turned, smiled, and pointed. "Just look in yonder, Christine, on my bed trunk. Bring it out, please."

Christine got up from where she was sitting by the widow's rocker. Quickly she was back with the quilt.

Alexandra ran her hand over it. "Why, it is beautiful. And so heavy! I bet you do not dread Old Man Winter now."

"Mercy, no! I just wonder about wanting to ever get out of bed from under something so nice!" Her laugh cackled like a hen. "She says she might make it out here this summer, if the Lord tarries. She has not seen her nieces or me in three years. I do miss her. I had her so young that we almost grew up together."

It seemed like each week of winter brought on more cold weather. Just before the beginning of February, the winds blew steady, and the temperatures were holding at ten below.

For late autumn, Alexandra's Monday morning talks with Ma had moved to the warmer afternoons instead. Now for winter, she had to settle for talking to Ma through the window facing the cemetery. While James was out doing morning chores, Alexandra would gaze out the window and tell Ma all about the past week and all the news from town. Somehow, it was not as comforting, but at least she still had her time with Ma.

As they entered February, sadness fell over their home. Lee and Christine could feel the tension and grief in the air but were leery of asking questions. Finally, at bedtime one night as Alexandra was brushing Christine's hair, the younger sister could not stand it any longer.

With fearful eyes, Christine turned around and looked up at Alexandra. "Is something wrong?"

Alexandra looked surprised. "Why?"

Christine looked down and chewed on her lip. "Well, for the last day or two, you and James have been real quiet and ... well ... sort of sad-acting."

Alexandra sighed. "I am sorry. I thought I was hiding it so well." She pulled Christine up on the bed beside her and hugged her close. "Tomorrow will be one year ago that Pa died. Then fifteen days later will be when Ma died. I guess I do not know what to feel or do about it all."

Christine gave a quiet "oh" in response.

Alexandra continued with a solemn tone. "I have not noticed James, but I am sure his reasons are the same as mine. Let us bring it up to the boys and see if they are thinking about Pa and Ma, too."

Together they went back to the great room to find the boys in front of the fire.

Christine approached James with her head down. She looked at James' feet, then up to his face with her innocent eyes. "Are you sad about tomorrow?"

James was caught off guard. He straightened up with a start, then after meeting her gaze, he dropped his shoulders and sighed. "Yes, I am. I did not think I should bring it up."

Alexandra smiled softly. "I was thinking the same thing, but it seems you and I have been wearing our hearts on our sleeves, so to speak. Both our brother and sister have noticed our sadness and thought something dreadful was wrong."

James scratched the side of his face. "Hiding our feelings sure will not change anything. I am sorry we worried you both."

Everyone sat quietly for a moment. Then Lee looked from each person to the next. "What about tomorrow?"

Christine took his hand into hers. "Tomorrow will be

the birthday of when Pa died."

Lee just looked at the floor.

Surprised, Alexandra smiled. "That is a good way of putting it, Christine. You could say it is like a birthday. I had not thought of it quite like that."

James nodded. "Does not seem right to be sad over a birthday. Yet, I had not thought about celebrating Pa's death."

"No. That is not right. But we do not want to think negative. So we could simply celebrate Pa's birthday of his new life in heaven." Alexandra searched James' face for a sign of encouragement.

Lee looked up. "Then we won't need to be sad no more?"

James reached over, grabbed Lee's arm, and pulled him to his lap. "No, my young man, we will not be sad. I am going to concentrate on being happy for Pa."

Christine's eyes lit up. "We could sing some of Pa's favorite songs tomorrow!"

Alexandra added, "We could all tell something funny or special that we remember about Pa."

James nodded. "That all sounds good. I will look through Pa's Bible and pick out something that was special to him."

"What about a treat? Everyone likes a treat for his birthday," Lee chimed in.

Alexandra laughed. "Funny you should be the one to think about a treat! If I remember correctly, Pa's favorite was pumpkin pie."

Christine clapped. "I know how to make that!"

"Pumpkin pie it is," James declared, and everyone went to bed feeling much better about the tomorrow.

CR

By the week's end, the weather had taken a turn for the worse. James awoke Saturday to a roar outside his window. At first, he thought it was a downpour on the roof, but soon realized it was a blizzard with a fierce wind. Lee was lying beside him with the covers pulled tightly to his chin. His eyes were wide with fright. James reached over and patted Lee's chest. "It is just the wind."

Lee's chin quivered a little. He swallowed hard and tried not to sound scared. "I know. Do you think it will blow the house away?"

James rubbed his own cheeks to warm them up as he began to rise. "Never has before, has it?"

Lee jumped out of bed and quickly pulled on his clothes. He did not want to be left in the room alone. "I ain't never heard it so loud and mean sounding," he yelled towards James.

"Haven't, not ain't, please." James shook his head as he corrected Lee.

Both boys looked up as a loud knock pounded at their bedroom door. Lee looked frightened. James laughed. "Oh, Lee. It is only your sisters. What did you think was on the other side of that door? A bear would not knock to come in, you know." James was about to shout over the noisy wind for the girls to enter but decided to save his breath. He went over and opened the door.

There stood Alexandra and Christine, wrapped in a quilt, shaking. "Good morning."

He grinned. "Up mighty early, girls, and coming to call in your nightgowns. Not very civilized, I would say," he teased.

Alexandra blushed and looked at the floor. "We were wondering if you were awake yet, that's all."

James laughed. "Since when? This blizzard woke you two with a fright, did it not?"

Christine was nodding her head up and down. Alexandra elbowed her slightly.

Lee stepped up beside James with wide eyes. "Us, too!"

James lost his grin, and now it was his turn to grow pink. "Err ... well ... it is pretty fierce sounding," James sheepishly admitted.

Alexandra slowly grinned. "Enough. It scared us all. Now, let's get dressed and warm this house up."

For five days, the blizzard raged. At noon each day, James fought his way to the barn. There were moments he thought he might lose the battle! Slowly, he would make his way there and back. He tried to tend to the stock well, for he knew once a day was all he could manage to make it out there in the weather.

By day three, the snow covered the open doorway completely! The house was much quieter and warmer. The snow acted as a blanket against the wind. James took all day to dig a tunnel to the barn. He missed the door but hit against a wall of the barn. Digging some more, he eventually found the door. The tunnel made chores a lot easier.

They remained in their snow cocoon for seven more days. Finally, the sun caved in spots of the tunnel.

After the children went to bed that night, James and Alexandra sat up drinking hot cider.

"I think we will see more weeks like this," James said solemnly.

"It gets tiresome staying inside, but I am sure we will manage, won't we?" Alexandra queried suspiciously. She was not quite sure why James was so concerned.

"I just like us to be prepared and be careful. I want you to fix only what we need to eat. Not anything extra or fancy," James began. Alexandra opened her mouth to protest, but James held up his hand. "That sounded wrong. I only meant I want our supplies to stretch until spring. Moreover, I am not sure how late that will be. Our cellar is bountiful, but I just want us to be careful. That is all I was trying to say."

Alexandra closed her lips and studied the table for a moment. Then she looked directly into his eyes. "Why are you so concerned?"

He slowly shook his head. He knitted his brow and chewed the inside of his mouth. Finally, with a heavy sigh, he whispered, "I do not know how to explain it. I truly do not feel worried. I just feel this tremendous burden to prepare. I wonder if this is how God spoke to Pa. Remember when he and Ma would sit up by the fire, and Pa would lean his elbows on his knees? He and Ma would speak in low, deep whispers. Ma would sigh and reach over and pat Pa's hand." James paused and bit his bottom lip. Alexandra could see him going back to one of those times in his mind's eye. James continued, "Once, after I witnessed it, I closed the book I was supposed to be reading there at the table. I sat until Ma went on to bed, though. I went over and asked Pa if everything was all right." James looked at Alexandra. "He looked troubled. I wanted to help somehow. Pa looked at me for a moment as if he did not know me, then he softly smiled. He told me to sit down; so I sat on his footstool. He rubbed his hands back and forth slowly for a time. He sighed and said, 'Nothing is wrong, son. I am just trying to do as I am told, and ... well ... it is not always so easy to understand the directions.'" James continued after a time, "Then Pa looked at me and smiled. I wanted to ask — what directions? Who is giving you directions? But I didn't." He paused. "I think I have the answers to those questions now."

Alexandra smiled and reached over and patted his hand. "I am sure you do. I will be prudent with our provisions, James."

TESTS AND TRIALS

The remainder of February and early March held three more blizzards. Everyone grew weary of being closed in for such long periods. Nature did not take well to the emptiness such a long severe winter caused. More than once James found footprints of critters around the barn in the mornings. On quiet, still nights, howling could be heard in the distance. On fair days, James kept busy making sure every inch of the barn was fortified against the starving beasts that roamed at night.

James was climbing the barn's loft ladder one morning to throw some straw down when his foot slipped and dropped through the rung! It was only the first rung of the ladder, but he came down hard on his ankle. Lee, who was in the back of the barn tending to his sows, heard James holler out. He dashed into the barn and found James sitting on the floor at the bottom of the ladder. James had his eyes shut tight and was breathing deep and slow.

"What happened?" Lee gasped.

James swallowed hard and with great effort hoarsely whispered, "Get me a pail of snow." With shaking hands, James began to unlace his boot while Lee ran out for some snow.

Lee was yelling towards the well where he saw Alexandra pulling up water. She dropped her bucket and came running. As she entered, breathing heavily and asking what happened, James was taking the snow from Lee and packing it around his ankle.

A pale James shook his head. "Clumsiness. I tried to climb the ladder by setting my foot through the rung instead of on it!" The color began to rise to his cheeks. "I came down on it, and it twisted."

Alexandra knelt down beside him and Lee. "Let me have a look." She gently brushed away the snow and gasped. The flesh was swollen a bluish-pink. "Oh, James!" She tenderly felt the bone of his ankle. James wrenched and gritted teeth.

Tears began to roll down Lee's cheeks. He brushed them away with his coat sleeve.

Alexandra shook her head. "James, it is so very swollen. I cannot seem to feel if it is broken."

"Can you get me a sip of water, Lee?" James leaned back, breathing heavily, against the stall door. He waited for Lee to disappear around the barn's door. "I cannot tell, either."

He was a greenish pale. Alexandra worried he would faint or be sick. Lee came rushing in with the bucket of water and its dipper. Alexandra took Lee's handkerchief and dipped it into the cold water. She wiped James' neck and brow. James sipped a little water.

"Well," Alexandra began as she reapplied some snow to his ankle, "we need to get you inside and then prop this leg up. We can decide what will come next once we accomplish that much."

They got James up slowly and awkwardly helped him to the house. A surprised Christine rushed to the door when she caught sight of them.

Once James was settled in his chair and his wraps put away, Alexandra sent Christine to help Lee finish the barn chores. Then she turned her attention to James. "You keep that foot propped up and the snow on it the best you can. For swelling, Ma always covered the area with clay. Until I get some, we'll use the snow. The coolness will help, I am sure." Once she had James settled, Alexandra headed out to the creek to dig up some clay.

By afternoon, James' ankle was a deep purplish blue. It throbbed with pain. Beads of sweat could be seen standing on James' upper lip through his thin mustache. Lee sat quietly by the fire, too frightened to play.

Christine brought a cup towards James. "Try to sip on this mint tea. Maybe it will settle your stomach some."

James cracked open one eye and barely shook his head. He whispered hoarsely, "No, thanks. My stomach is just fine."

Christine set the cup on the table.

Alexandra took a cold cloth from the basin at the sink. "You are sweating, James." She tried to wipe his face.

James reached up and took the cloth from her. "Stop, Alexandra! My ankle is hurt, not my face. Now just give it a little time, and I will be up and about. You all stop treating me like a baby."

Everyone stood staring at him for a moment. Finally, Alexandra broke the silence. "I did not realize it hurt so terribly bad."

James sat up a little. "I just got through saying it does not hurt so bad." He reached down to take the clay wrap off his ankle.

"Oh, yes, it does, or you would not raise your voice." She bit her lip. "Well, now I am worried. I am going to get

Doc Cannon. He surely needs to look at it." She went to get her coat and wraps on.

James protested, "Alexandra! I will not have you out in a winter like this. What if a blizzard comes up all of a sudden?"

Alexandra stood twisting her scarf in her hands. "I do not know, but we cannot have you mending all wrong. We rely on you, and to farm, you will need a good strong ankle. I am sorry, but I do not know what else to do. James, you are in a lot of pain. You are sweating. Your ankle is swollen and all shades of the wrong colors. What if it is broken?"

James sat back with a huff. He sat for a time with his eyes shut and his teeth clenched. Finally, he wet his lips and sighed. "All I know is I cannot let you go out. You are right about my ankle, but we just cannot take a chance with this weather. We all need to pray. God will send us help somehow. That is something I do know."

Lee got up on his knees. "I will pray! I'll do anything to make you not hurt, James."

James gave him a weak smile. "Thanks, buddy. You pray now. I will pray from this position, okay?"

Everyone gathered around James, and Lee led the prayer. It was simple and to the point. He prayed for someone to come and help James' ankle. He also prayed for James' pain to go away.

After the amen, James patted Lee on the head. "That was very nice. I just know God heard you. Thanks." Lee hugged James' neck. "I will try some of that tea now, Christine." James tried to steady his voice and smile a bit.

Christine jumped up to heat James' tea.

Alexandra stood up. "Christine, I will leave you to get supper on. Lee, you and I need to do chores. I take longer than James does to complete the animal chores, so we had better get started." Alexandra went on to instruct Christine on the preparation needed for supper. Then, she and Lee headed outside.

As she got to the lean-to door, James called out to her, "I am sorry, Alexandra."

Alexandra smiled and shook her head. "There is nothing to be sorry about. Accidents happen. Maybe this is God's way of making sure we appreciate all that you do." She laughed and headed out.

The night was restless for James and Alexandra. The slightest pressure from any covers was too much for James. By morning, he was feverish with pain and exhaustion. As Alexandra was coming out of the barn from doing the morning chores, a wagon was nearing. By the time she and Lee got to the porch, Alexandra could tell it was the Unruh wagon.

She quickly ran inside. "Help has come, James!" She hurriedly removed her wraps and instructed Christine to put on a large pot of coffee. Alexandra opened the door to find Doc Cannon, Mrs. Unruh, and Monica coming up the steps.

Doc removed his hat. "'Morning, Alexandra. What seems to be the problem?"

Alexandra shut the door. "James hurt his ankle some kind of bad. But, how did you know to come?"

Mrs. Unruh and Doc went straight over to James. Doc chuckled. "Widow Stephans sent me. Poor soul did not sleep a wink. She walked to my house first light today. Says the Lord spoke to her heart. Put quite a burden on it in your honor, son. Now tell me about this ankle of yours."

After an explanation and a painful examination, Doc declared it it was not broken but was one of the worst sprains he had ever seen. "How it is not broken, I do not know. I would say the Lord took care of you, though right at this moment I do not know that you would agree with me." Doc smiled at James, then left some medicine for pain and instructions on how to take care of the ankle.

Monica had been helping Christine clean and start a stew. Mrs. Unruh helped Doc wrap James' ankle, and then she coddled Lee for a while.

Doc and Monica offered to help finish any barn chores that needed tending, but James insisted they head for home immediately. "I would hate for you to be caught out in a blizzard due to my clumsiness." James offered a prayer of thanksgiving before they departed.

By the time Alexandra came in from saying her good-byes, James was sleeping soundly in his chair. Lee was wrapped in a quilt on the floor beside James ... also sound asleep! "I guess he did not sleep well with all his worrying about James." She smiled over to Christine.

They went about their remaining duties as the boys slept.

By night, Alexandra managed to get James settled in his bed. Doc showed them ways to arrange pillows beside the ankle to form a tent. That kept the heavy quilts from pressing down. The tonic Doc left for James' pain helped him rest, too.

After several days, James' swelling was improving. The pain was tolerable, and he was becoming restless.

"I think I will try to construct me a prop to lean on, so I can begin to get back to work," James said slyly one morning at breakfast.

Alexandra stopped eating and stared at him. "What sort of prop?"

James shrugged slightly. "Something to lean on, so I

will not put my weight down completely on this here ankle."

Alexandra went back to eating. Everything was quiet. Suddenly, she looked up again. "No."

Lee and Christine stopped, their spoons in mid-air, and gaped at her.

James looked offended. "What do you mean 'no?'"

Alexandra blushed but continued looking directly at James. "Doc said two full weeks of not touching that foot on the floor. Then he said another two weeks of taking it easy. I am about as tired of doing your chores as you are of having to sit around, but it just has to be. Larry, Luke, and Christoph were right kind to ride out day before yesterday, but they cannot do that all the winter. If you re-injure your ankle or it does not mend properly, we will be in a real pickle! Now, you have managed to be good-natured about all this for eight days; a few more will not kill you." She got up and took her plate to be cleaned.

James sat there for a minute. He looked at Christine and Lee. They were frozen in their places. Quickly, they resumed their eating. James sighed. "You win. Lee, after breakfast, please find me a real good piece of wood to whittle. I think I have read everything there is to read in this house already."

By late afternoon, it was obvious they were in for another storm. James sent Alexandra out early to tend to the animals. About the time Christine set the food on the table for supper, the wind and snow were raging outside.

"I am glad I am in here," Alexandra said with a shiver.

"Me, too, but I am sure you will be out in it eventually. It will be around for a while." James stared at the window.

"Well, the Lord will help you, Alexandra. Won't He, James?" Lee stated confidently.

Turning away from the window, James smiled. "Yes, I am sure He will. Alexandra, in the morning, set my coat and things close to the fire to warm. They will keep you warmer than your own. No rush to go out. Plan on a once-a-day chore time until the storm lets up."

Alexandra sighed wearily. "I think I will turn in early. Sounds like an adventurous day tomorrow."

❧

The blizzard raged on for two days with only a few hours' break before it took up again!

Once James' two weeks of recuperation were up, there was too much snow for him in his weakened, clumsy state. Alexandra tended to his chores a full extra week. In turn, he aided Christine in the household chores where he was able. Although his ankle was stiff and tender, James was very happy to be up and about.

When James finally did get to take back his chores, they took him twice as long to complete. He did not care; he was just content to be of some help. Alexandra was sore exhausted. She was more than happy to resume her job as keeper of the house.

One morning after James was able to start back to work, he woke and began the fires, but no Alexandra. He brought in more wood and some snow to melt into water, but still ... no Alexandra.

Christine soon came from their bedroom yawning and rubbing her hands by the fire.

"Where is Alexandra?" James inquired.

"She is still sleeping. She has been so weary lately I did not have the heart to wake her. I will get breakfast going," replied Christine.

James pulled his collar up on his coat and put his hat on. Picking up a bucket beside the lean-to door, he whispered, "Let her sleep. She has been doing the work of two people long enough. I am afraid she will get sick if she does not rest. Go hurry Lee and have him meet me in the barn."

Alexandra slept until the smell of coffee and baking beans made her stir. She quickly dressed and hurried out of her room.

"What time is it?" She looked around the room. The lamp on the table was lit, and the fire glowed throughout the room. Everyone stopped what they were doing and looked up.

"Nearing eleven o'clock. Seems you are just in time to help with the dinner preparations," James teased as Lee snickered.

"You do not mean it, James!" Alexandra's hands flew to her cheeks. "How could I have slept so long, and why is it so dark at almost noon?"

James shook his head. "Well, now, let me see ... you were probably tired, and to answer the second question, the snow is so thick, not a speck of light can shine through it."

"Oh, not again! Do you think spring will ever come?" She quickly went to help Christine in the kitchen.

"I do not know, but this storm came on quick and quiet. I was in the barn with Lee, and all of a sudden, the sun just blinked off. Lee ran over to the door, opened it, and the blizzard was here. By the way, there were claw scratches on the barn door this morning. I do not believe the wildlife is faring as well as we are this winter," James said as he placed another log on the fire.

As they sat by the fire reading aloud that evening, the cry of wolves could indeed be heard.

"I do not like it. For wolves to be out in this snow means they are starving." James went to the door and took down his rifle.

"Surely you are not going out now, James?" Alexandra asked nervously.

Christine gulped and watched him with wide eyes.

"No. I just want to prepare for trouble, though. That way I will not be caught off guard."

The night proved to be a long one. The howls of the pack seemed everywhere. The wind seemed to carry the cries all around the house. As the wind increased towards the dawn, the howls decreased. A tired James headed out with his gun at the first hint of light.

Anxiously, Alexandra and Christine prepared a hot breakfast while Lee made the beds and swept the floors. Christine was pouring the coffee and tea when they heard James enter the lean-to. Once inside, he walked over and hung his rifle back in its place. No one spoke until after the meal's prayer was said.

"Did you see any footprints?" Lee asked with raised eyebrows.

James shook his head. "That storm is raging on — wolves or no wolves. Even the footprints I made this morning are beginning to fill up." He continued eating. After a few moments, he looked up at Alexandra. "I have a bad feeling about this storm. Being so late in the season and coming up all of a sudden ... well, I hope no one was caught off guard."

Alexandra gave a small gasp. "Oh, James, you do not suppose someone could be caught out in this storm, do you?"

James sipped his coffee. "I pray not, but every year it seems to happen. This storm just seems to fit the circumstances that actually might catch someone unawares."

Everyone sat solemnly staring at their plates and moving their food around. James cleared his throat. "I did see evidence that our barn and house were attacked by the pack last night."

Everyone sat up to attention!

Alexandra spoke first. "Our house!? What do you mean?"

James took a deep breath. "Bloody marks on the lean-to door and by the barn's window. They clawed hard to tear their paws enough to draw blood. The shutters are sturdy and thick enough that they will not get into the barn. They cannot dig in, either — snow is too deep. I also feel the lean-to will stand any abuse they try to give it. I do not want anyone outside unless the rifle is with them. The wolves will only hunt when the snowfall eases up or stops. During the heavy downfall, they'll not venture out. Now during any snowfall, it will only be me going out, but afterwards, I need to definitely be there if anyone steps out." James finished eating. He looked up at all the scared eyes staring at him. He smiled. "No need to look so frightened. We are safe in this warm house, and the animals are safe in the barn. Once we have a little warm spell, the smaller wildlife will come out, and the wolves will be satisfied. This is just how nature works."

That night was a repeat of the previous night. A few hours before dawn, the storm disappeared as quickly as it came.

When James came in from doing the morning chores, his brow was drawn, and his hands were covered in blood!

Christine gasped, "James!"

Lee and Alexandra started towards him.

"Stay back," James softly warned. "I am not hurt, but there will be no more eggs for quite a while. The wolves got through the fence and into the coup."

Alexandra sat with a thud onto the bench.

Christine threw her hands to her face. "Not my chickens!" she cried.

"Every one of them?" Alexandra asked.

"The few eggs there were are in the nest. I counted three. Of the two dozen chickens we had, all except two were either eaten or torn apart. Those two must have flown out somehow. The cold got them right away. That I am sure. They are whole and frozen. They are in the lean-to, so see if there is anything you can do with them."

After washing up thoroughly, James threw himself in his place at the table. Everyone sat in their places silently. Every now and then, Christine would sniffle. James sighed heavily, sat up, and asked everyone to bow. After prayer, there was more silence.

"Come spring thaw, I will order some chicks from Jackson's Mercantile. Maybe someone with an abundance of layers will sell or trade a few to get us by until you can raise another flock." James tried to sound optimistic.

"It took two years to raise the fine flock of layers we just lost. And that rooster was the best," Alexandra sulked.

"Well, I am glad it was not worse." James sighed.

Christine looked up with her sad, puffy eyes. "How could it have been worse?"

"They could have made it into the barn!" James said.

"Oh, it will not come to that, will it, James?" Alexandra sounded desperate.

"I hope not. I have done everything I know of to see to it the animals are safe. I figured the chickens were all right, but I should have moved them into the barn. I am sorry, girls." James leaned his head into his hand. "We need to pray for some clear days, so the wolves can find food elsewhere.

Lee and I will bury the remains and try to clean up the mess they left behind."

A quiet group finished breakfast and went about their appointed tasks.

That night for devotions, James read Proverbs 16:20: "'He that handleth a matter wisely shall find good: and whosoever trusteth in the Lord, happy is he.'" James sat for a moment. With his eyes cast down, he slowly nodded. Looking up, he gave Christine a comforting smile. "God will provide. I am very sorry about our chickens, but the Lord will take care of us. I trust and go on faith that good will come out of all this. Let us kneel."

CR

Two days later, jingling was heard nearing the house. James got up from in front of the hearth where he was cleaning his gun to look out the window. There were Christoph and Luke in the Whiteds' cutter. James grabbed his coat and hat from the peg and went out to greet them. Right away, he knew something was wrong by the grim expressions across their faces.

"Morning, fellas. What brings you out this way?" James asked suspiciously.

Looking at each other, not knowing where to begin, Luke finally cleared his throat. "Bad news, James. This storm came on quick, and well ... Minister Paul's son Michael was caught out in it. Found him yesterday frozen just north of their land."

James tried to swallow but could not. He rubbed his face with his hand and shook his head.

Christoph looked up at James. "That is not all. Jason

and Caroline Esau and their little girl were on their way to town to visit Doc and his wife, it seems. Must have lost their way. We found them and their buggy just outside of town. Mrs. Cannon is taking to it pretty hard."

James closed his eyes and said a silent prayer for the families. All three boys took out their handkerchiefs and wiped their faces.

"What can we do to help?" James managed to ask.

Christoph shook his head. "Nothing anyone can do. Deacon Henry does not want you to try to come to town. We need to hurry back. These crazy blizzards come on so quick. We will give your sympathies to the families."

Luke added, "We know you and Alexandra would want to attend the funerals, but do not risk it. It is planned to be short and quick. Everything is so deep and frozen; I do not know how they will manage a burial."

Everyone shook their heads.

"I appreciate you letting us know. I had a bad feeling about that storm." James struggled within to control his emotions.

"Are you faring all right?" Christoph inquired.

"We are fine. Wolves took out the chicken coup last night of the storm, but we will survive."

"Sorry to hear that. We hope the storms are over for this winter. We need to head back." Christoph pulled up his scarf and waved as back to town they headed.

James stood in the cold watching them disappear into the horizon. He pulled his lips tightly together to try to stop their trembling. He turned to go back in. Alexandra needed to know.

After many tears and prayers for the families, everyone sat down to lunch. It did not last long; no one seemed to be very hungry.

Towards bedtime that evening, James and Alexandra sat before the fireplace.

"I feel so terrible for Tonya and her family, and for Doc and Ms. Susie. Four people gone." Tears started welling up in Alexandra's eyes, and her throat became dry and tight. She sat back and stared at the fireplace.

James sighed. "I know. You and I both know in time the good Lord will see them through their grief . I hate not going to the funerals. Matthew has always been helpful and such a good friend. I would like to be there for him when they lay his brother to rest. No telling how long it will take to dig some sort of grave. I just hope the snow for this year is through." James leaned back and closed his eyes. After a while, he looked over at Alexandra. "Last year, I had most of the plowing done by now. It will be a late crop this year."

They both sat up late, in silence, looking at nothing but memories. The pain of loosing ones you love was too near to their own hearts. Tears were shed throughout the night, some for Michael, Caroline, Jason, and their little girl, and some for Ma and Pa. With exhaustion and love, prayers were sent for God's mercy and grace to help ease the pain ... for their own and those newly burdened.

FIRE!

Winter had done its damage for the season. It meekly dissipated into spring. There were a few more frosts, but Old Man Winter brought no more snow.

The final weeks of March were busy for the Williams and their neighbors. Plowing and planting were on everyone's minds. The last Sunday of the month, the Williams family was finally able to attend church services. The void of the lives lost that winter was deeply felt. Outside church before the services began, Alexandra and Tonya clung to each other and cried.

After church, Matthew and James stood beside the wagon together. Their words were few, but their sorrow was plentiful. James laid his hand on Matthew's shoulder and prayed with him.

As they both wiped away their tears, James tried to clear his throat. "I am sorry about Michael. I want to be here for you, if I can help at all."

Matthew looked off and whispered, "Will it ever stop hurting?" His voice shook, and his jaw trembled.

James looked at the ground and let out a deep breath. "No, but with God's grace, it will be bearable one day. Just take one day at a time. Do not hold it all in. Share with Tonya, your parents, or one of us. That helps."

Matthew took James' hand and shook it. "I really do

thank you. I will try and remember your advice." With a weak smile, he headed towards his own family's wagon.

After an afternoon with the Unruhs and the evening service, James took his small family and headed home.

"It was nice to hear that Christopher is planning to come out and help again this year. Larry was saying he should arrive sometime next month," James recalled as they drove home.

Alexandra nodded. She did not feel much like talking.

CR

The family spent the end of March and beginning of April preparing their garden and fields. It took plenty of early mornings and late evenings to make up for the time lost to the long winter.

One afternoon while Alexandra was out in the garden, and Lee, along with James, was working in the field beside the barn, Christine was clearing ashes from the cook stove and hearth. As she was bent over cleaning out the hearth, a crackle and a whooshing noise came from the cook stove. Having just stirred the ashes, Christine had left the stove door ajar. She turned to see a ball of fire roll out of the stove and land on the rag rug! It instantly burst into flames! Christine froze with fright and let out a scream.

Alexandra spun around. She grabbed up her skirt and took off for the house. James came running from beside the barn with Lee at his heels when Alexandra yelled out his name. Alexandra reached the doorway in time to see Christine trying to beat out the fire with the apron that she had ripped off her body!

Alexandra grabbed Christine and pushed her towards

the door. "Go get water!"

Alexandra worked her way around the fire, grabbed a pot, scooped water from the corner barrel, and tossed it around the flames. By now, James was inside with two buckets. He doused the rug and the flaming sideboard cabinets. Alexandra grabbed the curtain down from the burning window and stomped out the flames. All the while, Lee and Christine were bringing in fresh water for James.

Finally, they managed to put out the fire. James made everyone go outside for fresh air. Once they caught their breath, they went back to access the damage. Tears streamed down their soot-covered faces as their eyes scanned one end of the house to the other. The kitchen was badly damaged. The shelves and sideboard were burned, along with the floor. Even the wall and window were damaged. The side bedroom and great room were filled with smoky soot. Their own bedrooms were not too bad because their doors had been closed.

James ordered everyone back outside to wash up and get some cool water to clear their throats. Alexandra and Christine cried the entire time they washed up. Christine's apron was burned to ashes, and her dress was charred. Alexandra finally noticed that her own hands and arms were blistered.

James came over with a cloth and began washing Lee's and Christine's faces. Lee gasped, "James! Your face is so red. Look at your hands!"

James looked at his hands and realized he, too, was blistered. "I will be fine. Alexandra, are you all right?"

"Depends on what you mean. I am alive. I thank God Christine is not burned, if that is what you mean."

James looked at her hands and his own. "Do you

remember what Ma used for burns?"

Alexandra shook her head and coughed. "I am lucky I remember my own name right this minute. Give me a bit to think on it, and I will come up with something."

"I reckon it will take most of the rest of the day to clean things out enough to sleep in there tonight." James turned to Christine. "What happened?"

Suddenly, a speeding wagon pulled up. Mr. and Mrs. Madison climbed out. Seeing too much smoke for just cooking a meal coming from their direction, the concerned neighbors had come to check on them. Christine related the events as she saw them happen.

Mrs. Madison helped fix up an ointment for the burns, and everyone pitched in to clean. Hot water and lye soap were applied to every nook and cranny of the house. Christine and Lee drug everything burned or charred outside in the yard. James took the stovepipe apart and scrapped and cleaned it. Alexandra opened all windows and doors and took all bedding material outside to air.

By bedtime, the house had been scrubbed clean from top to bottom. The burned flooring and wall kept the smell of the fire lingering in the air, but the soot had been removed. After they sat down to jerky and milk, James gathered everyone for a long, thankful prayer before turning in. "I can replace the floor, the window, and the other material things, but I am thankful God spared our lives. We must give thanks that we still have a bed to lie in and a roof over our heads tonight."

Two days later, the Unruh family paid them a visit. Word had gotten into town about the fire. The Williams family was busy working outside as the wagon neared. Fretfully, Alexandra pushed the loose strains of hair out of her face. She looked at her soil-covered hands and dress and knew what a sight she must be! The wagon stopped across the yard at the field where James was working. James stopped plowing and met Mr. Unruh and Larry at the end of the row.

Monica hopped out of the wagon and ran over to the garden where Alexandra stood. "Oh, Alexandra! Are you and the children all right?"

Alexandra held out her soil-covered, bandaged hands and arms. "Toasted, but alive." She smiled at her friend.

Monica hugged Christine tightly and kissed Lee's head. "When we heard last night there had been a fire here, we almost headed here right away, but Pa said we would come at first light. I did not sleep a wink. How much damage?"

Alexandra sighed. "Mostly the kitchen and eating area. We scrubbed the house thoroughly right away, and with the Madisons' help, we aired everything out. Christine lost her apron trying to beat out the flames, and James and I lost a set of clothes. We will grow back the hair that was singed, and I am sure the skin will heal, also." She paused to steady her voice as she gazed at the dirt at her feet. Taking a deep breath, she continued, "The curtains Ma made were burned, and some handiwork of Pa's destroyed, but James can fix everything else, I am sure." She wiped her cheek with the back of her hand.

"I am so sorry. Can I help in anyway?" Monica wiped her own eyes.

As the girls stood there talking, Mr. Unruh and Larry were questioning James.

James shook his head as he answered Mr. Unruh's inquiries. "No, sir. I will not worry with fixing the house until after the planting is complete. This long winter has thrown us behind schedule, as I am sure it has you, also. For now, I will concentrate on the planting, and then I will focus on the repairs. The weather like it is, we should not be bothered if the house is a little airy. I appreciate you worrying about us, but we are grateful it was no worse than it was. Alexandra and I got a might singed, but we will survive."

Mr. Unruh shook his head. "I understand priorities. Larry and I have been working double time to get things right at home, too. Since we are not needed for repairs today, once planting is complete we will come back out and help."

"I would appreciate that, sir," James answered gratefully.

Larry spoke up. "Ma sent word to plan on being with us come Sunday. Tell Alexandra we will take care of all the food this time."

"I'll do that, Larry. Send our thanks to Mrs. Unruh." James nodded a good-bye as Larry hollered for Monica.

After hugging Alexandra and the children, Monica scurried to the wagon.

THE PROPOSAL

By the following week, crops and gardens had been planted. Alexandra and Christine were doing the wash while James and Lee were tending to work in the barn. A wagon neared as the girls were hanging the first load out on the line. James came out of the barn as Minister Paul pulled up. After the two exchanged greetings, Alexandra watched as Minister Paul got down from the wagon and went into the barn with James. Soon, Lee came trotting over to the line.

"James says for me to help you girls until he calls for me," Lee said with a pout.

Christine wiped her brow and put her hands on her hips. "Good, you can help stir the clothes in the boiling water. I feel like I am melting over that pot."

Lee puffed out his chest. "Oh, I can handle that job easily."

Alexandra laughed. "I would like to hear you say that an hour from now."

They went inside to finish the next load. Alexandra had trouble concentrating on her chore out of curiosity over the meeting in the barn. 'What could possibly bring the minister out for a visit in mid-week, and so early in the morning?' she wondered.

She and the children were back at the line hanging out the colored clothes when Minister Paul was getting back into his wagon. He gave them a friendly wave and headed on his way. James stood by the barn and watched the wagon until it was clear out of sight. Alexandra sent the children in for a slice of left-over apple pie and some milk, while she headed to the barn. James had disappeared within the barn by the time she reached its doors. Before she could call out his name, she stopped, frozen in her tracks. There, in the middle of the barn with his back towards her, knelt James. Quietly, she eased away and made her way back to the house. She felt guilty for her curiosity. She knew she should have minded her own business. If James wanted her to know about the visit, surely he would tell her. She was determined not to ask him about it now.

She stopped on the porch and took and deep breath. "Help me, Lord, mind my own business and not be so curious. Amen." She entered the cabin to begin their lunch.

James went about the remainder of the day quiet and sullen. The meals were silent and the devotions short. After the children were in bed, he sat staring at the fireplace and rocking. Twice, he got up and went outside to walk around.

The last time he re-entered the cabin, he sat with an exhausted huff. "Alexandra, I need to talk with you." He nervously sat with his elbows on his knees.

Alexandra put her knitting in her lap. "I hope so. Your fretting about is making me a nervous wreck."

James twisted his fingers. "I am not sure where to begin." He ran his fingers through his hair.

Alexandra encouraged, "I take it this has something to do with Minister Paul's visit?"

James sighed. "Well, yes and no. I guess his visit sort of brought everything together."

Alexandra clasped her hands together to keep from

shaking. "Oh, James, out with it, please."

Still looking at his hands, James swallowed hard and began, "Well, sis, the last while, I have been having some strong feelings for someone special. I have been praying about it, but I did not know what to do. With you and me raising Lee and Christine, I just figured I would have to wait until you off and married and went to your new home. Nevertheless, the Lord has really put a heavy impression of this one person on me. Still, I just have not known how to handle the situation."

Alexandra looked at him with wide eyes and burning cheeks. "James, are you getting married?" Fear, joy, and confusion seized her heart.

James shook his head and held up his hand. "Just let me finish before you take over." He continued, "Minister Paul came to speak with me about you."

Alexandra's hand flew to her cheek. "Me!?" A million thoughts fluttered around in her mind. What had she done to bring the minister out about her? — she wondered.

"Yes, you." James gave her a weak smile. His cheeks were flaming red. He cleared his throat again. "Seems someone besides me has been thinking about marriage. Christopher Unruh has asked for your hand in marriage, Alexandra."

Alexandra's jaw fell open, and she stared in disbelief at her brother. A proposal! Her heart felt like it would jump right out of her chest!

James looked into her eyes. "I do not have to ask how you feel about him. Every time I mention his name — well, it is written all over your face." He gave her a sly grin.

Alexandra could not help the small smile that crossed her face. She quickly looked away from his gaze. Then, instantly, reality hit. Tears filled her eyes as with a trembling voice she replied, "Oh, James. I cannot marry. I could never leave Lee and Christine, and I would not think of taking them from you." Tears rolled down her cheeks.

"I told you to let me finish, girlie. Christopher wants to move out here. He proposes to help rebuild the fire damage and add onto the house. He offered to help work our land. As it stands now, I only utilize half our property. He offers to help here, so you will not have to leave. He, being the next to the youngest of eight, is not needed so much back at his home. I asked Minister Paul for some time to talk things out with you. Afterwards, he and I prayed and talked." He paused and took a deep breath. "Well, I sent a proposal of my own back to town." Relieved he had gotten everything out into the open, he sat back into his chair.

After a moment, Alexandra spoke. "Well, are you going to say her name, or will I find out at the wedding?"

"Oh, come now. You know me as well as I know you. I knew how you felt about Christopher seven months ago, so I am sure you know who she is." James smiled and blushed.

Alexandra grinned. "Well, I could not wish for a better sister-in-law than Monica."

James took a deep breath and exhaled. "I want both of us to pray over this. Tomorrow night, we will discuss things further. I need to go to town Thursday, so I told Minister Paul that we would stop in at his place then. Let us not mention anything to Lee and Christine until everything is settled."

"Agreed." Alexandra tingled all over with excitement.

After a long prayer, they retired for the evening. Alexandra lay in bed for the longest time staring at the ceiling. A marriage proposal. Christopher Unruh. She thought about all his endearing qualities; he was kind, soft-spoken, strong, and hard working. She remembered how he spoke respectfully and lovingly of his sister and mother. He had been very helpful when Lee took with the fever last summer and very nurturing when Christine had become so distraught. Alexandra remembered how earnestly he participated in the youth's Bible studies, and oh, what dark brown eyes he had. Alexandra quickly admonished herself, 'Shame, Alexandra! You should not even consider his eyes or his bright smile, warm laugh, or handsome looks.'

Shaking her head, she tried to clear her mind. 'Sleep? How can I sleep?' she asked herself.

She closed her eyes and prayed. "Dear God, please guide me in the direction you want my life to go. Help my thoughts be pure, and please help me get some sleep. Amen." She sighed. 'How can James sleep tonight? Boys have it so easy.' Before she could think another thought, her heavy eyelids closed.

In the other room, James tossed. A million thoughts swirled in his head. Life and its decisions seemed anything but easy to him. Finally, his mind gave way to his weary body, and sleep came.

❧

Thursday dawned bright and clear. Though Lee had fought the idea of a mid-week bath, he was awfully excited about going to town. While Lee and Christine chattered away in the back of the wagon, Alexandra and James sat silent and anxious in the front. Hardly a sound was uttered the entire trip from the front of that wagon. Lee and Christine were dropped off at Widow Stephans' house while James and Christine went to Minister Paul's.

Minister Paul and his wife, Vera, led them to their parlor. After everyone was seated, Minister Paul cleared his throat. "Well, James and Alexandra, I think we should get right down to the nature of your call. That way some color can come back into your cheeks!" He let out a laugh as he tried to ease the tension. Turning his attention to Alexandra, he said, "I understand by now that James has delivered Brother Christopher's proposal of marriage to you?"

In a small voice, Alexandra replied, "Yes, sir."

"Have you earnestly prayed over the matter, Sister?" he kindly asked her.

"Oh, yes, sir, I have," Alexandra responded in a nervous voice.

"And what word shall I send to our waiting Brother?"

Alexandra looked at James and took a deep breath. James gave her a little smile. She exhaled and blushed. Smiling at Minister Paul, she said, "Please send my acceptance."

With excitement, Ms. Vera grabbed Alexandra's hands. "Oh, congratulations, dear."

With a serious look, Minister Paul turned to face James. "Now, Brother James, I have a message to you from the Unruh household." He paused.

Alexandra held her breath, and James looked at the floor. After what seemed like an eternity to James, Minister Paul spoke. "Monica sends her acceptance, also." With that, the minister grinned and grabbed James' sweaty hand. "Congratulations and God's blessings on you, son."

James blushed and smiled. "Thank you, sir." The air in the room took a much lighter tone now that the pressure and anxiety were eased.

The minister's tone was much livelier and full of joy. "Did you and Alexandra talk over Christopher's full proposal concerning the living arrangements?"

"Yes, sir, we did. When Christopher arrives, I would like to discuss house plans and arrangements with him further. We believe it is the Lord's will, and we think we can make a go of it." James continued, "Neither one of us can bear the thought of leaving Lee or Christine. Ma asked us to raise them — not just Alexandra and not just me. Expanding the house and sharing the responsibility seems the best way to fulfill our promise to Ma."

Minister Paul nodded. "I think it will be a fine solution. That land of yours is a huge responsibility for a man of your age. I am glad Christopher will be able to share that with you. Once I hear back from Christopher, Alexandra, we will make wedding arrangements. I take it a double wedding is acceptable for you both? Or do you want to go ahead and make separate arrangements with Monica, James?"

James shook his head. "No, sir. One wedding should do. We will wait on your word from Christopher."

After a little more conversation about the weather and farming, James and Alexandra were soon on their way. Although still quiet, the mood was definitely different!

Once the shopping and errands were completed, they picked up Lee and Christine. Alexandra had to laugh when James started singing on the ride home. Lee and Christine looked at each other and shrugged. Whatever made their brother and sister in such a good mood was fine by them ... they just joined in the singing!

Minister Paul spoke privately with James on Sunday, just long enough to let him know that Christopher would arrive in ten days' time. They planned for the Friday following his arrival to meet at the Unruhs' home for an evening meal. All plans would be finalized at that time.

Alexandra did not know whether those were the longest or the shortest two weeks of her life. While she was living them, the days seemed to drag on forever, but now as she sat beside James on the wagon heading towards the Unruhs' it seemed the days were over in the blink of an eye! That morning, they had sat Lee and Christine down and told them about the upcoming marriages. Though the children were initially frightened, James assured them neither he nor Alexandra were leaving. Once this was clarified, the children became very excited.

As the wagon pulled into the Unruhs' yard, Alexandra could not tell whether she was hearing her own heart or James' beating so loudly. James helped Alexandra and Christine down from the wagon. Mr. and Mrs. Unruh greeted them warmly at the door. Once inside the door, Alexandra spotted Christopher standing beside Monica. She could not seem to keep herself from grinning. Oh, how she hoped she was not as red as she felt!

"Good evening, Alexandra." Christopher gently smiled at her.

"Hello," softly Alexandra managed to say. She only caught his eyes for a moment, but it made her feel better, for he looked as nervous as she felt!

James made his way in the door and exchanged greetings with a pink-cheeked Monica. When Mr. Unruh started chuckling at the four blushing young people, Mrs. Unruh elbowed him.

With a smile, she addressed them. "Would you girls mind helping me in the kitchen with the table? You men can go to the parlor until we call for you."

As the girls followed Mrs. Unruh, Monica leaned over and whispered to Alexandra, "Oh, Alexandra, I am so happy we will be sisters."

Alexandra smiled and looped her arm in Monica's. "I am also, but I am so nervous tonight. I do not think I can eat one bite of food."

Giggling, the girls disappeared into the kitchen.

Mr. Unruh helped the boys sketch out the plans of the house and to make a list of the needed building materials. As a wedding gift, Larry and Mr. Unruh offered to build the girls a new dish dresser to replace the one that was damaged in the fire. At length they also decided that a small sitting area would be added to the boys' room, and the spare bedroom would be enlarged to give some privacy to the two couples. The girls' room would be enlarged as well. A curtain would be hung across the room for privacy, yet Christine and Lee could still talk to one another through the curtain. The kitchen wall, window, and the flooring that had been burnt would be replaced. Once the wedding was announced on Sunday, construction could begin. Mr. Unruh felt it could be completed and ready in two weeks' time. Therefore, the date was set for the second Sunday in June!

Between nervousness and excitement, Alexandra went through Sunday in a daze. She felt herself stand to open her way to the congregation , but she could not remember what she even said. Tonya's and Mae's eyes flew wide open when the announcement was made. Then when James and Monica were announced immediately following, a few gasps of surprise were heard.

On the ride home, James rubbed his hands together. "My hand is sore from all the handshakes today."

Alexandra laughed. "Oh, don't I know it! I will be black and blue from all the hugs!"

CR

A busy two weeks followed with hammering, sawing, sewing, and baking. As a wedding gift, Mrs. Unruh sent over six layers and a rooster along with ten chicks. Christine was giddy with excitement.

The Saturday before the wedding found Alexandra up before dawn. Unable to sleep, she took her stool and went out to talk to Ma.

As the rooster began to crow over at the barn, Alexandra sighed. "Oh, how I am missing you and Pa right now, Ma. I am so happy, yet there are moments that I get choked on sadness." She wiped a tear from the corner of her eye. "So many prayers have been answered. You asked me to make sure I married a man of God. I am, Ma. Christopher is a good-hearted, gentle soul." Alexandra took a deep breath and exhaled. "But I have so many questions. I want to be a good helpmate, but I am so nervous. I feel dizzy just thinking about it all sometimes. These last three weeks, I have missed you almost as much as I did the first three weeks after your passing. Mrs. Jackson helped to fit your wedding dress to me. Did I tell you her baby is due to arrive in October?" She paused and reflected on all the things that had been occurring lately. "I hope you are not angry with me, Ma. I know I have called on you less and less these last five months. Do not think that I do not think of you every single day; Pa, too." She closed her eyes. "I will be thinking about you tomorrow especially. I wish Pa could be here to see us marry." Alexandra stood and picked up her stool as the first sunbeam streaked across the sky. "I love you both." She turned and walked towards the house.

CR

James leaned against the doorframe of the barn with his arms crossed as he watched Alexandra walking towards the back of the house. 'So that is why I did not hear you scurrying around this morning,' he thought to himself.

He stood and watched for the sunrise and thought of all the new responsibilities that began for him tomorrow. 'Oh, Pa, so many questions. What advice would you be giving me now if you were here?' he wondered. When the sun burst out of the horizon, James smiled and turned back into the barn to finish his chores.

CR

Earlier in the week when Christopher's folks arrived, they had presented the couples with a set of oxen. Mr. Arthur Unruh had patted Christopher on the back and said, "Son, if you and James are going to turn over that new soil, you will need to do it with oxen and not try and kill your horses."

By mid-morning the day before the wedding, Monica's parents, Larry, Monica, Christopher, and his parents all arrived to help settle the place for the newlyweds to come home to tomorrow evening. On the back of the wagon sat a huge lump covered by a quilt, several crates, and bulging baskets. Once everyone said their hellos, Larry asked Monica and Alexandra to step to the back of the wagon. He and his father slowly removed the quilt to unveil a new dish dresser. The girls gasped. It was lovely! Both girls gushed with thanks and even shed a tear or two. A blushing Larry was glad when his father finally put an end to the gratitude, and they began to unload the dresser. The men carefully took it into the house. The ladies went about unloading the baskets and crates. Monica's sisters, Faith and Hope, had sent new linens and embroidered tea towels as gifts. Monica and Alexandra had earlier sewn new curtains for the new rooms and to replace the kitchen window curtain.

That evening after supper, James and Alexandra sat at the table with Lee and Christine. Neither James nor Alexandra felt much like eating.

Lee watched as James pushed his food around with his fork. "What is wrong, James? You got a stomach ache?"

Puzzled, James looked over at Lee. "What do you mean?"

"Why, you keep scooting your food around, but you do not eat. It is good. You really should try it," Lee innocently encouraged.

James chuckled. "I am sure it is delicious, but I do not feel much like eating."

Alexandra sighed. "Me, either." She touched her abdomen. "Too many butterflies fluttering about."

Lee and Christine slowly looked about for the butterflies. Not seeing any, they looked at each other and shrugged.

The next morning, James was standing by the front door pulling at his collar. Lee was sitting in James' rocker, tapping his feet on the floor impatiently. Christine sat in Alexandra's rocker smoothing the front of her skirt. Every head turned when the bedroom door creaked open. Christine drew in a breath and Lee whistled as Alexandra stepped into the room.

James shook his head and smiled. "You are as pretty as a rose, Alexandra."

Christine jumped up and took Alexandra's hand. "Was that truly Ma's wedding dress?"

Blushing, Alexandra touched the collar of her pale blue dress and smiled. "Yes, it truly was."

"You look too nice to touch," Lee whispered.

Alexandra laughed nervously. "Thank you, Lee."

James walked over and handed her a package. "This is from the children, Monica, and me."

Alexandra stared at the package, and then looked into each face."I do not know what to say."

Christine giggled with excitement. "Oh, open it, Alexandra."

Alexandra walked to the table and opened it. "Oh, it is ..." With tears in her eyes, she looked at James.

James grinned. "It matches Ma's wedding day candlesticks."

Alexandra ran her fingers over the beautiful pewter platter.

Christine trembled with excitement. "Turn it over!"

On the back was engraved the day's date and "with love and prayers for happiness, James, Monica, Lee, & Christine."

Lee smiled. "I cannot wait to see it piled high with some of your fried chicken!"

Everyone laughed.

"Oh, thank you all so much. I will cherish it always," Alexandra gushed as she hugged each one of them.

Christine looked up at Alexandra. "Now?"

Alexandra nodded. Lee ran into his room and returned with another package, which he handed to James.

James smiled. "I guess I am not the only one who has been sneaking around." He unwrapped the gift and smiled. "I do appreciate this."

"I know Pa's Bible will always be special to you, but we thought you and Monica needed your own family Bible to record your family events in," Alexandra softly said.

James nodded as he looked over the Bible. "You are quite right. Thank you all. I promise Monica and I will use it daily."

Finally, they headed to town. God blessed them with a perfect June day. The sky was partly clouded at times, which helped keep the sun from becoming unbearably hot. As they approached the churchyard, James glanced over at Alexandra. He looked back straight ahead and laughed.

"What is so funny?" Alexandra turned to him and asked.

James shook his head slowly and teased,"I hope Monica does not look as scared as you do, or I might run the other way!" Alexandra tried not to laugh, but she could not help it. "That is better, sis. If I am to let you marry Christopher, I have to see that you have that smile on your face."

Alexandra poked James with her elbow. "Come now, James. You are a bit pale yourself. Anyway, I am not scared. Maybe a trifle bit nervous, but, well … don't you think I should be?" Alexandra sat up straight and took a deep breath.

James agreed. "I guess this means we hold a healthy dose of respect for the important step we are taking. Be nervous, but just do not look so scared. I would hate to have to go chasing after Christopher if he takes off running!"

The younger children laughed as Alexandra slapped playfully at his arm. "James Edward, you hush now!"

They were all smiling when James pulled up to the front of the church. Christopher, Larry, Monica, and Mr. Anthony were waiting there for them. Christine was helped out by Larry. She and Lee took some things over to where the ladies were setting out the food on the tables under the shade trees.

Christopher helped Alexandra from the wagon. "You look very pretty, Alexandra," he whispered in her ear.

She looked up in his eyes and whispered, "Thank you."

Larry took the wagon from James in order to care for the horses.

James nervously stood by Monica and her father. Mr. Anthony took James' hand. "This is a good day, son. Missus and I are very happy, but I can also tell you giving away my baby girl's hand is not easy, even though I love you dearly. She is very precious to me, and I ask you to treat her as our Lord has instructed. Take care of Monica. And if you ever find yourself in need of anything, I hope you will call on me, son."

James swallowed hard. "I promise, sir."

Mr. Anthony turned to Christopher. "Now, Christopher, I feel I need to say a few words to you. Alexandra's pa was a good friend of mine, and I know how he felt about his daughter. It saddens me to know that you never got a chance to meet him, but he was an upstanding Christian Brother. I expect you to treat Alexandra with the love and respect her father and her brother have always given her. She has seen enough heartache in her young life, son. On this day, I would like to think of her as my child, and I ask you to follow the Lord's leading and make her happy always. I will be here for you also if you ever need anything."

Christopher looked at James and then his uncle. "I

will, sir."

Mr. Anthony wiped his eyes, cleared his throat, and hugged all four of them. They all took a deep breath and walked into the church.

CR

Alexandra could not tell whether hours or minutes had passed. Her heart beat so hard and fast her head felt like it was swimming. There she stood looking at her husband! Someone was pushing a plate in her hand one minute; the next, they stood by a table opening gifts. Constantly it seemed like someone different was hugging her, shaking her hand, or squeezing her waist. She asked about Lee and Christine ever so often, but could never get an answer or see where they were.

Finally, Widow Stephans hobbled up with her cane to Alexandra. "Honey, you stop fretting over them babies. Enjoy your day. I have both my eyes on them. These old legs are not what they used to be, but my eyes are still clear. I will take real good care of them. Come Wednesday, I will have them ready when you and Monica come to fetch them."

"Thank you, Mrs. Stephans. It was so thoughtful of you to suggest they spend a few days with you."

"Well, now. It will give you lovebirds time to settle into your nest. And I have to be honest; I love their company!"

Next thing Alexandra knew, it was late in the afternoon, and Larry was bringing around the wagon. He, Christoph, and Luke had loaded the gifts and some last minute items from Monica's folks. The grooms helped their brides onto the front seat of the wagon. James and

Christopher sat at both ends with the girls squeezed in the middle. Everyone shouted and waved them off.

Once at home, they pitched in to unload the food baskets and gifts. While Alexandra and Monica were left to arrange all the new things, James and Christopher went to tend to the animals. After a while, the door swung open wide. In walked two quilts! Both girls stared wide-eyed in disbelief.

Monica found her voice first. "What is going on?"

Christopher and James set down each of their quilt-draped bundles.

Sheepishly grinning, they looked at each other. "You first, James." Christopher nodded towards James.

"No. You first, by all means." James' eyes sparkled with mischief.

Christopher laughed as he saw both girls staring at them. "How about we go at the same time?"

James returned the laughter. "Sounds good to me. One, two, three." At that, they both lifted the quilts off their gifts.

Both girls' hands flew to their mouths as they squealed in delight. Two new rocking chairs! Monica and Alexandra rushed over, sat in them gingerly and gently touched the arm pieces.

"Oh, what lovely work," Monica whispered. "It is so comfortable."

Alexandra took a deep breath and closed her eyes as she sat all the way back. Then they jumped up, hugged their husbands, and voiced their thanks. This left both James and Christopher blushing and speechless!

MARRIED LIFE

The next morning brought sunshine to match the joy of the new family. Both men had gone out to tend to chores. Monica was straightening her room while Alexandra was busy in the kitchen. Soon, Alexandra headed to tidy up her room, and Monica scurried into the kitchen. After a nice breakfast, the girls began to wash dishes, and the men went back to the barn. About that time, the wagon was heard pulling up to the house. Both Alexandra and Monica stood grinning, ready to burst with their secrets.

Christopher stepped into the doorway. "Do you have everything ready, Monica?"

The smile left Alexandra's face and a look of confusion took its place.

Monica ran giggling to her room and came out with a packed picnic basket and a blanket. "Here you go. Have fun, you two."

Alexandra looked from one to the other.

Christopher held out his hand for hers. "Well, are you coming?" He grinned.

Right at that moment, James walked in. "Everything ready, Alexandra?"

Now it was Monica's turn to look surprised!

Alexandra smiled. "All set." She went off to the children's room and came back with a packed basket! She handed the basket to Monica. The girls laughed and looked at the grinning faces of the men.

"Alexandra, I think we have been had," Monica huffed playfully.

Alexandra laughed. "I believe you and I will have to keep a close watch on these two!"

Together, they all loaded into the wagon. They drove to the lake and set out their blankets. They waded along the bank, skipped rocks across the water, told stories on each other, and laughed.

Finally, James sat up. "I am getting a might hungry. What do you have in those baskets, girlies?"

"Hungry?" Alexandra playfully admonished, "It is a good hour before lunch, I am sure."

Christopher sat up and touched his stomach. "Lazing around has worked up my appetite, too. Let us take a quick peek in those baskets."

Monica laughed. "A quick peek? Knowing you men, 'quick,' 'peek,' and 'food' do not go in the same sentence!"

The girls set out the lunch, and Christopher returned the thanks with prayer.

After everyone had their lunch, James wiped his mouth with his napkin and shook his head. "That was right fine. Thank you very much."

"I have to agree with you, James. That hit just the right spot. Thank you," Christopher added and pulled Alexandra over to him to kiss her cheek.

After a short rest, James stood up and stretched, "How about you and I walking some of that good meal off?" He reached out his hand to Monica.

Christopher stood also. "That sounds like a good idea. How about it, Alexandra?" He helped her up.

James and Monica strolled off in one direction down the riverbank, while Christopher and his young bride walked hand-in-hand in the opposite direction.

A while later, James and Monica came back to the picnic spot to find Christopher lying back in Alexandra's lap, napping. Alexandra was gently stroking his hair. She had flowers sticking out of the sides of her own hair.

She looked up and softly greeted them. "I like your flowers, Monica."

Monica smiled and looked at the bouquet of wildflowers she was holding. "Thank you."

"Well, if you can wake sleeping beauty," James teased, "I think it is time we headed for home."

CR

The next day, late in the morning, James and Monica took off for lunch out on their own. They came back by mid-afternoon. Christopher and Alexandra took a picnic for supper and walked to the creek. By the time evening devotions were at hand, all were at home gathered around the empty fireplace.

"I guess it is back to reality tomorrow," James said with a sigh. James looked from Monica to Christopher. "I want to ask both of you to be patient with Lee and Christine. They are good children, and they love you both, but this will be one more change in their short lifetimes. I am certain with a little time, they will settle in just fine."

Christopher nodded, and Monica gave him a reassuring smile.

Shortly after dawn the following day, everyone loaded into the wagon and headed to town. This time, the girls sat on a seat Christopher had fashioned behind the front one. They sang, laughed, and talked the whole way. James stopped the wagon in front of Widow Stephans' house. As Christopher helped Alexandra to the ground, Lee and Christine came flying out the door. Christine wrapped her arms around her sister's waist.

Alexandra laughed. "I guess I do not have to ask if you missed me!"

James chuckled. "Another day and I do believe you would have knocked me off my feet!" He rubbed Lee's back; Lee had both his arms wrapped around James.

Monica playfully put her hands on her hips. "Excuse me, but what about me?"

Christine smiled and hugged her, too. Christopher squatted and tapped Lee on the shoulder. Lee turned around with a bashful smile.

Smiling, Christopher spoke up. "Care to share some of that, partner?"

Lee reached over and hugged his neck.

Alexandra walked over to Lee and grabbed his shoulders. "Have you grown a foot in two days' time?" She squeezed him tight. "I have missed you guys something fierce. Have you minded your manners and helped Mrs. Stephans?"

Christine nodded. "Yes, ma'am. We have had a very nice visit, but I am sort of ready to go home."

James put his arm across her shoulders. "Well, this is your lucky day, then. After we help out over at folks-in-law's, we will be heading home; and if you do not come with me, I am sure to be some kind of sad. The house is too quiet without you."

James and Christopher went ahead and drove the wagon on to the Unruh farm to help for the day. Monica,

Alexandra, and the children planned to walk over after they visited with and thanked Widow Stephans. Mr. and Mrs. Unruh enjoyed having their Monica and her new family over for the day. Christopher's folks and his youngest sister Olivia were still around, so it made for some nice visiting. Alexandra was a bit nervous at first to be around her mother-in-law, but soon found herself at ease and happy. Ms. Rebecca was very friendly and loving. She had embraced Alexandra and the children upon their arrival that morning and continued to coddle Christine and Lee affectionately throughout the day. They all stayed through lunch and for a light evening meal before starting for home. Alexandra and Monica invited both sets of parents for a meal at Saturday's noon as they departed.

Heading home, the talk centered mostly on Widow Stephans. She had not looked well for months, and Christine told Alexandra how the widow had napped rather often during their visit.

Soon, they were home, and chores were completed. Now everyone could settle in for their first night home as a new family. Monica had helped so often over the last year that she seemed to fit in at the farm almost instantly.

Their first morning all together found them up early and busy bustling around. The men-folk were out tending to the crops. They had completed animal chores by sunrise. Christine and Lee were out in the garden weeding. Alexandra and Monica were scrubbing the house and tending to the laundry. They were off schedule for the week, but no one seemed to mind.

"We need to figure out our meal for Saturday," Monica mentioned as she scrubbed a grass stain off Lee's overalls.

Alexandra brushed a loose strain of hair out of her face. "I was thinking we could bake first thing in the morning

233

and do the ironing. Besides airing out the tick mattresses, that would put us caught up with all our chores for the week."

"Sounds good. What about baking gooseberry and blackberry pies?" Monica raised her eyebrows and smiled.

Alexandra raised a finger. "And a buttermilk pie, too. Christopher says it is his mother's favorite."

The girls worked and planned until at last their day was complete.

After washing up and getting ready to turn in that evening, James asked Christopher to lead devotions. They decided they would alternate devotions unless the Spirit had other plans. After prayer, the very tired family went to bed with the sun.

By the time the Unruh wagon arrived just before noon on Saturday, the girls had the table set with their new embroidered tablecloth, Ma's candlesticks, and one of Christine's bouquets. Each place setting was neatly arranged, and it was decided that the ham would be served on Alexandra's new platter. The girls had prepared wheat bread to go with the strawberry jam, ham, rabbit and dumplings, fried squash, baked carrots and turnips, corn, and the blackberry, gooseberry, and buttermilk pies. They had cooked yesterday afternoon mostly in the lean-to as to not make the house any hotter than it had to be for today.

Monica and Alexandra each wore one of the new dresses that had been made for them in the two weeks prior to their wedding. Christine kept smoothing the front of her new pink dress with the small white dots all over it that had been a gift from Monica's mother.

Christine looked up at Monica. "Do you think Mrs. Unruh will think it looks good on me?"

Monica knelt in front of her and grabbed her hands.

"I know she will, but she might like it even better if you remember to call her grandma like she told you."

Christine giggled. "I forget. She is not really my grandma, and she looks too young to be my grandma."

Monica stood up, smiling. "She is really a grandma. Remember Benjamin, Hope's little boy?" Christine nodded. Monica continued, "But I know it feels funny. She said she could not have you call her 'Mrs. Unruh,' so since you do not have anyone to call grandma, she thought she would like to have you as a granddaughter. Now run off and make sure the front steps are swept clean." Monica watched her go out the opened front door.

Alexandra came up beside her. "Your parents have been so good to us, telling Lee and Christine to call them grandparents. That shirt and dress your mother made them for the wedding were so thoughtful."

Monica smiled. "I think my folks have always had a special place in their hearts for you and your family. These marriages just added to that."

Soon Christine jumped into the door. "I see a wagon coming!"

Before anyone knew it, the house was full of company. The men-folk sat on the back porch in the shade, and the ladies set the food out. Finally, everyone was seated around the table. James and Christopher sat at each end of the table with their new brides to their right. Ms. Clara was beside Monica, next Mr. Anthony, and then Larry. Ms. Rebecca sat next to Alexandra, next Mr. Arthur, and beside him on the end of their side was Olivia. Lee and Christine sat behind them on a make-shift table by the empty fireplace.

Alexandra observed the conversation around the table. She smiled as Ms. Clara kept getting up to tend to Lee and Christine. The children were soaking up all the special attention. Alexandra's eyes rested on Ma's candlesticks. She let out a small, happy sigh. She could hardly remember how this room had not so long ago felt so empty and sad. Not any more. A laugh at the other end of the table snapped her out of her thoughts. 'Pa!' flashed through her mind. She swallowed hard to keep from choking.

Christopher touched her arm. "Are you all right?"

She smiled at him and nodded. "Just, um, swallowed wrong." She touched her hand lightly to her throat. "I am fine, thank you." She picked up her cup and drank some water. She looked down the table at James. 'Oh, how much like Pa he is,' she thought, before Ms. Rebecca distracted her with conversation.

After the dishes were cleared and put away, everyone sat around and relaxed. The men strolled out to the barn, and the ladies went out to the garden site.

Around five o'clock, Mr. Anthony announced their departure. "Children, I have enjoyed my visit today. The food was delicious, and your hospitality was great. It does this papa's heart good to see you all so happy."

Mr. Arthur nodded his head. "I will head home Monday with a lighter heart knowing my son is being left behind in such loving company."

Ms. Rebecca grabbed Christopher's waist. "But I will still miss my baby boy." She hugged him tight. Then she reached over and hugged Alexandra. "And my new daughter, too."

They all loaded up and waved good-bye until the wagon was out of sight.

At church the next morning, they learned that Widow Stephans had taken ill. James, Monica, and Lee went to eat with Brent and Faith after the service was ended. Christopher, Alexandra, and Christine went to eat at Minister Paul's. Christopher and the girls left the minister's house early in the afternoon to stop by and visit with Widow Stephans. Her granddaughter, Amelia, was there at Widow's bedside. It was she who answered Alexandra's quiet knock. She told them that all the family had gone back to their homes to rest. Her Aunt Ruth had arrived in town on Friday.

"She has gone to my house to rest a while," Amelia informed them. She showed them to the widow's bedside and let them have a little time with her grandmother. Pale and thin, Widow Stephans was sitting up leaning back on some pillows. Her head was leaning to one side, and her eyes were closed. Alexandra sat in the chair beside the bed, and Christopher stood behind Alexandra with his hand on her shoulder. Christine stood beside the bed and placed her hand softly on Widow's. Widow Stephans slowly opened her eyes and smiled.

She weakly squeezed Christine's hand. "Hello, precious."

Christine smiled and whispered, "Hello."

"I am so glad you have come to see little old me." She turned her pale, weary face toward Alexandra. "Oh, how pretty you are, missy." She reached out her hand for Alexandra's. Smiling, she looked up at Christopher. "I knew the good Lord would let me live long enough to see happiness come again to this child and her brother. Bless you, young man." She looked back at Alexandra. "Don't you shed any old salty tears on me, child. I have lived a long blessed life. Our Lord has been better to me than I have deserved. With a full and peaceful heart, I wait to be called home. You know, my Ruth came home to me this week. My! How I have enjoyed seeing my baby girl again!"

She stopped and closed her eyes and looked as if she had dozed off, except for the peaceful smile still on her lips. Soon she opened her eyes again and looked out the window beside her bed. "I have been waiting for her visit. It was a long winter, and I wondered at times if I would make it to lay eyes on her face one last time. The Lord gave me one more visit with her; for that, I am grateful. I look forward to telling Him face to face real soon."

Alexandra wiped her cheeks and cleared her throat. "I want to thank you, Mrs. Stephans. For helping us so many times, but especially the time you got through to James right after Ma was buried. You helped him live again. I will be eternally grateful."

Widow shook her head. "Girlie, all I ever did was to love you all. You have abundantly repaid me many times over."

Christine took Widow's frail hand into her own and touched it to her cheek. "I love you so much," she sniffled.

"And I love you, sweetheart. Now, you laugh and remember all the fun we have had; no crying and being sad over this old body. I am so happy. I want no part with tears." The old woman cackled and smiled. Christine wiped her eyes and gave her a smile. "That is much better." She gave Christine's hand a gentle squeeze.

Alexandra stayed just a little longer, then the new little family said their good-bye and headed to church. They arrived a little early, but so had a few others, so it gave them some time to visit. Tonight would be the hymn sing service. Alexandra loved to sing.

From her place beside Monica with the married ladies, she noticed Mae and Tonya sitting together a few pews up. Alexandra felt a little uncomfortable, and she shifted in her seat. She still felt like a little girl around some of the older ladies of the church. 'Oh, I hope I act older than I feel,' she thought to herself. She sat up straight and shared a hymnal with Monica and Christine.

Mr. Jimmy led the first song. After the opening prayer, two more songs were sung. During that last song, the door opened and closed in the back of the church. Alexandra wondered who was arriving so late. Then she saw Preacher Paul walk to the front and speak with one of the song leaders.

After the song was finished, Preacher Paul stood before the congregation. "Brothers and Sisters, I come before you with mixed emotions." He paused, bowed his head, and closed his eyes for a moment. Then he looked up and continued, "Our dear faithful sister, Ester Stephans, has gone to meet her Maker. While it saddens me to lose such a fine friend, I feel great joy knowing she was ready to go in peace to her heavenly home." He left the front of the church, walked quietly to the back, and took a seat.

Although Alexandra knew in her heart that Widow Stephans would not be much longer on this earth, she still felt surprised at the announcement. She withdrew a handkerchief from her sleeve and wiped her eyes and nose. She tried not to cry, but the tears came anyway.

Finally, Christoph rose and walked to the front. He led the congregation through "Amazing Grace."

On the ride home, Christine tapped Alexandra on the elbow. "How come everyone seemed so sad? Widow Stephans was so old, and she said she wanted to go to heaven so badly. Should we not be happy?"

Christopher looked back at her. "You know, Rosebud, we are happy because of all the reasons you said, but we will miss her, so we are sad to lose her company. However, I agree with you; she was getting on in age and seemed to be in such poor health of late. I will not be sad, but happy, that she is in heaven. What about you?"

Christine was smiling; she liked it when Christopher called her "Rosebud." He had given her that nickname last year when she wore a school dress with rosebuds all over it.

Christine asked, "Can we sing her some songs? She loved it when Lee and I would sing to her."

James nodded. "I think that would be nice. Lee, what do you think? You have been awfully quiet back there."

Lee shrugged his shoulders and kicked at the side of the wagon. "She was a real good checker player," he said in a small voice.

Christine grabbed his hand. "You always made her smile and laugh. She said no one tickled her funny bone like Lee."

Lee gave her a small smile. "She did say that, didn't she?"

Monica began to sing, and everyone joined in.

THE SUMMER HEAT

The following week, school began. Lee and Christine walked to school each morning and returned about an hour before supper was served. Lee was very excited to be learning to read this year. He had mastered his alphabet and some simple ciphering last term and was putting together words and sentences right at the beginning of this term. Christine's favorite subject was spelling. She studied her word list every day so that by Friday's spelling bee she would be prepared.

Monica and Alexandra were busy preserving the bountiful harvest from the garden. They found themselves working from sun up to sun down. Alexandra was grateful for the company this summer. She had been lonesome at times last year with the children in school. The work was a lot easier with an extra set of hands around every day! Little by little the cellar was filling up, and the pantry was beginning to bulge with jars and crocks of preserves. It was also nice to have fresh vegetables on the table.

About once a month, they invited someone over for supper. Sometimes, they found themselves heading to town, where they had been invited for a meal. At least two Sundays a month, they ate at Monica's parents' house. Sometimes, Ms. Clara let Monica and Alexandra prepare a most of the meal.

One night after clearing some of the land for next year's crops, the weary and worn men ate silently at the table.

Monica looked over at Lee. "How was school today?"

Lee swallowed his food. "Hot!"

James wiped his mouth and spoke sternly. "You should not sass, Lee. Now answer Monica properly."

Lee shook his head innocently. "I weren't sassing, James. It really was hot today. We did not even run at recess. Just sat under a tree and talked about cold things." He went on with his eating.

Christine tried to suppress a giggle. Monica tried to hide her smile, also.

Alexandra pushed around her food. "I have to agree with Lee. It was a powerful hot day. Once or twice, I found myself thinking about doing something cooler than stirring the clothes in that boiling water."

Christopher watched Alexandra picking at her food. "Aren't you hungry?"

She sighed. "I think I must have gotten too hot washing clothes today. I just do not have much of an appetite."

James drank the last of his water and set his cup down. "This August heat is one thing, but it is the dry spell that is wearing me out. Hauling water to the gardens and watching our fields fry under the sun's blaze is enough to wear a man thin."

Christopher nodded in agreement. "I pray rain comes soon. Many more days like this week's heat, and we will lose some crops."

After the supper dishes were put away, the men-folk came in from the animal chores. Alexandra helped Lee wash up. Soon, Monica was calling Christine's spelling words out, and Lee was doing some ciphering on his slate for Christopher.

By dark, everyone gathered around the table for devotions. The windows were raised with mosquito netting over them, and tonight James had opened the front and back doors to try to create a draft.

James walked over to the water basin and washed his face again. "It is so sticky tonight," he said as the cool water dripped down his face.

Christopher got up and stood in the doorway, looking out at the night's sky. "Too hot for night. I am not sure if it has even cooled down much since afternoon."

After a prayer for rain, they decided to turn in early, since no one felt much like doing anything else.

The next day held much of the same. By ten o'clock, the men were seen coming across the yard towards the house. They surprised Monica, who was coming out of the lean-to into the kitchen. "What are you fellas doing back at the house? Lunch is not for at least two hours."

James and Christopher sat at the table.

James wiped his face with his handkerchief. "Too hot and dry to function already. We thought about running over to the creek to splash around and cool off."

Christopher looked around. "Where is Alexandra?"

Monica motioned toward the bedroom as she handed the men their cups of water. "She is lying down. She was not feeling well. This heat has really bothered her these last couple of days."

James and Christopher looked concerned.

Christopher had just risen to go check on Alexandra when she appeared at her door, saying, "I thought I heard you two. Surely I did not lie down that long?!"

Christopher went over to her. "Are you all right?"

Alexandra smiled. "Yes. I am fine. Did I hear someone

say 'creek?'"

James laughed. "I bet you would cool down there. How about we all run down for a dip and then come back for a light lunch?"

Soon they were traipsing off towards the creek. Monica and James went to one spot while Christopher and Alexandra headed a little ways upstream.

Everyone's spirits improved with the cool dip.

Soon after lunch, a gust of wind blew through the opened front door. Monica and Alexandra rushed to the porch.

Monica shook her head. "I do not like the look of that."

Alexandra squinted and shaded her eyes as she peered off into the distance. "It is rolling in too quick to be any good." She saw that James and Christopher were walking towards them from the barn. "Looks like rain. What do you think, guys?" Alexandra called out.

James looked worried. "It has been so hot and sticky, now this wind comes out of nowhere."

Christopher looked at the approaching clouds. "Those look scary. I do not like the direction, either."

Monica turned to him. "What do you mean?"

"Those clouds will hit town and roll this way unless the wind changes," he explained.

Monica and Alexandra looked at each other. At the same time, they whispered, "The children!"

James waved his hand. "Now, surely Miss Erinn will not let them head out of town in such a storm. She will make them wait it out there."

Alexandra wrung her hands into her apron. "No, James. School let out after lunch today! Miss Erinn was going home for her quarterly visit. Oh, James, they will be walking home now!"

Monica grabbed James' arm desperately. "Could they beat it here?"

He shook his head doubtfully and looked in the direction of town. "We can only pray."

Immediately, they bowed their heads right there on the porch, and James prayed for direction, the safety of the children, and their own safety from the storm.

The sky began to grow darker, and lightening could be seen in the distance. James and Christopher went and hitched up the small wagon. It was decided that James would go out after the children, and the others would wait at home. As the girls watched James race away, Christopher went to secure the barn and chickens. Alexandra turned and ran inside to close up the windows, and Monica ran out to help Christopher. The two made it back to the porch just as the storm broke loose. The rain came down in sheets. Lightening flashed, and the thunder roared! The wind blew the rain horizontally. The three of them sat inside at the table ... waiting.

"Those poor children — they will be soaked. Lee is probably scared stiff," Alexandra worried aloud.

Christopher got up and paced around the room. "Surely James picked them up by now, or they might have run to the Madisons'."

Monica got up. "I will get some tea brewing. We need to get some towels out and have them ready to dry off the children the minute they step through the door."

Alexandra came back from the bedroom with some towels and set them on the table.

Christopher stopped and held up his hand. "Do you hear something?" he whispered. "They're here!"

They all rushed to the door. Christopher ran out to

help James. Monica held the door to keep the fierce wind from blowing it wide open. Soon all four were standing in the room dripping. Lee and Christine were both crying. Monica and Alexandra quickly proceeded to dry them off and try to comfort them. James and Christopher were talking urgently to each other.

James turned to the girls. "We seemed to be driving into the storm as we neared home, so I believe it should not last much longer."

Monica was taking off Lee's dripping socks and shoes. "James, you should get out of those wet clothes."

James nodded. "Come with me, Lee. You and I will change into something a little less squishy." He took Lee's hand, and they went to the bedroom.

Alexandra took Christine to change, and Christopher went to his room to change out of his wet things. By the time everyone gathered back at the table for some tea, the storm had blown past. Christopher and James went out to investigate the damage.

Monica looked at Christine. "Now, tell us what happened."

Christine's eyes grew big, "We were walking home. We did not get but just outside of town when the wind started to blow, and the sky was looking dark."

Lee piped in, "I was glad, 'cause it made it not so hot."

Christine nodded in agreement. "Well, we got all excited thinking it might rain. We knew how much we needed some rain. Anyway, we kept walking, and it kept getting darker! Then the lightening flashed! We kind of got scared then," she said meekly.

Alexandra patted her hand. "That is all right. I got a little fearful myself."

"Then all of a sudden out of nowhere it started to rain! And rain hard!" Christine continued.

Lee grabbed his head. "It hurt, it was raining so hard."

Christine continued her story. "I remembered a hollowed tree we had looked inside of once, so we made for it at the edge of our land. I shoved Lee inside, and I could get in most of myself. I figured we would wait it out in there. After a bit, something grabbed me! I screamed!"

Monica was wide-eyed. "What was it?"

Lee broke into a grin. "James!"

Christine nodded. "I thought it was a bear or something, but it was James. He grabbed us around the waists, ran us to the buggy, and we raced home!"

Alexandra let out a deep breath. "We were so worried."

James and Christopher came in as the girls were opening the house back up.

James sat at the table. "We had some limbs blow down and a little roof damage to the barn."

Christopher nodded. "You girls might want to work in the garden some. The rainwater will do the garden good, but the wind messed up some things. Your pole beans are down, but they can be put back up."

The girls went and put on some old dresses and headed through the mud. While the boys worked on the barn roof, the girls labored mending the damage done to their garden. The ground was thirsting so badly after such a long spell of dryness that it had soaked in the rain by the time the girls headed back to the house.

The sun was disappearing when everyone sat down for the evening meal.

DUMBFOUNDED

The end of August brought the end-of-school program, and September brought the harvest near. By late September, the temperatures were cooler and the days less hectic. The girls had finished the preserves and were ready to clean the house in preparation for Old Man Winter.

They began bright and early one morning. White and crisp from washing, the ticks were hung on the line. The older girls scrubbed walls and scoured the floors. Christine took everything from the cupboard to wash and scrub. For lunch that day, the girls served cold ham and cornbread from the night before and baked beans from over a fire pit outside. After the stove was scrubbed and polished, they threw in two blackbird pies for the evening meal. By evening, the ticks were re-stuffed and back on the bed frames, the cupboards were neat, clean, and orderly, and the house sparkled with cleanliness. All three girls yawned while washing the supper dishes.

Alexandra leaned over to pick up a spoon she had dropped. As she stood up, she threw her hand to her head and grabbed for the table.

Monica seized her elbow. "James!"

Both men spun round. Christopher reached Alexandra just as she collapsed. He picked her up and ran her to the bedroom with Monica and James fast on his heels.

Monica turned to Christine. "Get a cool rag, quick!"

Christopher gently laid Alexandra on the bed. He took the rag from Christine and softly wiped Alexandra's forehead.

Alexandra's eyes fluttered, and she looked up at Christopher. "What happened?" she whispered groggily.

He gave her a worried smile. "I was hoping you could answer that."

Putting her hand to her head, she took a deep breath. "Well, I remember drying the dishes. I dropped a spoon, then the room started to spin, and everything went black."

James stood with his hands on Monica's shoulders. "You have not been eating enough. All this physical work you are doing, yet you have picked at your food every meal for weeks now."

Alexandra smiled and nodded. "You are probably right. Now that things are cooling off and staying that way, I am sure my appetite will pick up."

She attempted to get up, but Christopher gently stopped her. "Maybe you should lie still for a while."

Alexandra protested, "I am fine now. I will try to turn in when the children do tonight and get some extra rest. I am sorry for scaring everyone, but really, I am just fine." Gingerly, she rose, and everyone returned to the great room.

James and Christopher kept a close watch on her the rest of the evening.

CR

A few weeks later, they gathered around the table at Monica's folks'. The atmosphere was cozy on such a blustery autumn day.

"I think we will be ready for apple picking by mid-week," Mr. Anthony announced. "We are planning on your help."

James nodded. "Yes, sir. You say when, and we will be here."

"I would like to begin just after sun-up Wednesday morning. We will provide a big lunch and supper. Of course, we will send several crates home with you to pay for your help," Mr. Anthony bellowed with his big voice that made Christine giggle. He winked at her.

Christine smiled and looked at Lee as he rubbed his hands together, licked his lips and said, "Apple picking time means apple cider and apple roasting!"

Monica laughed. "Yes, Lee. I think the same thoughts every apple picking."

As the women were washing and drying the dishes, Ms. Clara looked with concern at Alexandra. "Dear, I do believe you have lost some weight."

Monica nodded. "She has not been eating well since the hot spell in August."

Ms. Clara shook her head. "Child, what ails you? That was more than two months ago. Heat can not be bothering you now." She kept washing the pots. "You picked at your plate and turned down dessert today."

Alexandra blushed from the attention and shrugged. "I have not had much of an appetite. Things just do not taste good to me lately, and sweets make my stomach do flips!"

Monica dried the pots as she spoke. "She has had dizzy spells, also. James thinks her poor eating is attributing to her being so tired lately."

Ms. Clara dropped the pot back in the dishwater and looked hard into Alexandra's face. Suddenly, she broke into a wide grin.

Alexandra was startled. "What?"

Ms. Clara dried her hands in her apron and reached over to hug Alexandra.

Alexandra stood there confused with her arms at her sides throughout the hug. "What is this for?"

Ms. Clara laughed. "Why, it is for you ... little momma."

Monica gasped and hugged a stunned Alexandra. "Oh, why did I not think of it before? It makes so much sense."

Alexandra walked over to the chair by the wall and sat with a 'plop.' "I never even considered the possibility. But Mama Clara, do you really think it could be true? I am so young, and we have not been married but four months."

Ms. Clara laughed. "Yes, dear, I am sure. If you are old enough to be married, then you are old enough to be with child. You say you have had a sour stomach, dizzy spells, and been extra tired over at least two and a half months?" Alexandra nodded. "Then it all adds up to just one thing ... congratulations!" She reached over and hugged Alexandra again.

Monica grabbed Alexandra's hand. "Oh, will not Christopher and James be surprised!"

Alexandra smiled. "Oh, but let me tell Christopher alone first." She paused. "A baby! Oh, Monica, can you believe it?"

The women tried to stifle their excitement and to act as if everything were normal. As they entered the parlor, they found the men relaxing and talking.

The afternoon drifted by lazily. Christopher was playing checkers with Lee, Ms. Clara was re-braiding Christine's hair, and James was nodding on the sofa.

Mr. Anthony suddenly cleared his throat. "Alexandra, your cheeks are glowing today. Married life seems to agree with you."

Alexandra blushed warmly and shot a look to Ms. Clara, who was trying not to grin so obviously. Monica covered her smile and turned to get a book from the shelf.

At home that night, Alexandra told Christopher the wonderful news. He sat on the edge of the bed with his mouth opened and his eyes wide in surprise. Then he suddenly jumped up, grabbed Alexandra around the waist, and swung her in a circle!

"That explains so much," he said breathlessly. Then he gingerly sat her back onto the edge of the bed. "Oh, I should not swing you around so. I am sorry."

Alexandra laughed. "I won't break, but I might be sick; so maybe you should not swing me."

He sat back beside her and grabbed both her hands. "Wow, a baby," he whispered.

They talked things over into the night. Finally, exhaustion won out over excitement.

At the breakfast table the next morning, James returned thanks for the food. As everyone began to eat, Christopher cleared his throat. He took a deep breath and blushed before he even spoke. "Alexandra and I have some news we would like to share with everyone."

Alexandra put her hand to her warming cheek as Christopher gently took her other hand into his under the table. With all eyes staring at him, Christopher continued, "We are expecting a baby around next June."

Monica smiled, and Christine gasped.

Lee shrugged. "Aw, I thought it was something important."

Christine turned to Lee with her brow wrinkled and her mouth opened. "Why, Lee Charles, that is important! Just think — a baby in the house!"

Lee shoveled hotcakes into his mouth. "We get new babies every spring out in the barn."

Everyone laughed.

James cleared his throat. "Enough, Lee." He turned to look at Christopher and Alexandra. "Congratulations. I guess that answers the mystery of your illness, sis."

Alexandra smiled and thanked every one for their congratulations. "Yes, I guess it does at that, big brother."

And for the next two weeks, Monica and Alexandra went to Ms. Clara's on Tuesday to sew shifts for Alexandra. The following Sunday, Alexandra wore her first shift to church. Now everyone would share in their happy news! There were lots of hugs, handshakes, and well wishes.

CR

James, Christopher, and Lee spent the next-to-the-last week in October harvesting all the pumpkins and remaining potatoes. The weather was increasingly getting cooler, and they wanted to make sure to beat the frost.

One work-filled day, James was toting the last bushel of potatoes to the cellar, while Christopher and Lee gathered all the vines up to burn.

Christopher looked over to find Lee drawing pictures in the dirt. "Lee, this will be the fourth time I have had to ask you to stop playing and get back to work. We would like to finish this job today. James and I want to start working on finishing our wood supply first thing in the morning."

Lee put his hands in his pockets and kicked at a pile of twigs and vines. "I am tired of working," he mumbled under his breath.

Christopher walked towards him and sternly spoke. "I beg your pardon, Lee?"

Lee shrugged. "Nothing." He dropped to his knees carelessly and with little effort began to pull at the vines.

Christopher squatted beside him and gently placed his hand on Lee's shoulder. "Just a minute. Something is troubling you, son. Do you want to tell me about it?"

Lee looked up angrily with tears in his eyes. He jerked his shoulder away from Christopher's touch. "I am not your son!" he shouted. "You are always bossing me! Just leave me alone!" Lee stumbled, trying to get up, and dashed to the barn, leaving Christopher in the ruins of the garden with his jaw dropped.

James came walking up just as Lee disappeared into the barn. "Where is he off to?" Christopher stood staring at the barn. James touched his arm. "Is everything all right?"

Christopher sighed. "I am not so sure." He proceeded to relay the event that had transpired. They stood and talked for a few moments about the situation. Then Christopher took off his gloves, tucked them into his back pocket, and headed towards the barn. Lee was sitting in the loft by the back hay door, looking out over the pigs' sty. He had his knees drawn up with his arms wrapped around them.

Christopher poked his head into the loft. "Mind if I come up?"

Lee wiped his arm over his face and shrugged.

Christopher eased over beside Lee and sat down quietly. "I am sorry, Lee, for calling you 'son.' I meant it as a term of endearment. I fully understand that I am not your pa." He paused for a moment and took a deep breath. "But, I do love you; and I give you direction because I care about you. You are a good boy, Lee. All of us need some correction sometimes. The Holy Spirit directs us adults, and God gave you a family to lead and teach you in a Christian manner." Christopher did not know what else to say, so he just sat there.

Finally, Lee spoke softly. "I am sorry I yelled at you."

Christopher nodded ever so slightly. "Forgiven." He paused, then continued, "May I ask why you wanted to yell at me?"

Lee stared at the floor between his legs for a long time. Then he swallowed hard. "I guess I was mad at you."

"Is it because I scolded you?" Christopher prompted.

Lee shook his head slowly. "No, sir."

Christopher looked out the hay door and solemnly nodded. "I did not think so. You seem to have been angry with me for some time now. You have been short and sassy for the last few weeks." He turned his face to look at Lee. "I have missed my good night hugs for many weeks now."

Lee swiped his arm over his eyes again and tried to stop the trembling of his lip. He sniffled.

Christopher spoke lovingly. "Lee, can you tell me what has happened to make you feel angry towards me?"

Lee looked at him. "Alexandra does not have as much time to read and play with me since you came to live with us. Now everyone is fussing over this baby you told us about." Lee turned his head and tried to swallow the angry tears. "No one cares about me anymore!" Tears streamed down his small cheeks.

Christopher tried to hold back his own tears. "You are right about me taking some of Alexandra's time. That is the way it is when someone is added to your family. She still loves you just as much though, Lee. Moreover, well ... maybe you have grown up so much over the summer that you are getting too old to read to and to be coddled. Maybe you could read to Alexandra now. She would like that when she is cooking or knitting." Christopher searched his heart and said a quick, silent prayer for guidance over the next hurdle. "As for the baby, why, I am so glad my child will have a strong, happy, and loving uncle to teach him or her things."

Lee scrunched up his nose and looked at Christopher. "What uncle?"

Christopher laughed. "Why, you! You will be the baby's uncle."

Lee's eyes opened wide. "I will?"

Christopher chuckled. "Yes, you will. You will have to help teach him or her all sorts of things ..."

Lee listened with wide eyes of interest as Christopher explained how important Lee was to the expected baby and to the whole family.

With a small smile, Lee looked up at Christopher. "I am sorry I was naughty. I will try harder to not waste time."

Christopher smiled back. "Thank you."

Together they climbed out of the loft and walked back to work. James pulled the remaining vines into a pile as the boys walked up, then stopped and leaned against the rake. "Just in time to light the fire."

Lee cleared his throat. "I will stand watch with the shovel over the fire, James."

James pushed his straw hat back a little off his forehead and looked from Christopher to Lee. He took a breath and nodded. "Sounds all right with me. Then Christopher and I will head over to the cellar to square away this last wagon load. Watch for any sparks or fly-away embers."

Lee smiled as he picked up the shovel. "Yes, sir."

THEIR FIRST THANKSGIVING

Christopher and James spent the rest of October and beginning of November chopping wood and hunting. After last year's rough winter, they wanted to be well-prepared for whatever this winter brought. Between work and Sundays, they did manage to sneak in an apple-roasting with the Schimdts.

The first of November found them going to the Jacksons' for a pumpkin pie social. The little children bobbed for apples and played games while hot cider and pies were being served. It was a great fellowship time, made more precious since no one knew how long a family would go in the winter storms without getting to town to visit.

About ten days before Thanksgiving, Alexandra and Monica arranged for the Unruhs and the Whiteds to come out to their farm for a basket supper. Each family brought enough food to feed their own family and set it all out on a table. Then everyone helped themselves to each others' food. Everyone sat around and played guessing games after they ate. Laughter and warmth filled the house.

A cold air rushed in the door as the last of the guests filed out into the evening to head back home. Old Man Winter was not far away.

Less than a week before Thanksgiving, Christopher decided to take Lee and go check the traps that they had set out near the west end of the creek. Alexandra stood on the porch with her woolen shawl wrapped tightly around her shoulders, waving at the boys as they trudged off together. She squinted up at the gray sky and into the blustery air. 'I hope bad weather holds off until after they return,' she thought to herself.

She started inside ... then stopped. Reaching inside the door to grab her coat from the peg, she walked around the house, pulling on the garment. She reached down and picked up a wooden bucket from the back stoop as she descended the steps, then headed towards the cemetery.

Once there, she turned the bucket upside down and sat with a huff. "Hello, Ma." She took a deep breath and gazed out over their land. "I guess it has been a long while since my last visit. It is not that I do not think of you often, but well ... I guess I find myself talking to you as I do little things around the house, and I think of you so often that I do not realize how long I have been between visits." She paused and brushed a twig and some leaves from around Ma's cross. "I know I can talk to you anywhere. I do believe your soul is not here in this grave, Ma. But," she sighed, "every now and then, I just feel the want to be here beside you." Looking off to the distance, she pulled her coat a little tighter around her. "Things are working out nicely, Ma. I really have enjoyed Monica's company. No one can fill your place in my heart, but Monica has helped fill the loneliness around the house. When James and Christopher are out working and the children were in school, she helps fill the void I felt being home alone." She smiled. "Oh, Ma, a baby. I never dreamed about a baby so soon. It will be hard without you here to help me." She swallowed hard and wiped a tear from the corner of her eye. "Christopher is a wonderful husband. He is taking good care of us. I really know you would like him, Ma. The wind seems to be picking up," she said as she brushed the hair from her eyes. "I hope the storm holds out until Christopher and Lee return."

From behindAlexandra at the house, Monica had come out onto the front porch and was calling her name. Alexandra stood and turned to look towards the house. The wind seemed to be blowing stronger by the minute. Alexandra turned back to Ma. "I never did tell anyone I was coming out here. I guess they got worried." She picked up the bucket and gently touched Ma's cross. "I love you, Ma."

Holding tight to the front of her jacket, she started back to the house. James came off the back porch and met her halfway. He took the bucket and hurried her into the house.

Christopher and Lee made it home just in time to beat the rain. It was a cold rain, and the wind made it all the worse. Before morning dawned, it had turned to sleet.

Over breakfast, talk centered around Thanksgiving plans. James and Christopher were quiet while girls buzzed about how they could surely make it to town for the holiday.

James set down his coffee mug and cleared his throat. "There is no way the roads will be passable by Thanksgiving. Even if the sleet stopped right now, the road will stay a mess for several days."

Everyone sat there in silence.

Christopher touched Alexandra's hand. "I do not think this weather is good for you to travel in. The wet, cold, and wind are dangerous. James and I discussed it, and feel it would be terrible if any of us caught cold, especially you and the baby."

Christine looked up from her plate and asked in a tiny

voice, "Will we celebrate Thanksgiving at all?"

Alexandra took a deep breath and forced a smile. "Why, of course we will! I have a whole household of things and people to be thankful for and I, for one, intend to show it!"

Monica smiled. "As a matter of fact, today is the day we start cooking, baking, and cleaning for Thanksgiving."

The conversation quickly filled the room with all sorts of plans for their first Thanksgiving together.

By evening, the sleet had stopped, and the sky cleared of storm clouds. However, the chance of sunshine still looked slim. The men-folk decided to get up early the next morning and go hunting. Christine sat at the table with her chalk and slate and wrote out the Thanksgiving menu as it was decided. They decided to hold off on the meat until the men came back from hunting. Meanwhile, stewed potatoes with tomato relish, fried squash with onions, buttermilk bread with plum jam, snap beans, pumpkin pie, apple pie, hot cider, and coffee were added to Christine's list.

The girls set about scrubbing the house and airing the beds the best they could. Alexandra scrubbed the stove and cleaned out all the ashes from the oven and hearth. Christine scrubbed the floors, and Monica ironed the tablecloth. By nightfall, the house near sparkled.

Early the next morning, the men set out before sunup. Alexandra had a batch of bread rising and was rolling out the pie crusts. Monica was mashing the steaming pumpkin meat, and Christine was stirring the soaking dried apples. By lunch, the house was filled with the aroma of a bakery. Cinnamon, apples, pumpkin, bread, and onions filled the air.

Late that afternoon from inside the lean-to, stomping, rustling, and murmuring could suddenly be heard. The girls froze in their spots and looked at the door expectantly. Lee burst into the room holding a turkey by its feet!

Christine's hands flew to her cheeks. "Oh, Lee! It is as big as you!" she exclaimed excitedly.

James and Christopher poked their faces in the door. James smiled. "It will be turkey for Thanksgiving, girls! First, Lee, bring it back out to the barn, and we will dress it for the girls. Alexandra, how about something hot to take with us?"

"Right away!" Alexandra exclaimed.

As Lee handed the bird back to James, Monica hurriedly sliced some wheat bread and covered each slice with a thick slab of cheese. James and Christopher took the bird to the barn with them and left Lee to bring out the snack. Alexandra took the coffee pot off the back of the stove and wrapped it in a towel. Christine grabbed her coat and scarf so she could help Lee carry the snack.

After Lee and Christine headed out through the lean-to, Alexandra stood wiping her hands in her apron. "We have been so busy, and with all our singing, I did not realize the wind had picked up so."

Monica walked to the front window and looked out. "It is awfully dark. Yet the boys did not mention anything about bad weather. I guess it must not be too bad."

By the time the girls had finished their holiday cooking, the boys were coming in through the lean-to again. Christopher went straight to the fire and sat down. Next filed in Lee, rosy-cheeked and wearied. Lastly, James entered carrying the naked bird in a pan. He set the pan down by the dry sink and joined Christopher by the fire. Christine was pouring the coffee, Monica was ladling the baked bean porridge and salt pork into the bowls, and Alexandra was placing the blackberry jam beside the sliced loaf of wheat bread.

She turned to the boys. "We are ready when you are."

James scratched the side of his thin brown beard. "I am so hungry, I could eat that raw bird, but I am too tired to chew him."

Christopher chuckled and eased himself off the floor. "Well, you are a bit old to be spoon fed, so I suggest you'll have to find a little spoon-lifting strength and come to the table."

Monica went over and grabbed James gently by the elbow. "Come on, *old man*. We made bean porridge, so there is not much chewing needed," she teased.

The dinner conversation centered on the weather.

Christopher shook his head and spoke in between bites. "All the way home, we walked against that fierce wind."

James nodded. "I am sure there will be snowfall by morning."

Christine sat up straight in surprise. "Really, James?"

Lee nodded importantly. "I even helped by setting up the lead rope from the house to the barn."

Alexandra looked worriedly at James. "Do you think we will have a blizzard so early?"

James chuckled. "No. It just gave Lee something to do."

Everyone chuckled and sighed but Lee. Their little brother defended his actions. "Well, it is better to be caught prepared." That comment, or rather the important, grown-up tone he used, caused everyone to laugh even more. Lee just shrugged and went back to his beans.

James hung the scrubbed bird in the cold lean-to for the night. Come early morning, the girls would turn him into dinner's main course. Meanwhile, the girls finished putting the cleaned dishes away. Devotions were read, prayer was offered, and everyone turned in for an early bedtime.

True to James' prediction, a light snow was falling in the morning. The wind was so terrible that at times it appeared to blow the snow back towards heaven!

After chores, the men sat by the fire. They spent most of the day trying to sneak samples of the girls' cooking. Christopher settled down and read Lee and Christine a story while they waited to be called to the table. James talked Monica into a game of checkers in between her fussing around the table and basting the bird. Even Alexandra sat down every now and then to rock and pick up her knitting. Lee had his wooden horses in a corner waiting to be pranced around the room. Christine's dolly was wrapped warmly and "slept" soundly as she was rocked back and forth by the fire. Before the meal was quite ready, the men headed out to check on the livestock.

Monica worked beside Alexandra in the kitchen.

"You know, Monica, I am very thankful to have you in this family. I know God sent you to help fill the emptiness of our home," Alexandra remarked as she continued to slice the bread. "I would get so lonesome when James was out working and the children were out playing or at school last year. I still miss Ma and the wisdom she could share with me about life, but I am so thankful for your friendship and companionship."

Monica smiled as she stirred the carrots. "Thank you. I was very nervous when I received James' proposal. I have always admired how close you and he are, and I worried how you would feel about me moving into your home and family. You have made me feel comfortable and welcomed from the very first hour. I am thankful for being a part of this family." She paused to wipe her eye with the back of her hand. "This is my first holiday away from my mama and daddy. Even my sisters have been with us for every holiday since they married." She sighed, smiled, and went back to stirring the vegetables. "But I am very happy to have this new family to share Thanksgiving."

They hugged each other and turned to see the food onto the table.

Finally, when everyone was gathered and seated, James looked around at everyone. "Looks like we will be beginning our own little tradition this year. I was thinking we would each say a few things that we are thankful for, and then Christopher can lead us in prayer."

Everyone nodded an agreement. Lee was staring at the roasted bird sitting in front of his plate. James interrupted his thoughts. "Lee, we will start with you."

Startled out of his delicious imaginings, Lee sat up straight. "Oh, well ... I am thankful for the turkey!" He smiled big. However, it quickly turned to a frown as James looked at him sternly. Lee looked down at the table. "Well ... I am thankful for having a house full of people who love me and take care of me. And for my wooden horses." He looked up and smiled innocently at James.

James smiled back and ruffled Lee's hair. "Now you, Christine."

Christine looked at everyone slowly. "I am thankful for having food to eat, clothes to wear, and for having a happy family again."

Alexandra reached under the table and gently squeezed Christine's hand.

Monica spoke next. "I, too, am thankful for this bountiful table, my new family," she said as she looked from one person to the next, "a warm house to keep out the wind, and for my new husband."

James wrinkled his brow and looked serious. "What

happened to your 'old' husband?"

Monica blushed and playfully slapped James' arm. "Oh, you know what I meant!"

Everyone chuckled.

James smiled at Monica, and took her hand in his. "I am sorry. I should not tease at the table." He cleared his throat. "I am thankful for all the Lord has provided for us this year: bountiful crops, healthy animals, good health here in the house, friends, and especially our new family. Christopher, I am thankful for your help, your ideas, and your company. I am also thankful for the smile you have put back in my sister's eyes. But, I am especially thankful for my new wife."

Monica smiled and blushed again.

Alexandra took a deep breath. "I would like to say I am thankful for life." She laid her hand on her expanding waistline. "Our growing family this year has been a true blessing. I am so thankful for God's abundant grace and direction. I, too, am thankful for God blessing me with a tender-hearted husband." She laid her hand on top of Christopher's hand.

Christopher smiled affectionately at her, then cleared his throat. "I have given a lot of thought this week about what I am thankful for. I spent five days listing everything in my mind. I will try to shorten the list to the most important."

Lee let out of sigh of relief. James tapped him under the table and admonished him with his eyes.

Christopher continued, "I am thankful to be alive and well, to be warm and well-fed, to be loved, and to be able to love others. I am thankful I have the opportunity to know Jesus Christ and am thankful that He died for my sins. I am grateful for the many blessings God bestowed on me this year: a new family, a virtuous, loving wife, and for the baby we are awaiting."

There was a silence around the table as everyone reflected on what had been said. Finally, Christopher said, "Let us bow."

He returned thanks in prayer for their bountiful feast.

At the amen, Lee looked up. "Finally!"

James was going to scold him, but Monica touched James' hand. She was trying not to smile, but failing miserably. "I have to say after smelling all this food for two days, I am finally glad to taste it, too."

James smiled. "Then pass the carrots, please."

CHRISTMAS TOGETHER

Between Thanksgiving and mid-December, the Williams farm experienced only one more light snowfall. The house shook with excitement as Christmas secrets hid behind every stolen moment alone. Everyone worked hard at keeping the anticipation of the holiday alive. Alexandra so looked forward to sharing the holiday with Monica and Christopher.

One day, James came in through the lean-to with an armload of wood. Monica had gone out to help Christine with the chickens, and Lee and Christopher were still busy in the barn. Alexandra hummed as she kneaded some dough. James put the wood in the box by the hearth. He turned to head back outside, and Alexandra caught his eye.

James observed, "You sure seem very happy these last few days."

Alexandra looked over at him with a mocking, surprised expression. "Me? Well, why should I not be happy?" She went back to her kneading. "My appetite is back, which I wonder if I should be happy about." She laid her wrist to her expanding abdomen and laughed. "Oh, James, I am really looking forward to Christmas. It is always special, of course, to think of God's gift to us, but also I remember last year's holiday as a new beginning for us — and now our first Christmas with Monica and Christopher. I am very excited."

James smiled. "I am glad, sis. I have to admit that

I, too, am looking forward to Christmas. I know that you have been feeling better, but I do not want you to over-tire yourself. I saw you lifting water out of the barrel yesterday. You should call one of us to do that next time. I remember Pa never let Ma pick up heavy things or reach for heavy things over her head when she was expecting one of the little ones. So, it must not be good for you."

Alexandra smiled as she set the dough in its pan to rise. "Yes, sir." She knew he was speaking out of love, so she decided not to tease him.

James winked at her and smiled. "You know what I mean." He sneaked a cold biscuit out of the basket on the table and scooted out the lean-to door.

Christmas arrived on a very cold but clear morning. Monica, Alexandra, and Christine had worked very hard the last few days to do their share of the Christmas meal. The house was filled with the aromas of spices, fresh baked breads, and this morning's mulled cider heating on the stove. Lee had been up since the first hint of dawn. Christine giggled with anticipation. Monica dished out the corn mush as Alexandra ladled out the cider. The gifts were on the floor between the rockers. Lee kept stealing glances at the packages.

James teased, "Fidgeting will not cause the paper to fall off the packages, Lee."

Christine snickered.

Lee grinned and shrugged.

Once James prayed, everyone commenced eating.

Christopher looked up at James without a smile.

"James, I was thinking we should hold off on the gifts until we return from town. We want to be on time. I do not think we should be late to Uncle Anthony's."

Lee's mouth fell open, and his eyes went wide. Alexandra had to stare at her bowl to keep from laughing.

Christine held her breath and bit the corner of her lip as James slowly nodded. He thought, then finally replied, "Yes, I see your point. Mama Clara would not like us to hold up her meal."

Lee looked like he would cry.

Monica put her foot down firmly but playfully. "Boys! This is not the time to tease." She turned to Lee and grabbed his hand. "Lee, we will exchange our tokens of love as soon as the dishes are put away."

As Lee and Christine exhaled and smiled, Christopher and James laughed.

After what seemed to Lee like an eternity, the time came to exchange the gifts. Lee wanted everyone to open the gifts from him first. He had made leather belts for both James and Christopher.

Lee laughed. "Larry helped me!"

The men both took off the old belt and put on the new one. As they admired the workmanship, Lee beamed with pleasure.

Next, Monica and Alexandra opened their gifts. They each received a hair clasp made of a rectangular piece of leather with a hole bored in two opposite ends. A stick smoothed all over was pushed through the ends once the leather piece was placed over the gathered hair in order to hold it in place. Both girls promised to use their clasps when they took down their hair that very evening.

Lee smiled at Christine. "Now, you!"

Christine excitedly tore open her gift. Inside the

tiny parcel of paper she found two buttons! One was shiny and silver, the other was made of some type of riged, cream-colored shell. Christine held them out in the palm of her hand and examined them.

Lee leaned forward excitedly. "I picked them out. Ms. Susanne let me look at all her buttons!"

Christine smiled. "Oh, thank you, Lee! They are beautiful." She gently put them in her apron pocket. "Now, my turn to give out my gifts."

She rose and quickly went about handing out her packages. She had made embroidered handkerchiefs for Monica and Alexandra. Monica's had her initials in script lettering, and Alexandra's had a bouquet of flowers in one corner. Both girls were surprised.

Christine laughed. "Grandmama helped me every weekday we would visit." Suddenly, she playfully pouted. "I believe she made me take out more stitches than I sewed in!"

Monica laughed. "Oh, how well I remember. But, Christine, the end results are lovely. Thank you." She leaned over and kissed her.

Alexandra neatly folded her hankie and smoothed it. "You are doing so nice in your sewing, Christine. Thank you very much."

Christine beamed. Then she told James and Christopher to also open their gifts at the same time. They did, and each held up a new pair of knitted woolen socks.

James smiled as he examined his pair. "Just what I was hoping for. Thank you, girlie."

Christopher nodded. "I can go out in this cold with confidence! Thank you, Rosebud." He slipped his boots off, took off his old socks, and put on the new pair.

Lee and Christine giggled.

Lee opened his gift and gasped, "Oh, boy!" It was a pouch of leather for his marbles. Christine had run a piece of twine around the top so that he could tie it shut. She had even put his marbles in it! Lee laughed. "I had not even missed them! Thank you!"

Next, James and Monica handed out their gifts. For Christine, Monica had sewn three new dresses for Christine's doll, and James had made a box for storing them. Christine squealed with delight. For Lee, James had built a lidded box for the wooden animals. Monica had sewn a thin pillow for the inside bottom. Lee ran over to his room, got his animals, and laid them comfortably into their new home.

Alexandra and Christopher opened the gift that Monica handed to Alexandra. When the brown paper came off, Alexandra gasped. She looked at Christopher, and they exchanged a smile. "Thank you both very much," she said lovingly as she ran her hand over the cover of the new song book. "I know we will enjoy it for a long time to come." Alexandra handed it to Christopher to look through as she picked up their packages to hand out.

Lee opened his first ... a new blue flannel shirt! Lee rubbed it against his cheek. "It is so soft. Thank you!" He held it up. "Can I put it on right now?"

Alexandra smiled. "You are quite welcomed. You may try it on after everyone is finished."

Christine opened her flower press that Alexandra and Christopher had made. She could hardly wait for spring to arrive so she could press some petals and blossoms.

Lastly, Christopher reached under his chair and handed the last gift to Alexandra. She in turn passed it to James. With a smile, he handed it to Monica to unwrap. Once the gift was revealed, both Monica and James laughed! It was the same song book that they had given to Christopher and Alexandra! Everyone found amusement over the coincidence.

Christopher chuckled. "We will not have to stand in a tight group and share a book when we feel like singing now."

James nodded. "Yes. I hope we will feel free to sing more often now."

As he began to leaf through the pages, the girls left the room. They returned each carrying a parcel wrapped with a bit of twine. Monica handed her parcel to James, and Alexandra handed hers to Christopher. Setting aside the song books, the men both untied their package. Lee and Christine started laughing at the sight of the gifts. James and Christopher held up their new sets of long underwear!

James laughed. "I almost look forward to a blizzard now!"

Christopher added, "Let winter bring on its cold. I know these will keep me toasty!" He winked at Christine.

James stood and grabbed Monica's hands into his. He playfully led her to her rocker and sat her down. "Now you must close your eyes."

She smiled up at him, her hands in her lap, and squeezed her eyes shut tightly.

Christopher laid his hand on Alexandra's shoulder. "You, too, missy." She, too, quickly shut her eyes.

Christopher and James went into the lean-to. They re-entered the room with their gifts to the girls. They each laid their present on their wife's lap.

"Now, open!" the men said in unison.

The girls were speechless. Each one had a hand-carved shelf in her lap. Monica's had wildflowers and butterflies carved into it. Alexandra's had roses on a vine carved underneath the shelf.

"Thank you, James" Monica whispered as she ran her hand over the smooth shelf.

"Oh, yes, thank you. It is so beautiful." Alexandra quickly looked up at Christopher. She grabbed his hand and gave it a loving squeeze.

Both men smiled and blushed.

James rubbed his chin and pointed his thumb back towards the door. "We really should be on our way. Your mother will be looking for us."

Monica stood and kissed him on the cheek. "Merry Christmas."

He smiled. "Merry Christmas, Monica."

The remainder of the day was filled with songs, food, cozy fires, laughter, and prayers. Mr. Anthony read the story of Christmas from the Book of Matthew for the children. Then he presented each one with a penny bag of candy.

Once back home, the children were carried into bed. James went over to stoke the fire. Alexandra was putting away their things in the kitchen. Christopher remained out in the barn tending to the animals, and Monica had already gone into her room. Alexandra went over and sat on the stool beside James as he squatted in front of the fire. He was gazing at the flickering flames of the fire.

"Merry Christmas, James," she said with a contented sigh.

He gave her a small smile. "It has been that, little sister."

"So different than a year ago." She watched the fire as it popped and crackled, sending embers up the chimney.

James shook his head. "I do not know about that. Last Christmas held a lot of promise and peace for us. We had come through so much." He took a deep breath. "Looking on towards our future —" he looked over at her waist, and she blushed — "I see a lot of promise again this coming year." He looked back into the hissing flames. "I feel a great peace in my heart. I like seeing you happy, Alexandra." He smiled. "I know it would please Pa and Ma."

Alexandra turned to look at his eyes. She could see the orange glow of the flames dance about on his face. "I am happy. I, too, like seeing you so content. Pa would be very proud of you, James."

With a smile, he nodded. "Thank you."

Christopher came rushing in through the lean-to door. "It is really cold tonight. The stars are shining, but that wind is beginning to pick up." He came over to the fire to warm his hands.

Alexandra stood to excuse herself. She yawned and said her good nights. Both men remained by the fire.

Once in her room, Alexandra quickly took down her hair and brushed through it. Once in her gown, she hurriedly jumped under the down quilt and snuggled deep into her cocoon. With a smile, she poured out her heart to the Lord.

Finally, she whispered, "Thank you. Amen."

Just as she drifted into dreamland, she faintly heard James and Christopher say good night to each other.

THE NEW YEAR

The week following Christmas was cold and blustery. The fierce wind seemed to freeze one's breath in mid-air. James and Christopher kept busy working in the barn and making sure the coop and house were ready for whatever winter had in store for them.

January held three short snow spells. The first lasted just overnight. It left behind a wet, icy foot of snow. Lee and Christine were disappointed when Alexandra would not allow them to play in it. The wet and icy mix made for wet icy clothes, and she knew no good could come of another bout with fever or pneumonia. She and Monica tried to keep both children busy learning lessons, helping with cooking, and winter projects. Christine was working on sewing quilt squares together. James was slowly teaching Lee how to whittle. His project was simple: smoothing off the bark from a stick, hollowing it out, and boring holes to form a whistle. Lee would soon lose patience, return to his wooden figurines, and play happily by the fire for hours.

The second snow fell in soft, fluffy, large flakes. After four days, there were powdery, three-foot drifts. Bundled and covered, Christine and Lee romped and played a few hours in the white wonderland. On the second day after the snow had fallen, the older ones joined the little ones for an afternoon of snowmen and snowball fights!

The last snowfall came with a mixture of sleet. It left behind a world covered as if in sparkling glass. It made outside chores long, tedious, and dangerous. The weight of the remaining snow from the last snowfall and the ice from this storm caused the chicken coop's eaves to collapse. It took the better part of two days for Christopher and James to make repairs. Monica afforded any help the men needed. The women felt it too slippery and dangerous for Lee and Christine, and Christopher refused to allow Alexandra to step a foot outside. A fall could be more harmful to her than to the others. Alexandra was not exactly fond of the restriction, but she knew she did not want anything to happen to her yet-unborn baby.

Throughout the cold winter months, Alexandra and Monica spent time with the children playing jacks and marbles. Using the plain, brown paper they had saved from the Christmas wrappings, Alexandra helped Christine cut out paper dolls and clothes. Monica helped her decorate the clothes. Late in the afternoons, even the men found time for a game or two. Many a night found oil lamps shining light onto a checkerboard or a song book.

By the end of February, Monica had knitted two blankets and two pairs of booties, and Alexandra had found the time to make several tiny gowns for the baby.

Even though the cold was warmed with songs of praise, chores, projects, games, and friendship, after several weeks of winter's confinement, Monica woke one day feeling very lonesome for her family. James came in from morning chores to find her slicing carrots into a roaster and sniffling.

He walked up behind her and gently wrapped his arms around her waist. "Are you getting a cold, Mon?" He playfully squeezed her tightly.

Monica continued to slice the carrots, shrugged, and slightly shook her head. She replied in a soft, shaky whisper. "I don't think so."

He turned her around to face him. He gently took her chin and lifted it. A tiny tear slowly fell down her cheek, and her chin trembled. His heart seemed to skip a beat. "What is it, sweetie?"

Monica laid her head against his chest and swallowed her sob. "Oh, James. I miss Mama and Daddy." A small sob jumped from her throat before she could stop it. "I know it is foolish, but I cannot seem to help myself today."

James held her tightly and rubbed his hand over her back. "It isn't foolish at all. You have been cooped up for over a month. I bet everyone is missing folks and town about now. I wish I could take you into town, but the sky reads poorly now. Christopher and I were talking this morning, and we both agree the storm that seems to be brewing presently will be a bad one. We spent all morning moving wood into the lean-to and on the porch right beside the door. We are planning to bed down all the animals deep and tighten the line to the barn." He sighed and rubbed his cheek gently against her brow. "I am afraid we are in for quite a long stretch before I can take you home again."

Hearing the hurt in his voice, Monica lifted her face and looked deeply into his eyes. "Oh, James. I am home." She smiled. "I was missing folks and feeling pity for myself. I am sorry. I truly would like to see folks, but I am very happy to be cooped up with my new family in our home." She stood on her tiptoes and kissed him lightly. With a wink she added, "Girls act silly sometimes, maybe simply to finagle a hug or two."

James wiped the tear stains from her cheek and smiled down at her. "As much as I do not like to see you sad,

I do like comforting you." He squeezed her again, and she playfully pushed him away.

With a smile, Monica's face brightened. "You leave me be now so I can get this stew over the fire."

Reaching over and snatching a carrot, he crunched off the tip. "Yes, ma'am."

True to James' prediction, the first snow of February came in the form of a blizzard. The wind howled, and the snow poured from above for five days. James and Christopher had to dig their way to the barn. The snow piled up to the top of the doorframe. Each day, they had to pat down or dig out where the snow had fallen or blown down from the sides into the ditch they had burrowed. With no sunlight getting through the smothered windows, the family relied on oil lamps and fire for light. They found themselves rising later and going to bed earlier over the course of the next two weeks. It took that long for the snow to either blow or melt enough for some source of nature's own light to seep in.

In the midst of their imprisonment by the snow, one of the heifers gave birth to a beautiful calf. The men managed to help everyone make their way to the barn to witness the arrival. It offered a bit of excitement to a rather drab time in the cabin.

Alexandra seemed most effected by the loss of sunshine. She felt weak and sleepy most of the day. A few afternoons she dozing off over her knitting. Once she even fell asleep during the lunch meal! One moment she was stirring her bowl of soup; the next moment found her head bobbing up from where it had drowsily nodded! Christopher grew increasingly worried. Monica knew it was the lack of vitamins given naturally through the sun and the lack of physical work required of them from being inside so long.

The normally pleasant dispositions of Christine and Lee were worn to a thin line one evening before the fire. A game of marbles turned into a constant wave of bickering and harsh words.

Finally, James rose from the table where he had been reading. "Enough!" he stated firmly. "This is not the way I care to hear you speak to one another." Both children pointed and began to lay blame on the other. James cut them off. "I said enough! Both of you put away the marbles without speaking and go prepare for bed. Then I want you both to come back in here to me."

With jaws clenched and lips pouting, they picked up all the marbles and the string and went to their room. Once dressed for bed, they both returned to James, who was sitting in front of the fire with his Bible opened in his lap. No longer were their brows pinched and jaws clenched. Standing before him were two very sad and frightened, innocent-looking faces.

Christine spoke with a meek, soft voice. "We are sorry, James. We know we should not have argued like that."

Lee humbly nodded his head in agreement.

James nodded. "I understand that you both have been together a lot and that the weather has held you up inside for such a long time. Nevertheless, you both must understand that there is never a good excuse to be nasty to or hurtful to another person. Satan waits for moments of weakness on our part to jump in and take over." Both children stood looking at their feet. "Now, I want you both the sit by the fire and read aloud to each other these Scriptures that I have written on your slates. I want you to memorize them by tomorrow's noon meal. Not just the words, but I want you to be able to tell me what you have learned from the Scripture. Do you both understand?"

Each child took his or her slate. "Yes, sir."

Christine looked at her Scripture and quietly read, "James 4:7: 'Submit yourselves therefore to God. Resist the devil and he will flee from you.'"

Lee slowly sounded out each word written on his slate. "Luke 6:31: 'And as ye would that men should do to you, do ye also to them likewise.'"

James nodded. "That is correct. Now quietly sit over there by the fire and read them aloud and to yourselves until I call you for evening devotions." He watched as they went softly to their places. James returned his attention to his Bible.

After about twenty minutes, James sat back and closed his eyes in meditation. He opened his eyes to find Monica standing beside him. Quietly she had laid her hand on his shoulder. She silently pointed to the site where Lee had nodded off to sleep as he sat studying. "I believe we should go ahead with devotions. Everyone seems to be ready to retire."

James smiled and rubbed his hand over his eyes. "I think you are correct." He looked over to the table, where Christopher was reading an old church newsletter. "Excuse me, Christopher." Christopher lifted his head to acknowledge James. James pointed towards Lee. "I believe it is time to have devotions. The small ones, Monica, and I are ready to turn in for the night."

Christopher folded the newsletter and stood. Alexandra had closed her book and was already moving towards her rocker. "Sure. That sounds very inviting. Did you find anything in your reading tonight you would like to share with us?" Christopher asked as he took his seat in the sitting area.

James opened his Bible to the passage he had been reading and shared it with the others. Lee sat droopy-eyed in Monica's lap, and Christine knelt beside Alexandra's rocker. Once they had concluded with prayer, everyone retired for the evening.

Sixteen days after the last blizzard, the women bundled up warmly and headed outside to help the men with chores and any necessary repairs.

Christine was happy to brave the cold. She had missed tending to her chickens. They seemed glad to see her, also. She and Lee filled their basket with the few eggs, scattered the feed, and provided the hens with fresh water. James had taught her long ago to give the hens warm water in the wintertime since it helped with their body heat and cleansing.

Though the small, fresh-air excursion was exhausting, everyone felt better afterward.

The month of March arrived to clear skies. The sun was beginning to bring a small amount of warmth with it. The fierce winds blew the land dry. By the second weekend, James announced that everyone should prepare to head towards town on Sunday. The excitement rang through the house as if it were Christmas all over again!

Alexandra and Monica laid out everyone's Sunday best and checked for spots or any needed mending. Saturday found them baking two pies and making venison stew. Although Monica was sure her parents' table would be full, she wanted to bring something along.

Sunday morning, everyone was up early. The outside chores were completed and the breakfast dishes dried and back in their places. Christopher pulled the wagon up to the front porch, and everyone was loaded in. The pies and stew rested snuggly under the seat. The girls and children were tucked in tightly in the back, and James hopped up front beside Christopher.

When the church finally appeared in sight, Monica could feel herself shaking with anticipation. They arrived early and had time to ride by Monica's folks', drop off the food, and receive a quick squeeze from all.

When the congregation stood to sing the first hymn, Alexandra found that she could hardly sing. She was smiling so broadly she could barely form the words! She closed her eyes and drank in the words of the hymn. She quietly exhaled, opened her eyes, and found her place in the song. The long, cold, dreariness of the winter had somehow left her feeling so tired and weary. When the message was over and the congregation dismissed, Alexandra felt as if her strength had returned. She even noticed a rosy glow in Monica's cheeks.

The meal and fellowship that followed at the Unruhs' was a blessing, indeed. The house was lively with conversation, food, and people. Although the folks seemed surprised to see them walk through the door that morning, Monica noticed that there were already extra plates set out on the table.

As she was drying the dinner dishes, she tilted her head to one side. "Mama, did you know we would be coming today?"

Clara smiled and continued to wash the pans. "Oh, the roads finally dried, so I figured you could make it in. I have not seen my baby girl since Christmas. I was hoping she missed me enough to come out."

Monica went over and kissed her on the cheek. "I
have missed you so."

Clara handed the washed pot to Alexandra to dry.
"How have you managed this cold winter, child?"

As Alexandra dried the pot, she sighed. "It seems to
have dragged on forever. I have been so very tired lately, yet
have not done much of anything." She handed the pot to
Monica to put away and continued, "But after the beautiful
service today and the lovely sunshine along the ride this
morning, I do feel so much better."

Clara smiled and nodded. "Oh, how I do remember
the long, cold winter when I was expecting my own spring
baby. Spring is awakening, and being outside in the fresh air
always makes a body feel better."

Monica and Alexandra hung their towels out to
dry. They all went to join the men in the parlor. Despite
Alexandra's words, Monica watched as her sister-in-law
nodded off while leaning against Christopher's shoulder.
Monica rose and went into the kitchen. Clara followed soon
behind her.

"You have a worried look across your brow. Is there
something you would like to talk about?" Clara observed
as she sat down beside Monica at the smaller table in the
kitchen.

Monica looked into her cup of coffee. Her eyes
rose to meet her mother's. "I'm fine, Mama. I am just a bit
concerned about Alexandra. She seems to tire so easily. Also,
she does not appear to have put on much weight. She has
picked at her food since last fall."

Clara placed her hand onto Monica's and gave her
a comforting smile. "Some women never get their appetite

back from the first months of nausea until after the babe is born. In addition, it is quite normal to be tired during the pregnancy. Especially the first baby, when neither you nor your body knows what to expect. I agree, Alexandra does not appear to have put on great amounts of weight, but my dear, the last three months are just approaching. The baby does a heap of growing in the eighth month. She looks good in color and in spirit. Do not worry so much, all right?"

Monica smiled. "Thank you. I will try not to worry."

Clara got up and poured herself a cup of coffee. "Tell me, child, how you have fared this winter?"

Monica continued to sip her coffee. "Oh, I have had moments of longing for you and Daddy, but my sweet husband helped me through them. I have enjoyed having Christine and Alexandra with me. It has been like living with Hope and Erica. I feel very blessed to have sisters with me still. I think the winter would have been a lot harder to bear without them."

Clara chuckled. "I know it would. I have found comfort in knowing they were with you. Having your baby girl married off and knowing she is isolated through a winter would have been tough on me, also." She gave Monica a playful wink. "I am glad you missed me, though."

SPRING

The blustering winds of March blew away all signs of winter's designs. The warmth of April's sparkling afternoon showers caused the earth to sprout a world of green. The men left the house by daylight's first wink. Diligently, they worked at utilizing as much of their land as possible. The girls worked steadily in the garden. Their hope was to put up more than last harvest. Monica tried to keep an eye on Alexandra. She did not want Alexandra to over-exert herself.

Alexandra delighted in the refreshment of spring. She enjoyed being out under the sun's glow. She felt as if she was sleeping better since they had begun to spend so much time outside. The whole family labored hard to make the most of what God had provided for them.

This spring Christine could finally help prepare the school clothes that were needed. One of her dresses from last year just needed the hem let down. Lee, on the other hand, seemed to have grown by leaps and bounds. Last year's pants had only lasted until Thanksgiving. The pants made in December had already been let down twice. By April, nine-year-old Lee was only two inches shorter than was eleven-year-old Christine.

Until the last of the fields were planted, life consisted of morning devotions over breakfast, work, chores, an evening prayer as the sun closed its eyes behind the horizon, and then wearily climbing into bed.

One of those evenings, Monica sat on the edge of her bed brushing her long, wavy, brunette tresses. "James, how does Alexandra look to you?"

Lying on his back, James turned his head towards her and opened one eye. "Pregnant. Why?"

Monica stopped brushing and lay the brush in her lap. "I'm not sure how to explain it. She seems to wear out so easily still. I was hoping spring would revitalize her."

James sat up so that he was leaning on his elbow. "I know she is tired, but so are the rest of us. I guess I have been so tired myself lately I haven't kept a close eye on her. Is she overdoing it in her chores?"

Monica shook her head. "Christine and I have kept a close watch on her. We try not to allow her to lift anything the least bit heavy. Yesterday and today, I saw her rubbing her lower back when she thought no one was watching."

James lay back on his pillow and rubbed his hand over his eyes as he yawned. "I remember Ma complaining towards the end of carrying Lee. She said the weight was hard on the back."

Monica crawled under the covers while shaking her head. "That's just it. Alexandra has not gained that much weight. With ten weeks left in her pregnancy, she should be much bigger. I am sure she has but gained ten or twelve pounds. James, I am concerned about her."

James turned and kissed her on the cheek. "I'll pay close attention to her tomorrow. She ate so little last August through November. I am sure she lost weight back then. That is probably why it looks like she has not gained much weight. However, we must remember that she has a devoted husband to watch over her, also. Christopher has not mentioned any concerns about how Alexandra is feeling. Now, good night, dear," and he was asleep before he could turn back over.

Over the next few days, James observed Alexandra whenever the men-folk happened to be in from the fields. He examined her face and the shadows under her eyes. More than once, he noticed her stopping and rubbing her back.

One afternoon, he stopped beside her as she threw some bread crumbs to the chickens. "Sis, are you feeling all right lately?"

She brushed her hands off and shaded her eyes as she looked up at him. "Well, all right, I guess. I feel fat and hot, but I am sure that is quite normal."

James put on his hat and tucked his bandana into his back hip pocket. "Just do not over-exert yourself. If Monica cannot help you, just wait for Christopher or myself."

Alexandra smiled at her brother's thoughtfulness. "I will be just fine. But thank you for the concern."

James nodded and walked on his way.

As Alexandra turned and headed back onto the porch and into the house, a shriek came from the barn. Alexandra grabbed up her skirt and held her abdomen as she raced to the barn. Monica flew out of the house with her hands still dripping dishwater. But James beat both girls to the barn.

Just as they arrived at the entrance, they saw that Christopher had Christine in his arms. "Go back, Alexandra!" he called.

James grabbed both girls' arms and rushed them away from the barn.

Halfway to the house, Christopher laid a sobbing Christine on the ground. There were several visible whelps on her face. Alexandra whispered a throaty gasp.

Monica exclaimed, "Wasps!"

James turned to Lee. "Quick — get me a bucket of mud. Now! Run!"

Lee took off running.

Christopher was checking all over Christine to make sure the wasps were no longer stinging her. Not only did she have stings to her face, but also to her hands and arms.

Alexandra sat on the ground and leaned the hiccupping Christine onto her lap to try to calm her. Monica helped Christopher make cold mud cakes to ease the pain from each whelp. James took Lee with him to destroy the nest.

Christopher carried Christine inside the house. Although Alexandra had managed to calm Christine's sobs, sniffles still racked her thin frame. Monica made a pallet by the empty fireplace for Christine to rest upon. Soon, she sniffled herself to sleep.

Monica washed off the mud from Christine's body while Alexandra poured some apple cider vinegar into a bowl. Once Monica had cleaned off all the dried mud, Alexandra dabbed the vinegar onto each red whelp. Hopefully, that would aid in taking away the stinging.

Alexandra kept a close eye on Christine's whelps and breathing as she helped Monica finish cleaning the kitchen from the lunch. As she dried the dishes, she fought back tears.

Monica caught sight of Alexandra's shaking hands. She reached over and took the towel from Alexandra. "Here. Let me finish these last two plates. You go lie down and rest. That was too much excitement for all of us. Christine is resting. I'll keep a close eye on her."

Alexandra wiped the tear that found its way down her cheek. "Thank you." She went over to Christine, squatted clumsily, and touched her forehead. She rose and went to her room.

As she sat on the edge of the bed, she looked up. "Thank you, Lord. I know it could have been a lot worse. Please continue to be with Christine and heal her body." She closed her eyes for a moment and then whispered, "Amen."

She laid her head down on the pillow and pulled her legs up onto the bed.

When she awoke, she immediately thought of Christine. Hastily, she hurried out to check on her. As she entered the room, she saw Christine sitting at the table sipping from a cup of buttermilk. Alexandra tried not to gasp as she saw the whelps swollen over Christine's delicate face. Her right eye was almost swollen shut. Alexandra also noticed four or five whelps on Christine's right hand and forearm. The left hand had several, also.

She rushed over and gently picked up Christine's hand. "Oh, my. Do they itch or hurt?"

Christine wearily shook her head. "Not really. But they are hot, sort of a burning."

Alexandra reached down and lifted Christine's chin up. "Did you sleep well? Your eyes look so tired."

Christine sighed. "I tossed a lot. I do wish I could crawl back in bed. But I know there is the weeding yet to do."

Monica turned from stirring the stew. "The stings seem to have fever in them. I have some rags soaking in the apple cider vinegar. After supper, I thought we would use them for compresses. Once the fever is out of the whelps, she should feel better."

Alexandra rubbed the back of her fingers across Christine's cheek. "That sounds like a good idea. By morning, I bet we will see a smile back on this pretty face. As for the weeding, I will ask James to send Lee out to the garden. I will help, also. After my little nap, I feel very refreshed."

A look of concern masked Monica's face.

Alexandra looked at Monica. "Don't look so worried. I will take a stool and only do as much as I can. I promise not to overdo it."

Monica smiled. "All right. I'll make some cold ginger water to have when you need it."

After two more weeks of spring's work and fresh air, Christine's whelps had long since faded away, and everything was planted and growing. One morning as they were preparing for the men to come in for breakfast, Alexandra walked over to the dish cupboard to take out the dishes in order to set the table. As she reached up to take down the bowls, she felt a sharp stabbing pain in her lower abdomen. She froze! Slowly, she exhaled and rubbed the sight of the pain. She closed her eyes and tried to breathe normally. The pain passed. She rubbed her hand across her cheek. She looked around to make sure no one noticed.

Monica was slicing bread, and Christine had her head lying on her bent arm on the table. Relieved, Alexandra took the bowls down and resumed setting the table.

The girls had finished all the sewing and mending needed for the beginning of school. Berries had been harvested and many set up in preserves. Several times a week some sort of berry dessert garnished the table. New chicks and ducklings could be seen decorating the barnyard.

One evening after supper in mid-May, everyone sat out on the porch watching the sunset and the meandering of the barn life. Christopher drank in all the beautiful sights.

The garden and fields were blooming, and the barnyard was bustling with new life. The grass was green, and the wildflowers were vibrant colors. Everything and everyone seemed bursting with growth and vibrancy. Everyone, that is, except Alexandra.

Christopher watched Alexandra as she sat rocking and fanning herself. Her skin was tanned from working in the garden. But instead of a healthy glow, her face held a weary, drained expression. Christopher could see where Alexandra's face and body had filled out with her expectancy. However, he had thought she should appear healthier and more robust. He sat watching her, worrying what the strain of laboring for the baby would do to her. She seemed so fragile to him. With six weeks of her pregnancy left, he worried about her strength.

Alexandra sensed his eyes on her. She looked over at him and smiled. Christopher did his best to return her smile. He leaned back his head against the porch post and said a silent prayer.

CR

In the early morning hours of June's first day, Monica and Christine were stirring up a batch of flapjacks. Suddenly, a shrill cry came from Alexandra's room. Both girls dropped everything and ran to the bedroom. There stood Alexandra in her nightgown at the end of the bed. Her gown was pulled up to her knees as she stood with tears running down her cheeks and fear in her eyes. Monica looked at the floor and saw the puddle of water at Alexandra's feet.

In between sobs, Alexandra spoke in a frightened whisper. "It is too soon, Monica."

Monica went to Alexandra's side. "Do not worry." She

led her back to bed. "I'll send for Mama."

Monica turned to Christine, who stood frozen in her spot, eyes wide, mouth opened, and her chin trembling. "Run. Go get the boys. Now, Christine!"

Christine gathered up her skirt and ran out. Monica rushed into the kitchen. She filled the basin with water and gathered a couple of clean cloths. The men came running in from the barn with Lee and Christine on their heels. They burst in through the door as Monica was making her way across the room towards the bedroom.

Christopher and James spoke at the same time. "What's wrong?"

Monica steadied the basin of water. "Please, not so loud! James, you need to go get Mama. Alexandra's water has broken. Her time is come."

Both men shook their heads.

Christopher spoke. "This cannot be. She has four or five weeks yet."

Monica tried to reassure him with a smile. "Well, your baby thinks otherwise. Now, go in there and keep your wife calm." She handed him the basin. "Wipe her face, and remember to smile."

Christopher looked at the basin of water and then at the bedroom doorway. He swallowed hard and looked back to Monica. "Yes. Okay."

As he went into the bedroom, Monica turned to Lee and Christine. With a smile, she wiped her hands on her apron. "I need both of you to finish the barn chores. Then I will need some help in the kitchen."

They looked at each other, then back at her. "Yes, ma'am." They turned and slowly walked out the door.

Monica's smile disappeared as she turned to James.

"Hurry. Tell Mama to call on Doc Cannon. This is too soon, James, and I am scared!"

James gave Monica a quick hug and wiped his eyes as he turned and ran out the door. Within minutes, as she sat at Alexandra's bedside, Monica heard his horse rush past.

It took three hours for James to return, followed by Doc Cannon in his buggy. Mama Clara was with him. James helped Clara down off the wagon seat.

Christopher stood on the porch wringing his hands. Clara took his hands into her own. "How is she?"

Christopher cleared his throat and replied in a shaky voice, "Her pains are six minutes part. She screams out about her back." Tears fell down his cheeks. "She looks so pale and seems so scared, Aunt Clara."

She patted his hands. "We are here now. You go busy yourself and let Doc handle everything."

Christopher wiped his face and left to go help James put up the horses. Doc and Ms. Clara headed into the house.

As the hours of the day slowly elapsed, James, Christopher, Lee, and Christine waited restlessly. Christine made coffee and cheese sandwiches for lunch. Christopher stood looking out the front window.

James placed his hand on Christopher's shoulder. "Lee, Christine, and I will tend to the chores. Holler out to us if there is any change."

Christopher continued to look out the window and nodded.

Monica came out of the bedroom as James was heading out the door. He stopped and looked at her anxiously.

"I came out to make something for supper. No news yet," she said as she went to the kitchen, so the others continued on their way.

Christopher walked over to the kitchen. "How is she, Mon?"

Monica wiped her forehead with the back of her hand. "Doc says she is doing fine."

Christopher looked over his shoulder at the room. "But she sounds like ... well ... I mean, we can hear ..."

Monica touched his arm. "Mama says all that is normal. Childbirth is not easy, Christopher. Mama says it is going just fine. Try not to worry."

Christopher nodded, sighed, and went back to the window.

The moans and cries from behind the bedroom door were becoming more frequent and more intense. Monica, Lee, Christine, James, and Christopher sat silently around the table. There seemed to be more stirring soup around in the bowl than actually eating it.

Christopher pushed his bowl back and rubbed his hand over his beard. "I am sorry, Monica. I just cannot eat."

Monica looked around. "It does not appear that anyone has much of an appetite." She stood up. "Christine, please help clear the table. Lee, take all the leftovers from the bowls out to your pigs."

Christine stood to help, and Lee nodded and did as he was asked.

The men paced back and forth. Christine and Lee tried to concentrate on the checkerboard before them. Monica rocked and tried to tend to the mending. Suddenly — everyone stopped what they were doing. There was silence! All eyes froze on the door. Alexandra's moans had ceased.

As they stood frozen, waiting ... a wail came from behind the door.

"No!" Christopher could not stand the suspense any

longer. He burst through the bedroom door with James at his heels.

Doc Cannon and Clara stood crying beside Alexandra. Alexandra lay on her side holding the tiny baby, bundled roughly in a blanket. She buried her face in the blanket, muffling her cries. Doc looked up at Christopher.

He walked over and placed his hand on Christopher's shoulder. "I am sorry, son. She was just too tiny to make it."

Christopher's chin trembled as his eyes filled with tears. "And Alexandra?"

Doc took a deep breath. "She is weak and worn out. It will take time to rebuild her strength. Only God can mend her heart. She was very brave, but the delivery was hard." He looked over at the bed, then back to Christopher. "We will wait outside and give you some time with Alexandra and your daughter."

Everyone left the room. Christopher walked over and knelt beside the bed. Alexandra looked up at him with swollen, red eyes.

Through her crying, she whispered, "Look how perfect she is." She gently unwrapped the blanket. "See … all ten toes and ten tiny fingers."

With tears streaming down his face, he smiled. "She is beautiful." He gently touched his daughter's tiny cheek. "She looks like she is just sleeping."

Alexandra leaned over and kissed the baby's brow.

Christopher leaned over and did the same. He looked lovingly into Alexandra's face. "I am so sorry, Alexandra." He buried his face into the bed covers, sobbing.

Alexandra rubbed his hair. "Oh, Christopher, I am sorry. I must have done something wrong."

Christopher looked up. "Oh, no, Alex." He looked

down at the baby. "She simply was meant to be an angel." He tried to smile. "Look, she has your nose."

Alexandra wiped her nose with her handkerchief. "Do you think so?" He nodded. She took the baby's hand onto her fingertips. "She has long fingers like Ma's." Alexandra whispered, "What shall we name her?"

Christopher swallowed and took a deep breath. "Can I hold her?" Alexandra nodded and handed him the small bundle. He sat back on the floor against the wall as he held her in his hands. "I think it should be something beautiful and delicate, just like her."

Alexandra wiped at the tears pouring down her face. "What about Gracie?"

Christopher nodded and whispered to his daughter, "Gracie you shall be."

Outside the room, Monica was wrapped in James' embrace, crying. Ms. Clara was sitting in the rocker, calming Lee and Christine. Doc Cannon had walked outside to wash up and get some fresh air.

Christopher finally opened the bedroom door. He asked Monica for a basin of warm water, a towel, and a cloth. Silently, he went back into the room and closed the door. Monica gathered the items and knocked.

Christopher opened the door and accepted the items. "Once we have dressed her, Alexandra and I would like you to see her. Just give us a little longer with her."

Monica nodded and pulled the door shut. James lit the oil lamps, and Ms. Clara helped Monica make some tea. Doc Cannon went back into the bedroom to check on Alexandra.

After a few moments he re-entered the room. He took a deep breath. "Alexandra is doing as well as can be expected. I have advised her to rest for several days. Barring the funeral, I want her to remain in bed for at least a week. Lots of liquids for her, Monica." Everyone nodded solemnly. "Will you need a ride back to town, Clara?"

Clara dried her hands on her apron. "No, thank you, Robert. I think I will stay the night and keep an eye out on things. Grace is not here to do that, God rest her soul. Please take word to Anthony for me."

Doc nodded. "I would feel a bit easier with you here." He turned to James. "I will get word to Minister Paul tonight. I am sure he will be out at first light."

James shook his hand. "Thank you, sir."

Soon after Doc was on his way, Christopher opened the bedroom door and invited everyone in. Alexandra, though pale and weary, sat up against the pillows holding baby Gracie. They had dressed her in the pale pink dress that Alexandra had sewn. The gown was too big but was beautiful all the same. Gracie was also lightly wrapped in the white blanket knitted by Monica. Christopher introduced Gracie Unruh to her family. Alexandra held out the tiny bundle to James.

Nervously, he took Gracie into his hands. He and Monica gazed at the tiny being. James tried to clear his throat. "Sis, she is beautiful."

Monica leaned over and kissed Gracie's cheek as she cried silent tears.

James leaned down so Lee and Christine could see the baby.

Christine touched the baby's hand. "She is so tiny — like a dolly."

Lee looked wide-eyed and whispered, "She looks like an angel."

Mama Clara lovingly squeezed his shoulder. "She is,

love, she is."

James held her up to his face. He smiled through his tears. "Hello, Gracie." He kissed her forehead and handed her back to Alexandra.

Mama Clara led the children out of the room.

Christopher watched Alexandra for a moment and then turned to Monica. "Will you sit with Alexandra and Gracie for a while? I have something I need to do."

Monica nodded. Before anyone could ask, he was gone out of the room. Monica took a seat beside Alexandra's bed.

James followed Christopher. He caught up with him outside. "Can I help you with whatever you need to do?"

Christopher shook his head. With his hands in his pockets, he moved a rock around with the toe of his boot, then finally spoke. "No, thank you. This is the only thing I will ever be able to make for my little girl. I want to do it alone." He turned and walked to the barn.

James stood for a long time staring in his direction. He felt so helpless. He understood what Christopher meant. He had that same feeling when Ma and Pa had died. When he heard the sounds of sawing coming from the barn, it cut through him like a knife.

He turned away from the house and barn and walked. When James returned from walking, he could still hear Christopher working in the barn. He wanted so badly to help him. Then it came to him. He went to the lean-to and retrieved the shovel. Slowly, he made his way to the cemetery.

When Christopher came back to the house, Christine and Lee were sleeping. Mama Clara had cleaned the kitchen and retired to Christine's bed. James was on the back porch washing up. Christopher opened the front door. Under one arm, Christopher carried a tiny rectangular wooden box. Without a word, he carried it into his bedroom.

Alexandra, through exhaustion and tears, had fallen asleep. While Monica laid a blanket into the bottom of the box, Christopher gently lifted Gracie from Alexandra's arm. With one last kiss, he laid his daughter in her coffin. Monica tucked the white blanket around Gracie.

She stood and laid a hand on Christopher's arm. "I am so sorry." Christopher wearily nodded and patted her hand. She pointed to a pitcher and basin. "There is fresh warm water for you to wash. Ma brought it in hot a little bit ago before she retired for the night. If you or Alexandra need anything else tonight, please come and get me or James."

Christopher closed his eyes and inhaled. "Thank you." He exhaled.

Monica closed the door as she left the room.

CR

Minister Paul, his wife Vera, Doc Cannon, and his wife Susie arrived with the sun. By mid-morning, most of the congregation and town folks arrived. Everyone brought food for the noon meal, but few actually ate.

The funeral was held early afternoon. Christopher carried Alexandra to the grave side, where they had a chair waiting. The whole ordeal was hard on the young family.

Following the short service, Christopher carried the distraught Alexandra straight to bed. Mama Clara sat with her while Christopher accepted all the condolences. Most folks departed immediately following the funeral.

As the house emptied, Alexandra's cries could be heard through the bedroom door. James suddenly stood up and walked out of the house. Monica followed him as he entered the barn. She came up behind him as he knelt in the middle of the barn. She stopped where she stood. His head was down to his chest, and he was sobbing. Quietly, she walked up behind him and placed her hands on his shoulders.

He pressed his hot, wet cheek against her hand." I cannot bear to hear her hurt like that."

Monica whispered, "I know, but she has to grieve."

James blew his nose into his handkerchief. "I know. I have prayed and prayed for them." Monica pulled up a bucket and turned it upside down. She sat beside him. He continued, "I have always taken care of Alexandra in any difficult time. It is hard to stand back and not be able to fix this for her."

Monica reached over and brushed a tear from his cheek. "She has Christopher to help her through this; however, I think you will find that Alexandra still needs her big brother's love and prayers."

James laid his head into Monica lap and cried.

☙

Monica and her mother fixed everyone a light plate for the evening meal. Larry and his father stayed around for the afternoon. When Christopher came out to eat the food that his Aunt Clara had coaxed him into trying, James went to sit by the sleeping Alexandra. After a short while, she began to stir. She opened her eyes and looked around the room, finally focusing on James.

"It isn't a dream, is it?" James looked at the floor and shook his head. Alexandra closed her eyes and exhaled slowly. She turned her head back to James. "I feel so numb. I do not believe I have any more tears to shed."

James tried not to let his voice crack. "Sis, is there anything I can do for you?"

Alexandra smiled ever so slightly. "Oh, James. I need prayers. I know in my heart that only God can see me through this." They sat in silence for several moments. Finally, Alexandra spoke again. "She was beautiful, wasn't she?"

James nodded. "Yes, she was. Christine was right. She looked just like one of those porcelain dolls."

Alexandra quickly wiped the corner of her eye to keep a tear from falling. "Will you make her a cross marker?"

James nodded. "Of course I will. First light tomorrow morning."

Alexandra nodded. "Thank you."

As the quiet folded around them, Alexandra drifted back off to sleep.

EPILOGUE

Alexandra regained her strength, and the young family healed from their loss. Their life together was rich and full, not without its share of heartache, but blessed all the same. Two years after their loss of Gracie, Christopher and Alexandra gave birth to a healthy baby: a son. They would eventually have four healthy children in all: two sons, Charles and Dylan; and two more daughters, Leigha and Rose. Their fourth-born child, Benjamin, died shortly after birth, also.

Over the years, Christopher built his family a house on the south corner of the family land. He and James farmed together and eventually bought an additional one hundred acres adjoining their land on the west side.

A year after Gracie's birth, Monica and James gave birth to a son, Edward. Over the next ten years, they would have five more children: three daughters, Sarah, Denise, and Anna-Grace; and two more sons, Donavon and Michael.

Christine blossomed into a beautiful young lady. At fifteen, she taught the local summer sessions of school for three years before marrying Christoph Whited. Together, they raised three daughters: Grace Ann, Charlene, and Christina.

Lee grew to be a strong young man. He apprenticed with the town's blacksmith and eventually took over the business. At twenty-one, he married Kelsey Jackson. Together, they raised their son, Lee Jr., and two daughters, Susanna and Mary.

Through faith, love, and dedication, the families remained close to one another. Both heartache and joy bonded them with trust, love, memories, and loyalty. Their unified faith and steadfastness helped them stay founded in peace and harmony. All lived long, fruitful, and faithful lives.

Information about discussion and study guides for
Alexandra - A Williams Family Journal
can be found at:
www.pressworkpublications.com

LaVergne, TN USA
12 August 2010
193085LV00001B/27/P